(NEED)

BLIND AMBITION

———

KEVIN T. MYERS

**BEAUFORT
BOOKS**

(NEED) BLIND AMBITION

Paperback: 9780825309984
Ebook: 9780825308734

For inquiries about volume orders, please contact:
Beaufort Books, sales@beaufortbooks.com

Published in the United States by Beaufort Books
www.beaufortbooks.com

Distributed by Midpoint Trade Books
a division of Independent Publisher Group
https://www.ipgbook.com/

Book designed by Mark Karis
Printed in the United States of America

For those who lost their lives to addiction and mental health battles

1

THURSDAY, NOVEMBER 8, 2007

PARKER COLLEGE,

PORTLAND, OREGON

William James was beyond saving when the Parker College security guards discovered his body sprawled near the community garden by the border of the affluent South Parker neighborhood. William was a houseless vet, a recovering addict, and a regular fixture on the grounds of the small private college. He was conditionally accepted as part of the community, and grudgingly tolerated by the security guards who were often asked to "mitigate his presence" in warm, dry places on cold, wet days. The guards considered William an occupational annoyance, but a more affable one than the privileged South Parker gardeners, who constantly lobbied for protection against his unauthorized harvests. William would sometimes filch a tomato or a few snap peas during the productive gardening months, but this time of year there was nothing left to forage. It was the coldest November in decades, and the subfreezing temperature sapped all the joy from any vegetables remaining on the vine.

William was never welcomed in the South Parker neighborhood, and he especially avoided it at night. It was the least likely place to find him dead or alive. Standing over William's twisted corpse, the guards engaged in some mild speculation that led to no conclusions. His arms and legs were spread akimbo as if he fell dead while turning to run. He was missing a shoe, but his sock was dry, his jacket was unzipped, and his shoulders touched the ground with his arms spread perpendicular to his torso. His neck arched so the crown of his head rested in the freezing soil, making the gaze of his vacant eyes seem as if they were watching for the ferryman to come down the footpath and deliver him to his final destination.

Like many in the community, the guards called him "Willy the Sage." His nickname was given sardonically because of his claim to be able to "extract a book's wisdom by absorbing its aura through meditation," or as the librarians called it: sleeping. William enjoyed the moniker and wore it well. When the guards were called to the library to stop his snoring, he'd say, "I wasn't sleeping. You know why they call me Willy the Sage, right?"

His serious side made less frequent appearances. "I'm going to start a church," he told one of the guards who was watching over his body. "My church will have no rules; people will just come and look for God in each other's eyes. You won't find God in heaven if you can't find him in your fellow man." The guard thought about that exchange as she looked toward the road hoping to see the headlights of the medical examiner's van. She was cold and wanted to return to the warmth of her patrol car. Having not seen God in William's eyes then made her wonder where Willy was now. Then she thought briefly about her own mortality before raising the irony of his final resting place.

The guards joked, with a bit of spiteful glee, about which of their least favorite gardeners they hoped he'd haunt, and then shared jokes William told at the expense of the "So Park" neighbors. "Did you hear there was a blackout in So Park?" he'd wait for a reply. "It didn't last long. The neighbors called the cops to come take me away." When he was being more direct about the neighborhood's hospitality, he'd say, "It was illegal to be Black in all of Oregon until 1927, but now there's just a few neighborhoods."

Laughing at the stories felt too awkward, and they fell back into silence. Finding William dead on the grounds had a feeling of inevitability. *Of course, it would end like this for him.* Watching over William had become just another task, and his death would become just another line in their nightly incident report; it would take no more space than asking him to leave the library.

2

JUNEAU'S LANDFILL

Peter Cook drove to the landfill's summit to purge the flotsam and jetsam accumulated over a decade of living in Juneau, Alaska. His family was moving to Portland, Oregon, and his wife, Tessa, was determined for their "new life" to be simple and free from clutter. Their journey toward simplicity was inspired by a book she'd found by Googling "eliminating stress from family life." The couple agreed to follow the book's guidance, though Tessa adhered a bit more zealously. She boiled down the book's rules to one principle: Have you touched it today? Will you touch it tomorrow? If the answers are "no," then eliminate it from your life. She held so firmly to those rules that Peter asked if she was going to throw away his penis. It didn't go over well.

Peter was an engaged participant in the plan, even knowing he was the most complicated piece of clutter in Tessa's life. He feared her next Google search upon his arrival in Portland would be for divorce lawyers and he'd be swept into the dustbin with all the other items that had lost their value. Tessa and the kids were already in Portland, having timed their move to be settled by the start of Portland Public Schools. Peter stayed behind to sell the house, finish his job at the *Juneau Daily*, and tie up other loose ends. He was thrilled that he would soon be reunited with his children. The separation with Tessa, he hoped, would pull them back together, but momentum suggested a different outcome. Peter wasn't sure how to swing the tide back in their favor.

His trip to the dump felt like purging joyful memories and future accomplishments. He hated it. Growing up poor made Peter a bit of a hoarder. Discarding potentially useful things didn't come naturally; his drawers, closets, shed, and garage overflowed with items of *latent utility*. To escape the pull of each object's sentimental gravity, he quickly flung one item after another from the back of his Subaru wagon. Keeping a vigilant eye not to hit one of the ostentatiously patriotic number of scavenging bald eagles, he tossed the step stool his children had used to reach the bathroom sink when they were toddlers. Then he unloaded a perfectly good ax head that was attached to a splintered handle, a slightly warped bike rim, and a length of four-inch stovepipe that he was certain would make the perfect vent for an adobe pizza oven. Instead of adding value to future creations, his hoarded possessions were adding mass to the hill of refuse the locals called Mount Trashmore.

Swooping to claim a Costco chicken carcass, a bald eagle

flew near enough to Peter for him to duck his head and tense his shoulders. At the beginning of the family's "new life" in Alaska, such a close encounter would have inspired awe. But like the aphorism "never meet your heroes" warns, the raptors' grandeur quickly faded with the constant sight of them scavenging roadkill and rummaging through dumpsters. *They're resplendent pigeon rats*, he thought, then wondered why the raven, his favorite bird, had not been chosen as the nation's icon. *They're black and clever—that would have never flown in colonial America.*

Despite being inundated by the smell of methane while standing atop a hill of rubbish, Peter took a moment to appreciate the magnificence of the place he was leaving. He was thunderstruck by a sense of loss. Leaving the land felt like cutting off a limb. To his east, the trailing edge of Thomas Glacier draped over the chiseled mountain peaks it carved during its long retreat northward. Beneath the colossal expanse of ice, an emerald pool of glacial melt formed on a stone shelf. A weak stream meandered off the ledge so tentatively it seemed hyperbolic to call it a waterfall. The water did indeed fall off the ledge, but it quickly scattered into the wind, losing its form completely before reaching the treetops in the valley. He felt pangs of sorrow for the activities he'd miss doing with his children: sledding by the Mendenhall Glacier; picking berries while hiking to overnights at Forest Service cabins; and fishing off the rocky shores of Douglas Island when the silvers were running thick.

Juneau was the first place where the tendrils of Peter's heart took anchor. It was home. He loved the beauty and sense of community, but his own ambition, as well as Tessa's urging for him to meet his full potential, impelled him to swim into bigger ponds. He'd accepted a job doing media relations at Parker College—the Valhalla of higher education. Parker was the measuring stick for other colleges. Even those who worked at the Ivies envied Parker for its singular focus of intellectual pursuit.

Peter had worked hard to become editor of the *Juneau Daily*. It was the job he'd always wanted, but he'd reached his goal as the industry was being sedated and hooked up to life support. The mission of journalism was so deeply embedded in his DNA that he was willing to ride with the paper to the end of democracy. Tessa, however, wanted him to have a back-up plan and urged him to get his Master of Public Administration at the University of Alaska Southeast. Like many others fleeing print journalism, he took his new degree and went searching for work as a flack. The Parker job gave him an opportunity to grow his career, but, he wondered, at what cost.

After returning from the dump, Peter made one last sweep through the house and then had dinner with a few close friends at the Hanger restaurant. There were lots of hugs and a few tears before Peter towed the trailer of *useful things* to the ferry terminal in Auke Bay. He parked in the staging area, dozing in and out while waiting to board the Alaska Marine Highway ship *Columbia* for the thousand-mile voyage to Bellingham, Washington.

Fog froze to the windshield as Peter waited to board the ferry. The webbed patterns of ice created a kaleidoscopic view of the streetlamps, navigation, and traffic lights. When it was his turn to drive out of Juneau, he cleared the magical auras from his windshield, shifted into gear, and followed the instruction of the boat's boarding crew. The engines of the *Columbia* idled in a rumbling, powerful baritone, accompanied by the clanging of metal on metal as tons of cars and cargo crossed the loading ramp into the belly of the ship. Peter's Subaru wagon joined the assemblage of cars, trucks, and trailers driving onto the Alaska Marine Highway, the only road out of town.

3

PARKER COLLEGE

Monday mornings at Parker College began at 7:30 a.m. with an executive staff meeting in the president's office. Four vice presidents and the academic dean were greeted by the aroma of freshly brewed coffee and friendly conversation before discussing the pressing issues of the week. Unofficially, the meeting began when President Loch broke the pleasantries with some iconic wartime slogan or literary quote like "Once more into the breach, dear friends, once more!"

Arranged like dinner settings around the circular table were the meeting's agenda and the previous week's campus safety incident blotter, which was comprised of short reports from campus security guards: CSG #12, smoke billowing from dorm window, marijuana and bong confiscated. CSG #7, stopped argument over library carrel squatting, no action taken. CSG #2, underage drinking, confiscated case of PBR, freshman dorm. Most weeks the list was read silently and put aside without comment. Occasionally, the Vice President of Student Affairs Matthew Rosen talked about disciplinary measures taken in response to an aberrant incident. Rarer still was an entry that prompted spontaneous discussion, like William James' body being discovered near the community garden.

William James had been one of the few people who would reflexively greet all those he encountered on campus. Even if they didn't return his greetings, everyone knew him. The executives mostly commented on how remarkably put together he was for someone of his circumstance—though, most did not actually know his circumstance. Loch cheerfully shared the origin of the nickname "Willy the Sage," before asking if there was anything unexplained or unusual about his death.

"I hope students aren't expecting the college to pay for the vagrant's funeral," said Wells Farnum, treasurer of the college. Farnum's comment went mostly ignored, as they often were when emanating directly from his cold, dead heart.

Rosen, the only Parker College alumnus among the VPs, corrected Farnum's jargon, to houseless person, and begged him not to say "vagrant" when he was around students, faculty, or anyone with a sense of decency. Rosen went on to explain that James had served in the Army, and that Veteran Affairs was going to pick up the tab for his burial. Rosen then casually mentioned that John McMahon, an assistant district attorney, had called to let the college know that James had died of a suspected drug overdose, and not exposure, as the guards had assumed. President Loch perked up as Rosen continued. "McMahon said

James was the second fatal OD within a mile of campus."

"Did the DA say why *he* was calling, rather than the police?" asked Loch, with a curiosity that was leaning toward concern.

"He said he was letting us know about increased drug activity near campus," said Rosen.

"That still doesn't explain why the call would have come from the District Attorney's office unless they have a suspect and are building a case. Did he say anything indicating the drugs came from campus, or that dealers were focused on campus, or something of that nature?"

"He didn't," said Rosen. "But I suppose we can't rule it out."

"No, I don't suppose we can. Well, something to keep an eye on," said Loch.

The VP of advancement, Alistair Goodwin, made a show of clearing his throat and sitting upright in his chair. The others looked at him, but he didn't speak right away. Goodwin was tall, pale, slender, and shapeless. His octangular wire-framed glasses and sweater vest were the only characteristics distinguishing him from a weathered fence post. He had a series of nervous tics, most notably his neurotic behavior around Burt's Bees lip balm. He was never without a small round yellow tin. He kept stockpiles of them in his desk drawers, in his briefcase, in his squash bag, and in the glovebox of his beige Acura TL.

Goodwin didn't fit the mold for his job. Advancement chiefs are generally confident and gregarious. They tend to be the type of people who run political campaigns or advertising agencies. They're disarming and feel comfortable talking with all sorts of people, including members of the press. They're the rainmakers for the schools' endowments—the engines that fuel private education. Goodwin was none of these things. He was, however, as members of his staff secretly mocked, a Goodwin, of the Goodwin Pharmaceuticals Goodwins. The Goodwin family name was inscribed on the school's largest classroom building, the business cards of the endowed chair of chemistry, and on the resumes of graduates who received the Goodwin scholarship, the award for academic excellence in chemistry. To many, the Goodwin name was synonymous with Parker College. "Is this something for which we should be preparing?" Goodwin finally uttered while arranging his fingertips around his lip balm until the cap fit between all ten fingernails and the skin below.

"Prepare for what, exactly?" asked Loch.

Direct questions were one of many provocations that sent Goodwin into a ritualistic series of quirks. Rubbing his thumb over the beeswax tin to invoke an answer genie was the first step; then came the slow removal of his glasses and the deep-tissue eye massage, before drawing an exaggerated breath to summon a distant universe that he uncomfortably searched for beyond the walls of the room. "I'm just thinking proactively. It seems to me that it makes sense for us to come up with some sort of messaging strategy," said Goodwin.

"Good. Well, let's think this through. A houseless man with a history of drug addiction died on campus, apparently resulting from his addiction. I guess, additionally, we know that the DA is aware of increased drug activity *near* campus," said Loch. "It's a tragic story, Alistair, it really is, but unless the drugs came from campus, I'm not certain it's one in which the college plays a central role. Of course, it's possible you're seeing something I'm not."

The vice presidents are a well-educated and well-heeled collection of people. Refined. Their family trees shade the old monied neighborhoods of the country. Confrontation among the leadership group was considered crude. By using Goodwin's name to punctuate his disagreement, Loch not only questioned the validity of the idea but also the judgment of the man. No one in the room missed the Victorian smackdown.

"When does the new media relations director arrive? The Alaskan," asked Loch, emphasizing *the Alaskan* with zeal. "Perhaps you should consult with him."

* * *

Rattling the doorknob to the public affairs office always caused the staff to prairie dog. It was loud. The last time Goodwin caused that rattle and squeak, he was coming to fire the public affairs director, Rhea Smith. Jangling metal followed by the squeaking hinge had become synonymous with the swoosh and chop of the executioner's ax.

Goodwin called for Steven Collins, the latest in a series of public affairs directors. All previous occupants of Collins' office were qualified for the job and summarily fired for perceived encroachments into Goodwin's authority, such as asking questions of the president when he was in the room or responding to benign press inquiries without permission. Collins had few of the desired attributes and none of the professional experience required in the six previous job listings. To those he supervised, his hiring announced an end to the approach of employing competent professionals. As Goodwin entered the office, Collins flashed his most obvious qualification for the job, a special smile that conveyed obedience and a complete lack of initiative.

"When does the new media relations director get here?" Goodwin asked, waiting for a spark in the blankness of Collins' eyes. "Call him. Tell him to get here sooner."

Collins picked up the phone and began to dial. Displays of efficiency were also a specialty. Goodwin nodded his approval as he exited. Collins, however, was dialing his mother's landline. The only person at the college with Peter's cell number had been Rhea Smith. It took several hours, calls to Alaska, and then a call to Peter's wife, before Collins dialed Peter's actual cell number.

* * *

Steven Collins had replaced Rhea Smith as the public affairs director while Peter was packing the U-Haul trailer. Collins had been the department's office manager. His job responsibilities expanded from ordering copier supplies and collecting time sheets to being curator of the college's image and, until Peter arrived on campus, filling-in as point person for crisis communications. He was entirely out of his league, but he wasn't dumb. Collins had quietly observed the firing of six directors over the course of eight years and learned what drove Goodwin's expectations and triggered his anger. Alistair Goodwin was born holding a first-class ticket and thought it put him first in succession to command the ship. Collins understood this and found ways to make him feel like a captain. They had a symbiotic relationship like that of a suckerfish and a shark. Goodwin had money and connections, and Collins fed off those things; Collins attached himself and cleared the parasites that ate away at Goodwin's ego.

4

PETERSBURG, ALASKA

Collins' urgent calls went to voicemail as Peter sat on the bed of his 9x4–foot cabin reading *Grizzly Maze*, by Nick Jans. The ferry was a few hours out from Petersburg, so just as far outside of potential cell range. Even if the calls got through, the ship was two days from Bellingham, which is 225 miles from Portland. There was no faster route.

The Alaska state ferries are old, sturdy, and devoid of luxuries, but the views are priceless. Peter woke early and spent a lot of time walking the broadside decks. The bow cutting through waves created a cool, salty mist that collected on Peter's face, stung his eyes, and made him feel like an adventurer. His favorite ferry activity, though, was reading under the heat lamps of the solarium deck. The covered deck with open sides allowed

Peter to be warm and dry while still breathing the regenerative sea air. Some travelers pitched their tents and camped on the deck during their Alaska treks. Talking with these hearty souls helped shorten voyages and create joyful memories. For many travelers, it was their once-in-a-lifetime trip, and they spoke with the excitement of having discovered something new. He loved hearing their stories. His second-favorite activity was attempting to find the bottom of the bottomless coffee jug in the galley.

With negligible cell coverage along the route and the promise of solitude ahead, Peter's chest became tight, and he felt weakness sap his legs and arms. He struggled to catch his breath and the back of his neck got tense and sore. Peter would come to learn these as symptoms of posttraumatic stress disorder, but in this moment, he only knew them as harbingers of panic attacks that led to bouts of depression. If he couldn't call his children soon, his mind would spin with horrific thoughts. He checked his phone again for service as the ship began its long approach to the dock. No bars. Despair.

Being a father was Peter's greatest joy, but it was also his biggest source of anxiety. He desperately needed psychological help but didn't have the words to ask. When he was away from his children, his mind ran like a health class scare film on parenting—a constant montage illustrating the disastrous consequences of his poor decisions. Pleasant thoughts of his kids playing at recess would mutate into visions of abductions by pedophiles in windowless vans. Some days, the fear would become so overwhelming that he'd have to leave work to check on them. He'd cover for his anxiety by bringing them treats for their lunches or different seasonal jackets, so he could see them and know they were okay. It was not sustainable. If he was not able to stave off a panic attack while at sea, three days with no way to contact them was going to feel like a life sentence.

He would be lucky to get coverage at the dock in Petersburg and extraordinarily lucky when the boat reached Wrangel. The Ketchikan stop was in the middle of the night, and then the ship entered British Columbia, Canada, necessitating an international phone plan, which Peter did not have. If he couldn't reach his children in the next few hours, it would likely be days before he'd hear their voices and know they were safe. Peter's anxiety had him feeling like a wounded deer in a meadow as wolves stalked along the tree line. With his mug full of coffee and his book under his arm, he went back out to the solarium deck and waited for the approach to the dock.

During times of change or challenge, Peter longed for the guidance and assurance he was certain his late parents would have provided. Peter was raised by his aunt after the death of his parents. Growing up without them felt like being born without a rudder to guide him through life. He remembered very little about his parents and nothing about their deaths. The accident was a taboo subject for his aunt, which created many gaps in his family history. He knew their deaths likely shaded his perception of the world and were probably the root of his growing anxiety surrounding his children. An unavoidable family inheritance, perhaps: his predisposition for denial. He sidestepped most uncomfortable conversations with Tessa and ran from all forms of therapy, which he often regretted during the quiet times when his anxiety transfigured thoughts of his children's banal activities into catastrophic visions of their deaths.

Needing a safe place for his mind to wander, he turned his focus to Parker's leadership team. Peter had an oversized view of President Loch that dated back to when Peter was in grade school. They'd met during a campaign stop while Loch was running for mayor of Boston. Loch was one of the last hard-nosed liberals who championed the rights of unions and social justice causes at a time when "Democrats for Reagan" campaign stickers were being slapped on rusted car bumpers all around New England's dying factory towns. His opponent successfully painted Loch as an anachronism, giving himself the winning advantage in a close race. The impression of Loch as a man who used his privilege for the betterment of society stuck with Peter. One of Peter's *essential possessions*, which narrowly escaped Juneau's landfill, was a "Loch for Mayor" campaign button that was pinned to his father's work coat at the time of his death. Peter kept it in a wooden cigar box with a few family photos, Red Sox and Celtics ticket stubs, and other treasured childhood relics.

Loch remained an outspoken champion of equitable causes through his transition into higher education. His first act as Parker College President was to launch a $250-million fund-raising campaign to support need-blind admissions. In a mostly eloquent editorial published in the *New York Times*, Loch identified need-blind admission as a social imperative for the nation's top schools. Evoking the egalitarian spirit of Parker's founders, who imposed no restrictions on admission based on religion, race, or gender, Loch vowed to remove all restrictions to admission, including a student's ability to pay. He argued it was vital to the survival of American democracy to abolish all hurdles to higher education for those who exhibit dedication to scholarship, discovery, and independence of thought but lacked the wherewithal to attend the country's great institutions.

In true Loch form, the last third of his piece descended from eloquence into a barroom brawl. He took a few well-deserved jabs at elite schools who fudged their financial aid data to call themselves need-blind as a marketing ploy to attract more applicants. He went on to characterize many state colleges as minor league sports complexes with second-rate academic programs, referring to one of Oregon's most beloved public institutions as "a football team with an educational annex."

Working for Loch was going to be an exciting challenge, but Peter was equally excited to work with Rhea Smith, who came to Parker from the *New York Times*, where she'd worked as a metro reporter. When offering Peter the job, Smith, who did not hold nostalgic feelings for Loch, explained the position as, "adding context to statements made by the president. Make no mistake, you're not so much a mouthpiece as you are a bib," she joked. "But your job will never be boring." Peter didn't know yet that Rhea had been fired.

There was no cell coverage at the dock, but Peter's triggered state never transitioned into a full-fledged attack. He was relieved and found ways to keep himself manically busy throughout the day and into that night.

* * *

After breakfast the next morning, Peter finished reading *Grizzly Maze* and went searching for something else to distract him. The grab-all shelf on the observatory deck only had a few dogeared romance novels, and a 1,000-piece enchanted forest unicorn rainbow puzzle, so he continued his search elsewhere. Attempts at walking meditation along the broadside decks were waylaid by frigid gusts whipping off the ocean, checking his balance and stealing his breath. Retreating to the sanctuary of the solarium, he sat and gazed over the *Columbia*'s stern as she carved a placid wake through the choppy turquoise waters. From the view of his deckchair, Peter tried to calm himself by thinking of nothing at all. Closing his eyes, he turned his face toward the heat lamps, which radiated a penetrating woodstove-like warmth. Each breath of cold, salty air released a bit more stress into the wilderness. His body settled into a cozy, peaceful calm as he opened his eyes to a sheer mountainside only a few hundred yards off the portside rail. Jagged stone rose straight up from the ocean. Mature Sitka spruce, rooted in improbable cracks that seemed too barren to support life, flourished in contortions that stretched toward the sun. Low-hanging clouds rolled along a cliff at the back of an inlet. Below the clouds, a handful of mountain goats balanced on a rock face so sheer that Peter wondered if they had belayed down from the top of the mountain like rock climbers. Breaching in the ship's wake, a pod of Dall's porpoises popped up in a line, one after another, making the pod look like a single stone skipping across the surface. *Life finds a way to thrive*, he thought. The landscape reminded him of the Jack London stories he'd read as a kid and the wanderlust they'd inspired. But his childhood fantasies did not compare to the reality of the landscape.

A young dad walking from the portside deck struggled to corral his stubborn toddler into the dining area. Laughing, the delightfully spastic toddler ran toward the ladder-like stairs that led to the deck below, which caused Peter to jolt with fear. The panicked dad grabbed the child's arm with more force than intended, bringing a howl that sent a shockwave to the back of Peter's head. The ball of fear settled between Peter's shoulder blades before working its way forward into his chest, weakening his arms and legs, then completely enveloping his consciousness. His eyes dilated, and he blinked to protect them from a burst of light that only he could see. *There's no reason for this,* Peter thought as fear took root in his stomach. His shoulders slumped and his breathing became shallow. Strength fled his body as humming rang in his ears. He sat on his deckchair surrounded by warmth and beauty, but it felt like a gun was pressed against his temple while the triggerman counted backwards from three. Peter felt his mind being hijacked by a phantasm of fear. He was losing control. He didn't know how to stop it.

The *Columbia* was thirty hours from Bellingham. *That's too long to feel like this. Why is this happening?* He found no logical answer. *I've got to learn to deal with this,* he thought as he took a deep breath trying to calm himself. The cold ocean air burned in his lungs, making him cough. He focused on being eight years old in his home in Boston. Tremors of fear rumbled through his body as he tried to recall details from the day his parents died. His mind hummed like a high-voltage powerline. All he could remember about that day was his bike. *I must have been riding my bike when I learned,* he thought. He remembered the aftermath, being in his kitchen and a policeman telling him that his aunt was going to take care of him. He remembered riding in his aunt's car from Brighton to Milton, knowing he would never see his parents again. That was all he could remember. *It's just the unknown,* he decided. *There's too much uncertainty in my life right now. It's bringing it all back. That's all it is. My aunt was good to me. I had a good childhood. I was lucky to have her.*

Adrenaline pumped through his body, causing his extremities to tingle. He was about to lose focus. His untreated trauma was a cudgel swinging by his head so violently it whistled in his ears. He clenched his jaw and ground his teeth so hard they squeaked. Narrowing his focus was the only way to keep from having visions of his children in a car accident, as the victims of a home invasion, or being kidnaped. His unrooted feelings of terror would swirl with graphic images of his children in danger until his imagination could not be separated from reality.

If I could only talk with the kids, I would know everything's okay. Then I could be calm. All he wanted to do was hold his children. Hugging them, knowing they were safe, and telling them he loved them was always enough to tether him back to reality. He took out his cell phone, powered it up, and hoped beyond reason that he'd see bars. Seeing the "no service" message felt like being told his kids had died. He had become an expert at hiding these episodes and carrying on, but it was too much. It was getting too hard to cope.

This must end. Peter stood from his chair as tears flowed down his face. The vast wilderness had lost all its wonder as he walked toward the rail of the ship. Cortisol and adrenaline had his mind in a fog. His thoughts were being filtered through the fight-or-flight part of his brain. He saw no end to the fear; he couldn't even find a starting point toward de-escalation. Looking over the rail to the icy waters below, he thought, *I could end this right now. I'd be dead in a matter of minutes. This could all be over. It would be better for everyone.*

He could find no refuge in the future. No calm. No peace. There was nothing more real than the feelings of terror he was experiencing in that moment. *All I have to do is jump over this railing, and the pain would be gone forever.* He desperately searched for a reason not to jump. The flag flying from the stern twisted in the wind, and the grommets and fasteners clanged against the metal pole. The whipping wind and clanging gromets distracted Peter. He remembered standing by his parents' caskets, asking his aunt why they chose to die. Imagining his children asking Tessa the same question gave him pause. Knowing she'd have no answer, he backed away from the railing. "Why?" He said aloud. *I need help*, Peter thought. *I need to get better for the sake of the kids and Tess. I will get better. I can endure this for them.*

5

COLUMBIA

The urge to end his pain grew more intense throughout the previous day, overnight, and into the morning. Suicide emerged as the most expedient solution to quash the uncontrollable bouts of anxiety and depression. The thought of dying felt as comforting as stepping from the cold rain into a warm shower. He had never come as close to giving in to his suicidal ideation. Not trusting himself to leave his room for the last twenty-five hours of the voyage, he slept when he could and meditated when he couldn't, but he didn't leave his cabin. When the ship docked in Bellingham, Peter was showered, packed, and staring at his phone, trying to will it into cell range. At the announcement that the car deck was open to passengers, he bolted from his bed, rushed down the narrow stairwell, tossed his bag on the passenger's seat, and waited to drive off the ferry. He needed to see his kids like an addict needs a fix. The drive from Bellingham, Washington, to Portland, Oregon, was four and a half hours without Seattle and Olympia traffic. If he was lucky, he would be there in time to have a late dinner with his family.

Settled in the driver's seat, he looked to his phone for the umpteenth time that morning and finally saw bars. The relief was so intense Peter gasped as he listened for the dial tone: *beep, beep, beep;* he had ten messages. Three were from his children, Blythe and Ben, who called each night before bedtime to hear Peter's voice and to tell him they loved him, which filled his heart with love and loosened tears of relief. Six were from Steven Collins, all repeating the same message, "Peter, call as soon as you get this. It's important." Nothing else. Then there was one anxiety-filled rant from Tessa that began, "Who the fuck is Steven Collins and why does he keep calling me?" Those seven burnt a hole in the pit of his stomach.

Waves of regret washed over Peter like the plumes of diesel fumes filling the hull of the *Columbia* as the row of cargo trucks thundered to life. *Stay on the boat,* he thought. The last Peter knew, Steven Collins was the department's office manager. The urgency, he assumed, was either a missing HR form or the signal of a disaster like they had eliminated his position. Desperate to hear a friendly voice, Peter called Tessa. She only added to his trepidation by recapping her conversations with Collins whose only response to every question was, "It's very important that I speak with Peter as soon as possible." He said nothing else.

The first step in the plan for simplifying family life was Tessa quitting her job and not looking for another. It turns out that simple living requires a lot of time and energy and shares many traits with being poor. Peter was not an overly enthusiastic partner in the quest toward a "smaller-box lifestyle," but now he was hoping his family would not literally be living in a box down by the river. He decided to call Rhea Smith to see if she could shed some light on the situation. If it was bad news, he wanted to hear it from someone he respected.

"Good afternoon. Thank you for calling Parker College, you've reached Steven Collins." Peter thought he'd reached Steven's voicemail and checked his phone's screen to make sure he had called Rhea's office phone. He had. "Hello, this is Steven—" He continued to speak with an infomercial affect.

"Steven. It's Peter Cook." Peter was trying to not sound nervous.

"Why haven't you been returning my calls?" Steven didn't try to hide his annoyance.

"I was at sea. I told Rhea I would be unreachable until I got to Bellingham. I'm calling from the dock."

"Well, Rhea doesn't work here anymore. I've taken over for her and I need you on campus immediately," said Collins, sounding very much like a child mocking authority.

The news about Rhea chilled Peter's blood. Rhea was the most impressive staffer he had met in higher ed. She'd gone to Dartmouth and then Columbia School of Journalism. She was a reporter for the *New York Times* and a stringer for the *Atlantic*. She'd landed at Parker College because an investment banker lured her hotshot-chef fiancé away from Brooklyn to open his own restaurant in Portland. All Peter knew about Collins was that he could book airline flights, and when agitated he sounded like a tween boy whose balls hadn't dropped. *If Rhea could be impulsively fired*, Peter thought, *what chance do I have?*

"What happened to Rhea?" Peter tried to make his tone as nonjudgmental as possible.

"She no longer works here," Collins repeated.

What did I just walk into? wondered Peter. "So, they put you in charge while they do a search for her replacement, or—" Peter wasn't trying to be nice anymore.

"I'm in charge now," said Collins without a change of inflection.

"Well, okay, that's been established. So, what's going on?

"What do you mean?" asked Collins.

"You left six messages on my cell phone. I assume something happened."

"I'll tell you when you get here."

"Are you kidding?" Peter was at the end of his patience. "Steve, you left six messages on my cell phone, scared the shit out of my wife while trying to get ahold of me, and now you're not going to tell me what the fuck is going on?"

"It's Steven, and mind your language. I'm in charge now. I'll see you by five," snapped Collins.

"I'm six hours away, in moderate traffic. I'm not sure what you want me to do," replied Peter and the line went dead. *This must be a joke. Rhea must have put him up to this*, thought Peter. *Nobody really acts that way.*

Peter didn't want to call back Tessa. He was barely holding himself together and didn't have the energy to manage her anxiety as well. His heart sank as he dialed. They rehashed the call and tried to speculate what it meant for their future. Their combined anxiety ramped up the conversation to the point where it sounded like an accelerating turbine engine. He wasn't sure if he would have a job when he showed up to campus the next morning.

"This isn't good, Peter," Tessa's speech became even more rapid. "He would have told you if they eliminated your job, right? They wouldn't let you move your family fifteen-hundred miles for a job and then take it away before you got there. Would they?"

"I don't know, Tess, but it doesn't feel great, either way," Peter tried to think of something that would calm Tessa. "Maybe there's an issue brewing and they're worried it might blow up. Rhea's gone, and clearly there's no one else there who knows how to communicate. I mean, I can't imagine they would trust him to speak for the college. He seems like the guy you hire if you want to make things worse." The cars at the front of the ferry began to exit. "Hey, traffic's moving. I got to hang up. Are the kids okay?" Peter finally asked.

"Um, yeah, for the time being," said Tessa, buzzing with anxiety.

Peter drove off the end of the Alaska Marine Highway into Bellingham, wishing he'd never left Juneau.

6

PARKER COLLEGE, EAST LOT

Parker College is surrounded by residential neighborhoods on the outskirts of Portland. It's hard to find with good directions and familiarity with the city. Peter had neither. He gave himself thirty minutes to travel the seven miles from his apartment.

Among the sparse information shared in his new-employee packet was a single-sided 8.5x11–inch sheet explaining the healthcare and dental options, but there were three separate communications regarding parking on campus. One explained how to get a parking permit and registration sticker—neither were required, but "registration claimed many privileges," though none were enumerated. The second sheet was a full-color tri-fold brochure encouraging carpooling and alternative modes of commuting. The third and most forcefully worded communique included a map identifying the three main parking lots, and the appropriate use for each. The West Lot was primarily for campus guests. The North Lot was for staff members, and the East Lot was for faculty and students and was not to be used by staff members at any time and without exception.

By the time Peter found campus, he was so confused he couldn't tell east from a slice of Key lime pie. As he wandered onto the grounds searching for his office building, he noticed his shadow stretching out before him. *Oh no, I ignored the warnings against parking in the evil East Lot*, thought Peter. *Don't look back, or you'll turn to a pillar of salt.*

* * *

Pausing before carefully pulling on the brass doorknob of the public affairs office, Peter thought, *I'm here because I believe in the power of education. Education breeds confidence. Confidence breeds hope. Hope breeds peace.* He wasn't much for positive affirmations, but just as there are no atheists in a foxhole, there are no Stephen Covey skeptics in a shithole.

As Peter entered the room, he found the reception desk vacant. He walked around an Empire bookshelf that had legs adorned by carved roses which rested atop metal animal feet that dug their claws into the carpet. It was the most ornate piece of furniture Peter had seen outside of a Greek Orthodox Church. It was in sharp contrast to the putty-colored state surplus desk and file cabinets that furnished his office in Juneau. Hoping for a friendly word or gesture, Peter crept around the monstrosity to where a receptionist would sit. The main office housed four cubicles, two on each side of the room with desks facing windowless walls that were separated by six-foot-tall partitions. The interior design seemed intended to isolate and punish the employees. Nobody turned to greet him. Peter walked toward the two offices that were opposite the main entrance. The plaque above one door read, "Steven Collins." *It's in writing; it must be true*, Peter thought as he replayed his conversation with Collins from the day before. Worry.

Peter made it to Collins' office without being greeted. He poked his head through the door and knocked. Collins looked up, smiling, springing from his chair. His welcome was as stiff and self-conscious as a failed community theater audition, which gave Peter hope that Collins was acting, and Rhea would pop out from hiding, shouting, "Got you!" She did not. Collins turned Peter around and walked him back into the main office.

"Everyone! Help me welcome Peter Cook!" Collins put his hand on Peter's shoulder. "Peter, take a few minutes and say hello to everyone. I'll let Angela, our publications coordinator, do the honors. She replaced Alice. One must have an A-name to do that job, evidently," he finished with a fake laugh and a mechanical doubling over. Then he pointed to the office next to his, which had Peter's name above it. "That's your office. And, oh, we're also looking for a new receptionist. Come see me right away—as soon as you're done."

The staff exchanged uncomfortable looks as Collins went back to his office. Peter shook hands with Angela, who seemed to be weighing his mettle as she leaned in and whispered, "and you must be the a-hole who accepted this job." Peter laughed, because it seemed like a better option than crying.

"Did he say you were new? We met during my interview," Peter said in a hushed voice.

"No, he didn't say I was new. He said I replaced Alice. That was more than three years ago," Angela smiled dryly. "He doesn't have many jokes, so they get recycled—a lot. He also has no idea what I do. I'm pretty sure that's his mnemonic device for remembering my title."

"Well. That's—weird," said Peter.

"Buckle up, bucko," said Angela putting on a cheesy smile and giving Peter an attaboy punch to the shoulder. "It only gets weirder." It was the start of day one, but coming to Parker already felt like a disastrous mistake. Finding a potential comrade in Angela, however, was a bonus. He finished his hellos and headed back to Collins' office.

Feeling slightly more confident after making a new friend, Peter went to find out if he still had a job. Collins swiveled his chair to face an empty seat, he patted the cushion where he wanted Peter to sit. He sat. "Two things: one, don't ever talk to me like you did yesterday, again, on the phone, or anywhere else. And two, I saw you walking in from the East Lot this morning. That lot is forbidden to staff. It is reserved for students and faculty."

The few life-lessons Peter remembered from his father were all sports metaphors about protecting your turf. His job was his turf now, and he could not let Collins brush him back from the plate. "Look, I took this job to work with Rhea Smith and Loch. The only thing I know about you is that you're not Rhea. There's something going on here, and they clearly don't think you're the one to handle it. We can get along or not. That's up to you, but understand this: you need me!" said Peter as he glared.

"I have Alistair's full confidence," Steven snapped back.

"No. You don't. You tried to reach me fifteen times over three days," Peter countered. "Whatever Goodwin might feel for you, it's not confidence."

"Staff members are not to park in the East Lot for any reason, and without exception. That lot is reserved for faculty and students."

"Have they not told you what's going on?"

Collins' shifted gears slowly. He wasn't sure how to handle conflict.

"There was a homeless man found dead on campus. He died of a drug overdose," Collins paused for a big reaction, which he did not get.

"When was he found?"

"Four days ago, maybe five now."

"So, are we worried that he got the drugs on campus?"

"What are you suggesting?!?" Collins snapped.

"Well, why else would we be worried—unless there's some reason to suspect foul play or negligence by the college. I could be missing something, but I can't imagine what." Peter raised his eyebrows, frowned, and shrugged one shoulder.

"Alistair said to come up as soon as you got settled. We should head to his office now." Collins was not willing to concede anything until he saw how Goodwin responded.

* * *

Goodwin's office was in the president's suite on the east end of the administrative building, one floor above public affairs. Collins and Peter were ushered from the outer office by Goodwin's assistant to sit at the conference table while

Goodwin finished typing an email. The two went completely ignored. They sat like church mice. Forced to choose, Peter preferred the authenticity of Goodwin's rudeness to Collins' synthetic pleasantries. After several minutes of pauses and taps on his keyboard, Goodwin finally turned his chair toward his visitors and stared into the empty space between them. Peter smiled politely as he thought he should. Goodwin responded by returning his attention to his computer.

"Shall we come back?" Peter asked.

Without looking from his screen, Goodwin asked if Peter had parked in the East Lot.

Peter held onto the 3 percent chance that this was the most elaborate practical joke ever played and scanned the room for places where Rhea might be hiding. Then he was told for the second time that morning that the East Lot is for faculty and students. No exceptions. The North Lot is where staff park, and he was told to move his car when the meeting was over.

"Did Steven fill you in on our situation?"

"He told me about the houseless man." Peter was more comfortable as the conversation got towed out of the East Lot.

"The *dead* homeless man." Goodwin paused briefly on the word *dead*. Peter wondered if the emphasis was going to lead to more information. It did not. "I would like us to be prepared if the press inquires about his death." Goodwin sat forward in his chair.

"Absolutely! But I'm just not certain what we're preparing for, exactly." Goodwin stiffened with frustration at this question, rubbed his eyes, and let out a long breath—but again, he said nothing. "I'm just wondering if there's something I should know, is what I'm trying to say. I feel like I would need to know more to prepare myself." Still no acknowledgment from Goodwin. Peter took a beat to refine his statement further. "I would need to know what we're afraid of."

"Why do you say that?" Goodwin look at Peter like he'd asked for the PIN to his bankcard.

Really? Peter had a bias for journalists, believing they were a little quicker than the average bear at connecting dots, but the combination of Goodwin and Collins made him wonder if college administrators belonged to a subspecies of extra slow bears, admin-a-sloths, perhaps. It was tragic that somebody had died on campus, but there was no news value to the details as they were being shared with Peter, especially not several days after the body was found. They were either omitting a major piece of information or they were completely overreacting. "If there's something I should know, it would be better to hear it from you rather than being surprised by a reporter. That way I could be prepared for how to frame our answer—"

Goodwin inhaled melodramatically, rubbed his eyes again, and swiveled his chair toward his computer. He paused before tilting his head and looking at the ceiling. He stiffened his back until his ass lifted from his seat. His body was rigid as he slid his hand into his pants' pocket. *Pop, pop,* went the cap of his Burt's Bees lip balm tin. He pulled the small, round, yellow container from his pocket and twirled it between his thumb and index finger. Goodwin's world seemed to consist of his thoughts and that tin—nothing else. It went on for so long that Peter wondered if Goodwin thought the tin made him invisible; it was part magical orb and part comfort blankie. Peter was mesmerized. Watching Goodwin make decisions was like watching an exotic bird perform a mating ritual. He wanted to be more amused by the odd display, but this was his life now, and he was disheartened. *He's either inventing an alternative story or he has no idea what's important for me to know.*

Goodwin swiveled back. "Steven, would you excuse us please?" Collins left the room. Goodwin became instantly hospitable. The change was drastic, as if Peter had revealed the password to Goodwin's secret society. "I realize I haven't even welcomed you. Please, forgive me. This *situation* has absorbed all my attention," said Goodwin. "Can I offer you anything: coffee, tea, water?"

"No, thank you." *Hard sell is coming.* "I'm fine."

"You know, Peter, Parker College has a dreadful reputation among certain members of the press." Peter began to interrupt but was quieted by a slight hand gesture. Goodwin stood from his desk and put the yellow tin back in his pocket as he walked past Peter toward the coffee pot on the credenza. He filled a Parker College logo mug, held four sugar packets by their edges, shook them with a flick of his wrist, tore off all the ends at once, and dumped them into his coffee. "Naturally, this reputation is a myth, but like most myths, its origin contains a modicum of truth. In other words, I'm not trying to hide the fact that Parker College has struggled in the past to curb the use of drugs on campus. That's been well documented. I'm just concerned that the college's progress in this area will be overshadowed," Peter watched Goodwin stir the sugar into his coffee without allowing the spoon to touch the sides of the mug, and he waited in vain for the informational part of the statement.

"By what?" Peter asked. Goodwin tasted his coffee as he looked to Peter with a puzzled expression, then reached for a fifth sugar. "You said the college's progress may be overshadowed.

Overshadowed by what?" continued Peter. "What are we afraid
the press will find out?"

Goodwin's demeanor took another sharp turn. Subordinates
do not ask questions. They take orders and provide answers.
"This institution means a lot to my family, and it means a lot
to me," he said, marching back to his desk. "We need to be
prepared." He sat. "Understood?"

Peter did not understand. He was just as confused as when
he was sitting on the dock. *Dreadful reputation for drugs, overdose on campus, be prepared. Is it students, gangs, the mob, are the
security guards selling drugs; is it just a safe place for users, have
students overdosed?* he wondered. "I'll do everything I can," Peter
said as he straightened his back, hoping that sitting taller would
make him more reassuring—less dispensable.

Goodwin swiveled his chair until he faced his computer,
then began typing. Peter wasn't certain if he should leave. He
stood to see if it would provoke some reaction. It didn't. He
walked to the door. Feeling compelled to say something reassuring but having no clue what it should be, Peter said, "Mr.
Goodwin, you hired me to protect the college's reputation. I
intend to do that."

Goodwin turned his head, his glance not quite reaching
Peter before he looked down at the keyboard again. He took
another deep breath and stiffened his back; Peter waited for the
words he assumed it would fuel, but there was only an exaggerated exhale as Goodwin raised his gaze to the computer screen.

* * *

Peter went back to his office, shut the door, and called Tessa to
share the college's *big secret*. He told her the top brass seemed

more concerned with where he parked than with the death of the houseless person—and they were very concerned about the death of houseless person—only nobody seemed to know why. Glad he still had a job, Tessa provided no comfort, telling him to play along and to go move his car.

7

THE HILLSIDE APARTMENTS,
PORTLAND, OREGON

Blythe and Ben were doing their homework at the dining room table when Peter got home. Being the new kids from Alaska made them celebrities in their sixth- and fourth-grade classrooms. Guess What Someone Asked Me? was the kids' favorite new game to play with Peter. They loved sharing the odd or antiquated myths their classmates believed about Alaska. Blythe jumped from her chair and found a path through the clutter of useful things to hug her dad. She maneuvered around stacked boxes, unassembled bed frames, and furniture stacked with more boxes. Seeing his kids and hugging his daughter was the best part of his day.

"Daddy! Mom's getting Taco Bell," Blythe said with the excitement of trying something new and exotic. McDonalds and Subway were the only fast-food chains in Juneau, and the kids were looking forward to trying all the advertised delights that carried the disclaimer *may not be available in Alaska and Hawaii.* "She said it's too messy in here to cook dinner." Then Blythe's eyes lit up, and Peter knew it was time for her to share the day's busted myth. A boy in her class was surprised that Juneau had electricity, which caused her to ask if he thought she moved from a different century.

"A kid asked me what kind of money we used," Ben added.

"Did you tell them we traded in beaver pelts and whale oil?" Peter chuckled and added, "Well, you guys be good ambassadors, okay? Don't make fun of the other kids for not knowing about the country's largest and most awesome state," Peter winked as the apartment door opened.

"Tacos!" Blythe called out as Tessa entered with fast-food bags. Blythe quickly cleared the table to make way for the new world delicacy. Rather than saying hello, Tessa immediately complained about the state of the apartment. Passively avoiding his passive cue to offer help organizing, Peter took the bags of fast food from Tessa and carried them to the table. The family was learning that small-box living was the same amount of stress compressed into a smaller space. Tessa was feeling the weight of disappointment, but Peter didn't have a lot of sympathy for her plight. Engaging with her inability to organize the Tao Te Ching's Ten Thousand things felt like a task best reserved for another day. Tessa got plates and glasses from the cupboard. Peter got milk from the refrigerator. The parents put on happy faces for the children and got through another meal.

* * *

The kids were bathed and tucked in their beds. Peter waited at the table for Tessa to finish her nighttime routine before discussing "something important." Since the couch was not deemed necessary, the table was the only place where people could sit close enough to use their indoor voices. Peter looked at his watch like he was keeping time by the movement of a retreating glacier. The couple had been drifting apart for a while, but he still loved her. Peter sank into dread wondering how Tessa's important announcement might upend their "new life." Shiny faced and refreshed from having scrubbed and massaged with regenerative anti-aging potions, Tessa looked beautiful. Peter wished she could see herself as he saw her. Sitting in the chair next to him, she reached for his hand. That was different. He was pale with worry.

"Peter, I've been seeing someone," she revealed before catching herself at the sight of Peter's bulging eyes. "I've been seeing a psychiatrist."

"Jesus Fucking H. Christ on a popsicle stick, Tess." He waited for his heart to start beating again. "What about?"

"Gardening tips," she joked, with an *isn't it obvious* laugh. "You know, about how unhappy I've been, about our marriage, about all sorts of things." She was oddly relaxed and conversational. The feeling wasn't new. Tessa was always trying to tilt the world in a direction that would cause happiness to fall her way, and Peter was often an adoring and willing participant. Contorting their world to live in Juneau, he'd hoped, would bring her a deluge of joy. It never did, but Peter fell in love with the place, which caused Tessa to treat it like a mistress. She blamed the distance in their marriage on Juneau and convinced herself that leaving would help bring them back together. She was wrong, of course. Cheating, even with a municipality, is usually a symptom and not the problem. Conversely, Tessa didn't see the extent to which her jealousy was deepening the divide. By the time Peter accepted the job at Parker College, he was more in love with Juneau than he was with his wife. The wilderness was unforgiving, but at least it was consistent in its expectations. The forest and ocean brought him the kind of peace that eluded him everywhere else.

Peter was only half listening as he fully braced for the D-word. He wouldn't blame her for wanting to leave. He had built a wall that sealed her off and he didn't know how to take it down, get past it, or move around it. They weren't connected anymore. Peter wasn't feeling very hopeful, but he wanted to make it better. They both wanted that. It felt like a last chance.

"Where do we go from here?" Peter asked.

"Peter, I love you, and you're a great father, but I can't deal with you retreating every time I want to talk about our relationship or how you're feeling." She spoke with the confidence of someone who'd made up her mind. There was no tenderness in her voice, no wishing, only resolve. "You have to commit to reconnecting."

Yearning to jump over the railing of the *Columbia* into the frigid waters of the Inside Passage had fundamentally changed Peter. It was a wakeup call. He never wanted to feel that pain again, afraid the next time it happened he wouldn't be able to resist the urge to end his life. It was triggering to remember the moment he decided to jump. Tingling began in the back of his head. He tried to tell her about the episode on the boat, but he didn't know where to begin. His mind was so scattered that trying to follow a thought was like searching for a melody in the hum of a white noise machine. "I don't mean to shut you out, Tess. I can't do it on my own," was all he managed.

Tessa could see that Peter was lost between worlds she didn't know or understand. He had never talked about his panic attacks, fearing that if she knew how severe they were, she might take the kids and leave.

"I need to know that you're serious about doing something this time," she continued. "Dr. Franklin, the psychiatrist, *the guy I've been seeing,* recommended someone he thought would be good for you." The longing returned to her voice. "He thought you'd do well with someone whose approach is based in Eastern philosophy, but who isn't all mystic new-agey," she said with a smile.

"Is there a directory of Eastern philosophy–based non-mystic-new-agey types?" He was hoping she'd laugh. He got a small one.

"It's who he sees." She became more hopeful. "Will you go? If I make the appointment, will you see him?"

"I will."

Tessa hugged Peter. Comforted him. She was 80 percent hopeful and 20 percent skeptical that he'd see it through.

8

DAY TWO

PARKER COLLEGE

Finding the North Lot on his first try felt like a major victory. Staff parking was a five-minute walk to the nearest administrative building from the back side of campus. Servants' entrance. Commuting from his apartment brought him through an industrial zone: freight yards, bus depots, and warehouses. It was an area through which commodities moved, but nothing was created. It was depressing. Adding to the doom-and-gloom parade, NPR offered only stories of the Fed's timid actions to curb global financial concerns, the volatile stock market, and signs of weakening credit markets. The dominos were being set for a worldwide economic collapse. Not a good time to be job hunting.

By contrast, his morning drive in Juneau had followed along

the Gastineau Channel. He'd often see seals and occasionally orcas. The drive brought him by waterfalls and views of Lynn Canal and the Chilkat Mountain Range. The *Daily*'s parking lot overlooked the Salmon Hatchery, where he'd see countless spawning salmon that in turn attracted salmon sharks, seals, fishing enthusiasts, and tourists. He never tired of it.

Peter and his new work friend Angela arrived at the same time to the duly sanctioned lot. Peter waved to her as he got out of his Subaru. She ran to him like a grade-schooler spotting a friend during recess. Goofy. Adorable.

"I wasn't sure you'd come back!" She laughed. "And you waved to me! It's almost like we're humans. No one here has ever treated me so well! I'll miss these moments after they curb stomp your humanity and replace it with the life of the mind!"

Confused by the punchline, he ignored it, and looked around to make sure there was no one else within earshot before responding. "You make this place sound like a Russian Gulag, except for the you-chose-to-come-back part," Peter said without breaking stride.

"Yeah, I don't know; they get free potatoes in gulags," she shrugged. "We should strike for that. What do we want? Free potatoes! When do we want them? Now!" Angela playfully shouted, and then asked him about Alaska.

Peter cleared his throat to make a path for his playful announcer's voice: "Alaska became our nation's largest state when it was voted into the Union in 1959. Many Alaskans loathed the end of prostitution and gambling, and the addition of all types of regulation, particularly environmental. The state is abundant in natural resources, such as crab, salmon, oil, and minerals like gold, silver, and copper. Its people are independent and believe their politicians should be as dumb as the minerals they pull from the earth."

Angela enjoyed Peter's infomercial. The two were becoming fast friends, but Peter interrupted their bonding session because he was curious to know what happened to Rhea. He hoped to find some clue about her disappearance before getting within earshot of Collins. Anxious to know if her sudden departure had some connection to the secrecy surrounding William James' death, he said, "So, I really wanted to ask you. . ."

"I do have a boyfriend," Angela interrupted," but I'd totally cheat on him with you. What? That's not what you were going to ask? *Awkward.* Just kidding, what?"

Blushing through the entire spectrum of the Pantone color chart before settling back on Irish Ruddy White, Peter asked about Rhea. Angela assumed the countenance of a veterinarian having to break the bad news about his old sick dog. Rhea was the sixth director fired in the past eight years. Most of the others were sacked for trying to maneuver around Goodwin's incompetence or saying something flippant to him, near him, or while in the presence of Collins. But the cause of Rhea's dismissal, she told him, was a mystery to her.

"Six directors in eight years! And HR is just cool with that?" Peter was dumbfounded.

"You must know that Alistair Goodwin is a Goodwin of the Goodwin Pharmaceuticals Goodwins. Right? So yes, when your family gives tens of millions to the endowment, you get to act with impunity, which he does. He could use one of us as a sex doll and keep us imprisoned in a box under his desk, and we'd get punished for not keeping the box clean." She waited for Peter to stop laughing, which took a while. "I'm pretty sure that how's Collins got the job, by the way. He keeps a clean box!"

They laughed hard enough to attract the attention of others, which caused Angela to warn that if Collins heard them, he'd go straight to Goodwin, and they would both be fired. Miming locking her lips with a key, Angela ended the conversation as they got near the building. As they came inside, Goodwin was walking toward them on his way to the stairwell. Peter smiled and waved. Goodwin looked directly through them, showing no reaction as he turned and headed up the stairs.

"Is that normal, or should we be worried?" Peter asked nervously.

"You're gonna want to adjust your definition of normal, but yeah, that's Goodwin's normal," she said, stepping outside of her deadpan delivery so Peter would know she was being serious. "At Parker College, it's always advisable for the staff to be worried."

9

PRESIDENT CHARLES LOCH

Waiting on hold with the computer helpdesk to authenticate the myriad passwords that would grant him access to his work software felt a lot like being trapped in a box under a desk. Collins broke the monotony by announcing like a town crier in a public square that he and Peter were needed in the president's office. Such declarations were intended to boost Collins' stature among his staff. It was a failing strategy. Peter was frustrated that the fifteen minutes spent holding for a technician were for naught, but he was excited to finally be meeting President Charles Loch.

Butterflies tickled his stomach, and his palms began to sweat. Trying to keep from trembling, Peter told himself that *he's not the president of the United States. He's the president of the college.* Which reminded him of advice he got while working as a cub reporter covering the 1996 Democratic Primary in New Hampshire. *Keep your guard up. Politicians are regular people, they're just better at bullshitting than everyone else.*

* * *

Conversation stopped as Peter and Collins entered the president's office, which looked like it was modeled after the movie set for *Goodbye, Mr. Chips,* or *Dead Poets Society.* Darkly stained wood, floor-to-ceiling bookshelves, and the enormous paned windows gave off a vibe just shy of parody. Standing to greet Peter was the 1970s stereotype of a college president: male, WASPy, fit but not athletic, slightly bookish, and tall enough to survey a crowd to find the heavy donors without being obvious. Loch had strong symmetrical features beneath a flourishing head of red hair and bright eyes that projected confidence through his trademark circular tortoise shell glasses. "Charles Loch." His voice put Peter instantly at ease. "I'm the guy you're here to clean up after. Welcome. It's nice to finally meet you."

Wanting to make an impression, Peter told Loch they shook hands once before in a Dunkin' Donuts' parking lot during a campaign stop when Loch was running for mayor of Boston. There was a moment of reminiscing, but the business at hand didn't allow the conversation to linger. During introductions, Vice President Rosen tilted his head slightly and gave Peter a side-eyed glance accompanied by a barely perceptible clinched cheek. It was a familiar look. *The stench of poverty lingers. I'll never be totally clean of it,* thought Peter.

From the moment his aunt brought him across the tracks from Brighton to Milton, Peter felt like a gatecrasher into the world of the privileged. He wasn't like the Milton kids. The most obvious giveaway was his nearly impenetrable Boston accent. Deciphering his sentences was like trying to read *Ulysses* through a bowl of New England clam chowder. The sting he felt as a kid created a chip on his shoulder as an adult. No matter how far Peter climbed from being a poor Boston kid, nor how articulate or accomplished he became, he would always feel like an outsider in certain circles. His value to the college depended on earning the trust of the decision makers. Rosen's barely perceptible expression went unnoticed by the others but glowed like a warning flare to Peter. He needed to be sharp. Peter and Rosen shook hands and took their seats.

"The college is being sued." Loch dove right in. "A former security guard is saying we covered up a drug operation in the dorms and is accusing us of forcing him out for not colluding in our coverup. Peter, what questions do you have?" Loch waited.

Peter tried to gauge the others' reactions. He was in unfamiliar territory and wondered how direct he could be with the president. If he could be fired for laughing at a joke, what would happen if he got this wrong? He looked to Goodwin for a cue—some subtle change of body language, widening of his eyes, flaring of his nostrils, a slight gesture of warning. Nothing. Baptism by fire. *Six directors fired in eight years* bounced around Peter's head.

"Don't look at them." Loch didn't turn from Peter. "I asked you."

Loch's directness could make people feel uneasy. It made Peter trust him. "Is there any truth to the allegations?" Peter's nerves caused his intensity to be a bit high and put too fine a point on his question. Goodwin tensed and reached into his pocket for his beeswax tin.

"That is the obvious question, isn't it? Funny you're the first to ask," Loch nodded his approval to Peter. "No. The whole thing is manufactured. He wasn't even fired. The allegations are outrageous, drugs and copious paraphernalia, blood and gore. I can't imagine the absurdity of the claims is going to matter much, however, to certain press outlets."

"If he wasn't fired, does he even have a case?" asked Rosen. "Couldn't we just get it dismissed?"

"The suit accuses us of constructive discharge, which is a claim that we forced him out by making his work life intolerable. Given that, it would be very difficult for us to get it dismissed before discovery. The press will be all over it by then."

Peter asked for a copy of the complaint, which caused Goodwin to bristle and reject the idea—as if Peter's reading it would cause it all to be true. "He's being proactive," said Loch wryly. "It's a public document, Alistair. Any reporter who calls Peter will have it. It makes sense for him to have it as well." Returning his attention to Peter, Loch asked, "How will this be covered by the press?"

"They'll report on the allegations, just as his lawyer assumes they will," said Peter. "They'll be careful not to call them facts, but they'll also be careful to choose the most eyepopping charges."

"Which is why the suit reads like a '50s crime novel." Loch continued, picking up the complaint and reading aloud. "'He told me to clean the blood from the walls and kitchen floor. I asked him if we were going to call the cops. He turned to me slowly and said,' and I'm reading verbatim now, 'around here, we take care of things ourselves. That's the Parker College way.' So, Peter, did you know you were coming to work in a Mickey Spillane novel?"

It was a relief to be working alongside Loch instead of through Goodwin. It felt like his first breath after being held underwater. Peter was trying to hide his relief from Goodwin, *six directors in eight years*, but he was almost giddy.

"Alright, what are we going to say to the press?" Loch changed gears.

"Oh." He caught Peter off guard. "The allegations in this lawsuit are baseless, and we plan to address them in court, *if we do*. The college has no further comment," Peter looked for Loch's approval.

"The college is being accused of covering up a crime," said Loch continuing to play the role of reporter. "That's a very serious allegation." Goodwin became increasingly uneasy as the conversation went on. Goodwin's discomfort was troubling to Peter, but not as troubling as Collins' wolfish grin.

"Those accusations are coming from a former employee who is suing the college for a lot of money. They are not coming from law enforcement," Peter said confidently.

"So, are you saying that Mr. Noon is inventing these accusations to extort money from the college?" Loch made a got-you face.

"I don't care to speculate on motive. I was simply pointing out that the allegations were not coming from law enforcement." Peter was enjoying the repartee.

"Don't you think the public deserves to know the truth?" Loch turned aggressive.

"I do. We'll let the truth come out in court, and I'll look forward to reading your article exonerating us when it does. But for now, you're asking me to speculate on the motives of someone who's suing the college, someone I've never met. I'm not going to do that. The college's stance is that this lawsuit is baseless, and we plan to fight it. That's really all we have to say. If that changes, I'll be sure to give you a call," Peter turned his glance from Loch. "Thank you."

"But . . ."

"Thank you."

"This guy's good," Loch said to the gallery. Rosen smiled cautiously. Goodwin fidgeted, and Collins glared. "Good job, but let's not commit ourselves to going to court. Let's just say, the allegations in this lawsuit are baseless and the college has no further comment. Everything else was spot on."

"I've not had a chance to read the complaint closely," said Rosen. "Are we certain that all the allegations are baseless? His direct supervisors are gone, as is most of the department, so certainly it's not beyond the realm of possibility that one of them applied, what was the phrase, constructive pressure?"

"The legal phraseology is constructive discharge or constructive dismissal," said Loch, quickly traveling in and out of contemplation. "But sure, we don't know what the precise claim is. We don't know if they made him come in on his day off or if they made him juggle fire, but whatever the claim is, it would have to be pretty extreme, and they would have to demonstrate proof. I don't know, I feel comfortable in calling the suit baseless."

"He's accusing us of covering up a crime," said Goodwin.

"Right, but that's not the legal crux of his argument. There's no legal obligation to report a crime that takes place on private property," said Loch. "He's saying that's what motivated the behavior of his supervisors to make his work life intolerable— our only legal liability is the accusation that we forced him to quit. Everything else is window dressing to get us to settle quickly." Being a Georgetown Law graduate, Loch reveled in the opportunity to explain the origins of search and seizure laws, and protections against self-incrimination, beginning his dissertation with the Magna Carta. He was shocked at how little his subordinates knew about this part of the law. He asked Peter if he knew about the right against self-incrimination.

"I plead the Fifth," Peter said hoping to be funny, not flippant. Loch was amused and ended the meeting.

Everyone stood from the table. There is a hierarchical coordination/competition in how staff members leave the president's office. Generally, the highest-ranking member leaves last, unless that person wants to show disapproval for something that happened during the meeting, then they would leave first. When staff members of equal rank are confronted with the dilemma of who exits first, it generally defaults to seniority. No matter how it plays out, it's always preferable to leave last. It signifies to the others that you are nearest to the Alpha. Collins was closest to the door but waited for Peter to catch up and gestured politely for him to exit. Loch was behind his desk but not yet sitting.

"Dunkin' Donuts," Loch said with good cheer. "God, we ran a good campaign. It still stings to think about that election night. I can't believe you remembered meeting me. What were you, ten years old?"

"More like seven or eight, actually. My father was a big supporter. He was a union guy," said Peter, creating a logjam in the doorway. "We had a yard sign, "Loch for Mayor," in blue and green. In fact, I think I may still have a campaign button laying around." Peter knew exactly where the button was.

"I can't believe I lost with such a clever slogan."

"I would have voted for you if I was old enough," Peter said, meaning it.

"Early and often, I hope," said Loch.

Collins and Rosen slid through the door gingerly. Goodwin waited. He would have stood there until his feet bled, rather than let Peter leave the office last.

"Did you need me for something, Alistair?" asked Loch without needing an answer. Goodwin disapproved of fraternizing between castes. "I'm going to get to know Peter here a little bit," said Loch. "I was on the road during his interview, so—"

Loch asked Goodwin to shut the door behind him and waited until he heard footsteps walking away before he spoke again. "I just wanted to let you know that if this thing breaks badly, I am available to you at any time. You don't need permission from anyone else to come to me. Understood?" Loch looked deeply for a spark of understanding, which he got along with a bit of confusion. "But, why would it break badly if the case is baseless? I know," Loch continued. "His supervisors were all fired for cause. It was a real shitshow here for a while and we're still dealing with the fallout. It was one of the first things I had to address as president. It's possible that things went on that I don't know about. Not this," he said, pushing the lawsuit on his desk.

"I get it," said Peter. Normal behavior seemed out of place. For the first time since the ferry docked in Bellingham, Peter felt like he was on the proper side of the looking glass. He was helping to solve problems. He took comfort in the trust Loch placed in him. If there was no other reason to stay at Parker, he could believe in fighting for Loch, just like his father had all those years ago. "Thanks for that," Peter said as he opened the door. "It means a lot."

10

HOW DO YOU EAT
AN ELEPHANT?

Crossing the street to his new therapist's office, a converted four square in a recently gentrified, upwardly trending neighborhood, Peter imagined Dr. Redmon as an old hippie who'd stumbled into his Buddhist practice at a Berkeley commune while tripping on acid and listening to the *Concert for Bangladesh* album. Hinting that the stereotype might be apt were the Tibetan prayer flags hanging from the porch fascia, and the sage vaporizing from the good juju machine on the waiting room coffee table. The combination of trendy and woo-woo would have sent Peter back to his car if he hadn't promised Tessa that he'd gut it out.

Practicing Zen and living in harmony with Buddhist

philosophy were virtues Peter had been attempting to incorporate into his life, with varying degrees of success, since he was in his twenties. He saw it as an ultra-practical path. Zen was old school, not new age, and he was leery of anyone who tried to mystify it. Peter's meditation practice was about making peace with uncertainty; he needed to get better at that. The combination of Buddhist practice and therapy seemed like a winning one, but he was dubious they could be combined successfully.

Breathing vaporized sage, Peter waited for a groovy, paunchy, poncho-wearing, pony-tailed artifact of the man's movement who would try to sell him on a self-centered Americanized Boomer-version of Buddhism. The man who greeted him was a stereotype, but not the one he imagined. Redmon looked like he'd stepped out of a 1970s Alan Alda movie that was filmed in Northern New England during the Autumnal Equinox. He was short, thin, balding, and bespectacled. He wore layers of earth-toned wool, tweed, and flannel. For a frail looking man, he moved quickly and purposefully. His eyes were clear and focused. His gaze was piercing. Shaking his hand felt like holding an assemblage of balsa sticks that were loosely wrapped in wax paper. Peter was careful not to grip too firmly.

"Peter?" asked Redmon.

Peter nodded affirmatively and they walked into Redmon's office without another word between them. The office was furnished spartanly, a leather chair, a leather couch, a coffee table, and a discreetly placed copy of Redmon's unfortunately titled book, *A Path through Pain*. They sat. On the coffee table between them was a manila folder with Peter's name handwritten on the tab; it contained the answers to a questionnaire Peter had spent several hours completing online. Question topics ranged from educational and health background to political, social, and religious beliefs. Redmon made no reference to it.

As the session began, Peter was standoffish. He was testing Redmon, but the doctor saw through it. He put up with it for a few minutes before calling bullshit. "For therapy to work, at some point, you need to answer my questions directly," said Redmon in an even tone that was accompanied by an unforgiving stare. "Its effectiveness generally correlates with a patient's openness. Avoidance isn't helpful, and it's not something I tolerate for very long." Peter's concerns about joining a two-man drum circle were alleviated, but he wasn't sure he liked this alternative better. Peter apologized and went on to explain the anxiety he felt when he was away from his children. He admitted that his panic attacks were getting worse and that his biggest fear was falling so deeply into anxiety that he wouldn't be able to find his way back. Peter could feel the back of his head tingling as he exposed his worst fears.

"Stay in the moment, Peter. Be more aware of your surroundings. How so?" asked Redmon. "What triggers your attacks?"

"Can't all fears be boiled down to a fear of death?" Peter began to speak faster. "Fear of flying, fear of snakes, aren't they all implicit fears of death?"

"What are *your* triggers, Peter?" His eyes focused more intensely.

Questions and answers continued in rapid fire: question, deflection, question, rationalization. Redmon continued to toss aside Peter's defenses like a black belt in therapy as he zeroed in on Peter's vulnerabilities. As they veered off the path of his rationalizations, Peter's posture changed with the flow of the conversation until he was slumped and seemed lost. Redmon softened his approach and asked Peter to describe how he was feeling.

"Like I was shrinking, like maybe I wanted to get smaller," said Peter, his voice thin and uncertain.

"Like you were a child? Stay in the moment and know that feeling is not you, but rather it belongs to some other time and place. You're holding it, but it doesn't belong to you. It will be important to remember that. *It's not you. It's not yours to hold.* Okay? See these feelings from a distance now." Redmon leaned forward in his chair. "Why did you want to get smaller?"

"I don't know."

"You said all fears are implicit fears of death," said Redmon. "How does that fit?"

"I didn't know what else to say," Peter chuckled. "I thought it was clever."

"You didn't know what to say," Redmon kept the conversation moving quickly. "So, why do you think you chose to talk about death? I don't think it was a coincidence. You could have said anything, but you chose to talk about unarticulated fears of death."

Peter started to well up. He crossed his legs and pulled his shoulders in toward his ears. He dropped his chin to his chest. His nose began to run slightly. A tear rolled onto his cheek and hung for a moment before falling on the leather couch. It made a surprisingly loud thump against the taut leather. Peter's first thought was that his tear would leave a stain. *Long after I'm gone that stain will be there, and no one will remember where it came from.* He wiped it away with his thumb. Redmon was quiet. The two sat in silence for a few moments.

"I'm afraid for my children. Ben's the same age as I was when my parents died."

"Tell me more," Redmon said softly.

"Sometimes the depression hurts so bad—" Peter felt like he was about to lose control. He didn't want to cry. One tear was enough.

"Depression; your son being the same age as you were when your parents died; feeling anxiety when you're away from your children; loss of control," said Redmon. "How are these connected?"

"Yeah, I get it," said Peter. With the force of being hit with a twelve-pound sledgehammer, Peter believed he had arrived at the conclusion that the origin of his trauma was his childhood, involved his parents, and very likely how they died. Redmon cautioned him from hanging the "mission accomplished" banner prematurely. Finding the right location is different from finding the problem, which is different still from addressing it. Peter admitted feeling dumb. "I've been avoiding dealing with this for a very long time, it's caused me tremendous anxiety over the years, and it took you about ten seconds to get me there," said Peter with a laugh.

"Talk to me about your fear."

Peter talked about growing up with his aunt. He loved her, but he always felt like a burden. He didn't remember much before living with his aunt, other than his parents had frequent shouting matches. He spent a lot of time alone. He rode his bike a lot. He loved his bike. He talked about wanting to be a strong presence for his kids. He wanted his kids to know they were safe and protected.

"Wanting to make your kids feel safe? Where do you think that comes from?" Redmon continued to volley Peter's rationalizations back at him in a way that made it obvious to Peter that they were only beginning to peel back the layers.

"I don't know," said Peter as he drifted deeper into thought. "I have this fear of them being without me, of not being able to protect them. That's what I feel like overwhelms me at times. That something will happen to them, and I won't be there to help them."

"What happened to you as a child, Peter?"

Peter began to cry much harder this time, but he didn't know why. "My aunt was good to me. She was there for me as much as she could be," Peter could only spit out the words in chunks.

"What about before that?" asked Redmon. "Before your aunt was there for you? Who was there for you?"

"I was just small," uttered Peter. "I don't really remember much before moving in with her. Why? What do you think happened?"

"I'm just asking questions. Questions that seem to follow the direction you're bringing us."

Peter slumped. His breathing was shallow, and his eyes betrayed his attempt to look calm and fearless. Inside he felt like a lost, frightened little child. Redmon eased up. They talked about Peter's meditation practice. Redmon encouraged him to sit in meditation every day. There was a caring in Redmon's voice that was absent at the beginning of the session. "This type of therapy is not for the faint of heart, and I don't agree to move forward with everyone. I pushed you hard today, much harder than is usual for a first session. No one cries during their first meeting. Frankly, it's a mark of courage. It shows me you're ready. You're going to need to confront some things that I think you've been avoiding for a very long time. It's going to be hard, and we can't do all the work in here. I'm going to need you to continue to focus on these issues during meditation with the same ferocity as you showed here today. Can you do that?"

Peter nodded. For the rest of the session, they talked about techniques he would use during meditation. They talked about how each of them had become interested in Eastern Philosophy, and they set a date for Peter's next appointment. Peter left feeling energized by optimism but emotionally drained.

Progress is exhausting, he thought.

* * *

Remembering his promise to report to Tessa if he made it through the session, Peter pulled out his flip phone as he rushed down the stairs. Her voice was intertwined with excitement and trepidation when asking how his session went.

"It was the emotional equivalent of getting my dick caught in my zipper," joked Peter as he checked for cars on his way across the street.

"Is that good? That doesn't sound good. That sounds painful."

As he stepped off the curb, Peter heard the swoosh of bike tires accelerating against the pavement and the tension of the chain in the gears. A cyclist struck Peter across the back with a forearm shiver that sent his phone into the street. The impact was followed by stars and confusion. He never saw the cyclist but gauging by the impact he expected to see the rider collapsed on the ground; he was about ten yards away, however—upright, flashing Peter his middle finger. "The bike lane is for bikes, asshole!" shouted the cyclist as he sped off.

"Nice fuckin' leotah'd!" Peter shouted, surprised by the reemergence of his Boston accent. He never understood why grown men commuting on bikes dressed like they were racing the Tour de France. Watching the cyclist speed away seemed like the ideal time to share his observation. At 6'2" and 215 pounds, Peter was sturdy, unlike his phone that was now scattered in pieces. The day Peter was reconnecting with his inner child, aka the Boston Street Kid, was the wrong day to provoke him. The cyclist seemed to understand his mistake as he brought his bike to a sprint without looking back.

Peter's phone was broken beyond repair. *Everything's coming apart,* he thought as he got in his car. *The media relations guy can't be unreachable during a lawsuit.* He started the car and rushed out of his parking spot. *Not as bad as parking in the East Lot, but still pretty bad.*

11

STD

Driving back to campus through the patchwork of gentrifying neighborhoods had Peter discombobulated. There was no continuity: vacant lots next to peep shows, across from fancy restaurants, next to quaint homes with chicken coops and a goat, next to architectural monstrosities designed to maximize every inch of buildable space. Whatever, and whomever, old Portland represented, it was disappearing and being replaced by something more efficient, more expensive, more homogeneous, and less interesting.

Once again, Peter's lack of an internal GPS brought him to the wrong side of campus, and once again, he parked in the forbidden East Lot. Jogging to his office, he pleaded with the rulers of the universe to forgive his great imprudence and offered a vague sacrifice if his sins would go unnoticed by Collins and Goodwin. He had one voicemail from a *Stumptown Weekly* reporter. During the '80s, the paper had been a shining example of investigative journalism. Its writers won boatloads of local, state, and national awards for journalistic excellence. It was a stalwart example of top-notch journalism told from a specific viewpoint—until it wasn't. By 2007, its stellar reputation had been buried in the bygone dustheap with other forgotten societal touchpoints like *Spy Magazine* and the Social Compact. The beginning of the end came in the mid '90s, when an ambitious young reporter lied about having a Deep Throat–like source inside the Oregon governor's office. He wrote a quick succession of articles exposing alleged graft and kickbacks. The stories went national, and the media lionized the young reporter, before the *Washington Post* did its own investigation and found that the stories were fiction—obvious, easily debunkable fiction. It destroyed the paper's reputation. That was back when being intentionally misleading was disqualifying for a news source.

After all the serious journalists quit, the paper found a new niche with oddball stories peppered with off-color language. To supplement for lost revenue, the *STW* started accepting classified ads for escort services, phone sex vendors, and skilled laborers whose ads were worded to narrowly circumvent the prosecutable definition of prostitution. Up until that point, the paper had been known as the *STW*, but readers began replacing that acronym with the one for sexually transmitted disease. The *STD* became the paper of choice for the young and irreverent to discover new bands, read funny horoscopes, and find movie times. Having been aware of the paper's early reputation, Peter felt a mix of emotions, but mostly consternation, upon receiving the call.

Googling the reporter's name didn't return much information. *"Vince Craven, that's a made-up name, and a bad one,* Peter thought as he typed. *Porn star name. Perfect for the STD.* Craven had only three bylines, for stories titled "Dog Park Hook Ups," "Food Cart Détente," and "Naked Cyclists Chafe PDX Popo." As Peter dialed the phone, he wondered what the headline would be for the Parker College story: *"Campus Pig Turns Rat." Oh, that's good! Maybe I should suggest it,* thought Peter as Craven answered the phone. Assuming the call was about the lawsuit, Peter anticipated it would be short. Craven admitted that after he was unable to reach Peter on his cell, he assumed he was being dodged. Peter shared the story about the cyclist who caused his phone's destruction.

"Keep Portland weird," Craven said, snickering at what seemed like an inside joke that left Peter on the outside. They chatted politely for a few minutes before Peter asked why Craven had called. It's best to let a reporter disclose why they're calling. In the one-in-a-million chance Craven didn't know about the lawsuit, Peter didn't want to be the one to tip him. "I'm doing a general story about the different approaches colleges take when dealing with drugs on their campuses. So, policy stuff," said Craven.

Peter was dubious and tried to draw out Craven's real angle. The two sparred for a few rounds, both aware of the game the other was playing. It would have been an obvious opportunity for one of them to bring up the lawsuit, but neither did. Peter was still clinging to the long odds that Craven might not know about it. The call was getting tense and going long, because Peter was too wrapped up in *winning the game.* He didn't like to lose, but neither did Craven. Finally, Peter gave an ultimatum:

"Vince, if you can't tell me what your story is about, then I can't help you, and I'm gonna hang up," Peter said loud enough to attract Angela's attention. She turned her chair toward the action and pretended to eat popcorn.

"I told you, it's about when Parker involves the police in crimes that involve drugs," Craven slipped.

"I'm not trying to be difficult, Vince, but that's not what you said," Peter adopted the tone of a scolding parent. "So, is it a general story about how colleges' drug and alcohol policies differ, or is it about what triggers police involvement at Parker College?" The back-and-forth escalated for a few more minutes before Peter told him to call back after he got his story straight. Craven never mentioned the lawsuit, and Peter wasn't inclined to help him write his story. Angela popped her head in the office door as soon as the call ended.

"Who was that?" she asked.

"My wife," Peter joked. "It was a press call."

"Do all your press calls go like that?" she asked.

"Not usually, but he was lying to me. I was trying to get him to tell me why he was really calling," said Peter. "And I had to show him I'm top dog."

"Oh! So, are you going to drive over to his office now and piss in his cubicle?"

Peter laughed and changed the subject, telling her the about the bike rider who broke his phone. "That is so Portland," said Angela. "The cyclists here are more aggressive than biker bikers. They're always punching people and kicking cars and stuff. Stories like these really don't make me want to share the road. They make me want to remove their bike seats when they're not looking. Anyway, I'll catch you tomorrow because I have something really important that I need to ask you, so don't blow me off. Okay?" said Angela in a serious tone. "It's personal, so we'll go somewhere private."

"Ooo-kay," Peter said with a tinge of worry. He drew out both syllables as if to say, you could tell me now if it's that important. Angela shook her head, smiled, winked, and left him to his work.

Am I about to be invited to have an affair? wondered Peter.

*   *   *

Protocol dictated that Peter alert Goodwin of a press call and let him decide if they should elevate the situation to the president, but Loch's counsel and common sense were compelling reasons to break the chain of command. Peter was tentative as he approached Loch's assistant, Sally, not knowing she had been instructed to let him interrupt whenever practical. It's good to be friendly and polite with the president's assistant. They know more than most people could imagine and are the gatekeeps of the president's time—at a small private college access to the president is the key to getting anything done. Peter knocked as he tentatively poked his head through the door. Loch gestured for Peter to come in.

"Shut the door," said Loch. "Keep Sally on your good side. She's got a memory like an elephant, and she knows where all the bodies are buried. So, what do we have?"

They talked through the best-case and worst-case scenarios for engaging with the *Stumptown* reporter. The language in the lawsuit was like catnip to members of the press. They weren't going to leave it alone. There was almost no upside for the college to cooperate, but the downside was likely a story accusing

Parker of hiding felonious activities and then firing everyone who wouldn't collude in the cover-up—with no counternarrative coming from the college. Since Craven had called under the pretense of doing a more general story, it gave them an opportunity to broaden the narrative to explain their drug and alcohol policies—countering the claims they didn't have any.

"Normally, I would say we should send a statement, but we can't say 'the lawsuit you didn't ask us about is baseless.' We could say we can't comment because of ongoing litigation in that area, but then we tip the suit to every other press outlet that isn't combing through court filings," warned Peter.

After a few more rounds of bad-press ping pong, they decided to invite Craven to interview Matthew Rosen, overseer of the adjudication process for the college. He was most knowledgeable about the drug-and-alcohol and enforcement policies and could speak to their strengths. If Craven pushed the conversation into the area of the lawsuit, Peter would be there to end the interview.

"Well, let's go with that," said Loch. "I don't love it, but it seems like it's probably our best option." Loch let out a big sigh, put his hands atop his head, and swiveled his chair to face his phone. He stared at the receiver like it was a Magic 8-Ball about to reveal if he should make a call or not. "We offered Noon ten grand, and Sophia thinks he's going to take it."

"Ten Grand? What, is that about two percent of what he was asking for?" Peter wasn't sure if he was more surprised at how little Noon might be willing to take, or that Parker College was willing to offer him anything.

"What would it do to the story to tell him we settled for two percent?" asked Loch.

"Kill it, I suspect. I can tell the reporter that we have nobody available until Monday. Can we accelerate Noon's deadline?" asked Peter.

"I'll have Sophia call Noon's lawyer. Get time with Matthew to work on talking points, just in case." Loch accompanied Peter to the door. He wanted to run interference if Goodwin was in the common area. Loch put his hand on Peter's shoulder as they walked, "I'm really glad you're here," he said as he opened the door. Goodwin was hovering by Sally's desk, and let his angry gaze fall on Peter. "I'll fill in Alistair, now that he's free. Thanks again for your work on this, Peter," said Loch.

12

IPHONE, A LOVE AFFAIR

The children greeted Peter from the table as he stepped onto the apartment's two square feet of linoleum tiles—the foyer. Their voices carried the joy of relief, which cut through the dense tension in the room. Nothing from Tessa, who remained slumped over her soup. The simplified life promised feelings of gratitude and fulfilment, though her hours of solitude and household labor brought only resentment. During their previous "new life" in Alaska, happiness was promised in the form of a dream job as a US Fish and Wildlife Service biologist, but the position never made her feel better than the dark and rain made her feel gloomy. Somehow, Juneau's damp unhappiness got mixed in with all the useful things and threatened to saturate the family's new "new life" in Portland.

"Daddy!" Blythe shouted, causing tomato soup to drip from the corner of her mouth and down her chin. Jumping from her chair while wiping her face with her forearm, she took advantage of a newly cleared pathway to greet Peter. She glanced back momentarily to see that dropping her spoon in the bowl had splatted a bit of soup. Tessa blotted the table with her napkin and snapped at Blythe.

Noticing the slick black box in Peter's hand from the Apple commercials, Ben shouted, "iPhone!" as if Santa had walked through the door. As Blythe arrived at Peter's feet, her open arms suddenly narrowed and moved in the direction of the box. Peter put his free arm around her and kissed the top of her head as she pulled the box from him.

"Whoa!" said Blythe. "Seriously? Cool! Sierra's mother, Sierra, from my class, her mother, she has one and she let us look at it during free time today. It was so awesome!"

"Yeah, it's almost as cool as Dad, huh?" said Peter pretending to have hurt feelings.

"It's exciting," said Blythe.

"Can we get iFart?" asked Ben, giggling.

"Benjamin, we are at the dinner table," Tessa could no longer hold her frustration. "Peter, what were you thinking? We can't afford that!"

As Dr. Redmon had suggested, Peter listened for the sound of his breath to calm himself before responding. Ignoring Tessa's condemnation for the moment, he winked at Ben as a sign that things were okay and took an exaggerated sniff. Bread seared in garlic butter. "Tomato soup and grilled cheese. My favorite." Blythe asked meekly if Peter would sit next to her while pulling his hand to aid his decision. "The college paid for the phone, Tess. And when we're not at the dinner table, we'll talk about downloading iFart."

Ben and Blythe laughed quietly. Having not listened to Peter's message that therapy went well and he'd be late because the college was buying him a new phone, Tessa was a bit sour. For at least the third time that day, Peter delighted in telling the story about his encounter with the hostile cyclist. He added a few flourishes he knew the kids would enjoy, starting with "I was attacked by a biker!"

"Like a motorcycle gang biker?" asked Ben, matching Peter's excitement.

"Ben! My God, don't believe him," said an exasperated Blythe. "Dad, tell the truth!"

"I am telling the truth. It was a guy on a ten-speed bike!"

"Like, a bicycle, biker?" asked a disappointed Ben.

"Yes," Peter said defensively.

"Did you beat him up?" asked Ben.

"No!" Peter said. "He came flying at me out of nowhere and slammed me in the back because I was walking in the bike lane to get to my car."

"You're making this up," said Blythe. "You just wanted an iPhone and so you made up this story! Did the people at your work believe you?"

"Yes, because it's true!" said Peter. "The bikers in Portland are crazy!"

"Are you sure he wasn't riding a unicorn?" questioned Blythe, her eyebrows raised.

"Yeah, even if that story's true, you need to make up a new one, or everyone's gonna make fun of you," said Ben.

Laughing with his children was the best part of his day.

Tessa redirected the conversation for the children to share their highlights from school. "It was boring," said Ben. Blythe said she got to play with an iPhone, which made Tessa angry. She sent them to bathe and read in their rooms before bed. They did as Tessa asked. Peter waited for the kids to get in their room before asking her what was wrong.

"I don't know," said Tessa, before admitting to being angry after thinking Peter hung up on her. Having nobody to talk with all day had Tessa needing to let off steam. The invitation to share was like throwing the release on a pressure cooker. "I'm feeling like I'm in this by myself. You're at work all day, and I'm left at home to worry about what's happening. Are we going to have enough money, are you going to quit your job, are you going to get fired, did we make the right move in coming here? And then on top of it all, I have to organize everything and clean and cook, drop the kids off at school and pick them up, help them with their homework—"

"What did you think being a stay-at-home parent was going to be like?" As the words were leaving his mouth, he realized they were the wrong words—possibly the very worst words. Tessa's back got rigid, and her chin jutted out. She was getting her Irish up, and all that remained was to scrap. Staring past Peter's face into his medulla oblongata, she had detached his humanity. He was simply an idea that needed quashing. This is how they fought; Peter never backed down, but this time he didn't have the energy. He wasn't being altruistic; he was just exhausted.

"We don't need to do this, Tess," said Peter. "Look, I know it isn't easy. It's not easy on anyone. It's also a little hard to hear when I feel like I'm working inside a dog's dream."

Tessa chuckled, which surprised Peter. They saw an

opening back to toward civility.

"A dog's dream?" Tessa immediately began to relax. "Okay, I'll bite. Explain before I remember why I was so angry," said Tessa with a forced smile.

"It's like Parker College exists in an alternate reality that was created by something that's familiar with human behavior but doesn't have the intellectual capacity to understand it. Things look normal. But nothing *is* normal. It's like I'm always waiting for someone to sniff my ass rather than say hello."

"Give me a different example."

"Good point. Nobody actually says hello anyway. Okay, hiring Steve Collins to replace Rhea Smith is the equivalent of giving a MacArthur Genius award in history to someone because they watched an episode of *Hogan's Heroes*. The whole thing just feels like an experimental theater project."

"Is that what you talked about in therapy today?" asked Tessa with a giggle.

"No. That was a different kind of painful. But I'm glad I went," said Peter. "The doctor was totally no-nonsense, which I liked, and we talked about my needing to meditate more regularly and what I should meditate on and how I should do it. It was good."

"So you're happy you went?" asked Tessa.

"I don't know if happy is exactly the right word, but yeah," said Peter with a sincere smile and a bit of relief in his voice. "I feel confident that I'm moving in the right direction. Thank you for encouraging me and finding Redmon. He is definitely the right therapist for me."

"That's great to hear," said Tessa. "I'll tell the guy I'm seeing."

Peter stood from the table and kissed Tessa. "Now I have to go say goodnight to the kids and show Ben how to use iFart."

13

TALKING POINTS

The only time Rosen could prep for the *Stumptown* interview was before normal work hours. The strategy was to match Noon's allegations with the applicable policy that would counterbalance the lawsuit's narrative that Parker College was brazenly lawless. Institutions generally won't comment on active litigation, which is why the reporter lied about the nut of his story. Presumably, the reporter would ask questions about how the college would handle certain events that resembled the allegations in the lawsuit, and Rosen would reply with the appropriate policy prescriptions. Because the lawsuit leaned into Parker College's reputation for having no rules, Loch saw this as a good strategy to help educate the public on their policies and procedures. It was not without risk, but it was all they had.

There was a fresh array of Voodoo doughnuts in the reception area, and fresh in this instance also means naughty. Scanning past the voodoo doll with frosted X's for eyes and a pretzel stick through its heart, the self-explanatory cock 'n' balls, and the vegan maple blazer blunt—*ironic given the circumstances*—Peter reached for the old-school chocolate coconut cake and took a quick bite before realizing his meeting had begun. Rosen was standing behind Peter, extending his hand, but both of Peter's were occupied with coffee and a doughnut. Smiling humbly while resembling a pelican swallowing a whole fish, Peter forced a giant bite of mushy dough down his gullet before it was ready. Balancing the remainder of the doughnut on his coffee mug, Peter brushed his sugar-and-coconut–coated fingers on his pants leg and shook hands.

"Thanks for making time for me on such short notice. I know you're a busy guy," said Peter as they walked into Rosen's office.

"Did I have a choice?" asked Rosen with a blank stare and ironic grin.

"Not really," Peter smiled. "President Loch thought you were best equipped to respond."

"Did he? Well, I understand how important it is to *construct* a good image of the college for the press." Rosen's emphasis on the word "construct" was intended as an insult. People are not always precise with their language, but Parkies, as students and alumni call themselves, tend to say exactly what they mean. The implication was clear: Rosen believed Peter had been hired to create a fiction for the media. But did it also mean that Rosen believed the accusations in the lawsuit? *Maybe I can flesh that out*, Peter thought while deciding whether to address the slight. He took another bite of doughnut, wishing he trusted Rosen enough to ask directly about the lawsuit. Rosen motioned for Peter to sit at the table in the meeting area of his office.

"Matthew, I know the idea of media relations is new to Parker College. It may seem frivolous or undignified as a profession, and maybe it is, but I want to assure you that it's not about creating fiction. It's a bad idea to lie to the press. I'm here to help tell the college's story through its strengths, not to lie about its weaknesses—or failures."

"Even big ones?" asked Rosen.

"Especially the big ones," said Peter. "Everyone makes mistakes. But we can be principled and reasoned in owning them and responding to them."

"Interesting," said Rosen as he leaned back in his chair. Peter summarized his conversation with President Loch, letting Rosen know that *Stumptown* would run the story with or without their cooperation. Given that, it would be best to counter the allegations that Parker tolerates, accommodates, or *facilitates* extreme drug use. Without their counter narrative, the story would be something like: Parker College is a secretive, corrupt, and cloistered drug den, with the college responding, "no comment."

Reading through the lawsuit, they flagged the "clickbait-y-est" allegations and talked through how they would respond during the interview. Rosen was sharp, he quickly got the hang of what they were doing and eventually started having fun. As the task wore on, they got a little punchy and began joking by giving horrible answers. For instance, in response to the proposed question, "What do you do if someone shows up high or drunk to class?" Rosen quipped, "Faculty have complete autonomy to do as they wish in their classes." It went on like this until Rosen asked in earnest, "But what if we don't always follow our own policies and procedures?" The drastic change in tone brought the worry from Peter's gut to show on his face. *Is he about to reveal the allegations are true?*

"I'm new to how all this works," Rosen continued, knowing he'd stumbled past denial and touched something real. "So, I guess I'm just asking hypothetically. What if these accusations have merit and the motive was to cover up a crime to avoid headlines that might get in the way of a fundraising campaign?"

"Then the college would have been better served by calling the police. The cover-up is always sexier than the crime." Peter concluded.

"Interesting," said Rosen with a mischievous smile. "Well, I'm certainly glad we're not engaged in a cover-up."

"Yeah, me too. Hopefully not hypothetically—" Peter said dryly as he headed to the door. He had the feeling he was being tested. But tested for what? Competence? His ability to keep a secret? Was he about to be brought into the inner circle of those who knew what really happened? Peter's final advice was to only say what he knew to be true. "If you're not certain of something, it's okay to tell him you'll do some research and get back to him. It is always safest to assume the reporter knows the answers to the questions he's asking."

"Peter," Rosen softened, "I've heard rumors, which you'll come to learn are Parker College's version of intramural sports. I thought a person in your position might know if the rumors were true."

"A person in my position should know where the landmines are buried, but since I don't, I can only assume there are none," said Peter with a wry smile on his way out the door.

* * *

The rattle of the public affairs doorknob caused Angela to jump in her chair. She scowled at Peter as she rushed to tell him that Collins had been looking for him before he went up to Goodwin's office. She thought something bad might have happened because when Collins is nervous, "he walks like he's holding a deck of cards in his ass cheeks," she said, then told Peter she was afraid he'd already gotten fired. Her genuine relief was oddly comforting to Peter. They made plans to have lunch, so Angela could share her "really important thing."

"It's a date." Angela smiled, winked, and swirled her head with comedic flare as she turned to go back to her desk. She took a few steps before turning to catch Peter's reaction. He was amused and blushing.

14

ROYAL BENGAL
INDIAN BUFFET

Sitar music gently plucked through the Royal Bengal Indian Buffet's sound system, sweetly dominating the ambiance. The restaurant was in a boxy, glass-and-steel strip mall a few miles from campus, situated between a tattoo parlor and a head shop. The interior was unexpected in its grandeur. It had white linen tablecloths with comfortable crimson velour upholstered booths. Brightly colored, intricately woven tapestries adorned the walls and ceilings. The scents of cumin, coriander, and cardamom mixed with the comfortable smells of breads and meats cooking in tandoori ovens. The aroma coming from the kitchen was so rich it almost provided sustenance. It was Angela's special quirky place, and she invited Peter there to share her secret special thing. As Peter dipped naan into red curry sauce, he felt like a commando who'd strapped on a parachute, climbed into a small plane, and was ascending toward an uncharted destination to perform a secret unspecified deed.

When nervous, Peter focused all his attention on the task at hand. His current task was eating. What was making him nervous was Angela's "really important secret thing." What was making him particularly nervous was the idea that Angela's *thing* might be an invitation to have an affair, which is something Peter had never seriously entertained—not until he'd met Angela. At best, affairs were deceitful and messy, and at worst, they were devastating to families. Those had been his thoughts before being invited to a clandestine meeting at the Royal Bengal Indian Buffet. He wasn't seeking it out, he convinced himself, but he was very interested in hearing what she had to say. Peter continued to eat, and Angela continued to watch him like she was at the zoo, flirting with a gorilla through his cage.

"Okay. You're killing me with this, *thing!*" Peter finally blurted.

Angela dropped her head on the table. "I feel silly because now it really has become *a thing*. I didn't mean to build it up so big. It's not big. It's stupid. Can we start over?" Despite her protest, it was clear Angela did want it to become *a thing*, and she delighted in Peter's uncomfortable anticipation. That Peter was blushing, laughing awkwardly, and ready to explode made Angela giddy with joy. Still, she asked him to pretend he hadn't built up her "thing" into something colossal. After he agreed, she opened an emotional vein and bled out her work misery, which went on for a while before she finally said, "that's why you have to be my work friend!" Then she admitted to having had her heart broken by Rhea after the faculty cool kids befriended her first and occupied all her time. Angela's face turned so red that it blended into the upholstery. Peter wasn't sure if he was more relieved or disappointed.

She made him pinkie promise to be her work friend before she would share the actual thing. Even though it was just their pinkies intertwined, Peter had a rush in his chest. He missed human contact. But the *thing*! Collins had been trying to sneak the Dictionary.com Word of the Day into casual conversations for months. She had written off his awkward use of uncommon words as Collins being Collins, until he used *ruction* in response to something that had happened in a faculty meeting. He said, "Ha, that will be a *ruction* upstairs." Everyone just stared at him, mostly because they hate him, but also because it was another use of an unusual word in an odd way. Later, when she went to look it up to see if he used it correctly, she accidently searched *dictionary* instead of *ruction* and clicked on Dictionary.com— and there were all the words that Collins had been uncomfortably cramming into sentences: zwieback, wildcatter, insouciance, and ruction.

"Zwieback? The cracker bread?" asked Peter

"Yes!" said an animated Angela. "I'm hankerin' for some zwieback, right about now."

"He did not say 'hankerin' for some zwieback,'" said Peter between chuckles.

"I swear to God!" she said, giving the scout salute.

"I think I might be starting to understand this keep-Portland-weird thing, but c'mon, there's something kind of awesome about this. Maybe I have to reevaluate him," said Peter. "So, what, you want to hack the Dictionary.com site and change the words of the day to erotica, fisting, and smegma?" Angela laughed so hard she cried a little bit. She shook her head "no" but confirmed that Peter was the right man for the job. Her thing was that she wanted to use the Word of the Day in front of Collins before he did. Peter loved it, and he was all in, but he was also slightly depressed that his affair was shorter lived than his mango lassi.

"What did you think *my thing* was going to be?" asked Angela with a mischievous grin that grew wider as Peter grew redder, trying to come up with something plausible that didn't involve them tearing off each other's clothes in a fit of passion.

"I don't know, I thought maybe you had a secret or something," said Peter, "I hear rumors are like a sport at Parker," Peter lied poorly.

Angela's disappointment surpassed Peter's, she knew where he was directing the conversation. "Are you about to ask me about Rhea again?" She was jealous of how Peter and Rhea talked about each other. "I knew it! She talked about you the same way. *Oh, it will be so great when Peter gets here.* I was like, 'those two are going to sneak off for nooners, and I'm going to be stuck in my cubicle, listening to Collins go on about his hankerin' for zwieback,'" Angela stopped herself and rolled her eyes. "All I know is she came back from a meeting, mumbling something about stumbling into a rat's nest. I asked her what was going on, hoping for a funny story. Anyway, minutes later, Goodwin stormed in. They went into Rhea's office, shut the door, and maybe ten minutes later, Rhea came out carrying her personal belongings."

The only thing Angela knew about that morning was that Collins was also in the meeting. A few days after Rhea left, Angela bumped into her on the street. All Rhea would say was that she was working at her boyfriend's restaurant, Morton Park, in the Pearl.

"I forgot her fiancé has his own place," Peter said as he made a show of pulling his iPhone from his pocket. "Morton Park, in the Pearl District. Let me make a note of that in my new iPhone."

"O-M-G, are you serious?" She was excited to see an iPhone up close and personal. "Let me see that! Do you have any apps yet?" She swept her finger across the lock screen, quickly covering her mouth, and laughing herself into a fit as a loud cartoonish farting noise squeezed out of the phone. She could barely talk. Angela wiped away tears. "You are the director of communications at the fanciest pants-ed college in Oregon, and you now have the most sophisticated communication tool ever created, and the first thing you do is buy a fart simulator!"

"My son made me buy it," said Peter.

"Of course, he did." She was still laughing while sampling all the exotically named farts. Neither could stop laughing. "What? Did he threaten you with the taser app?"

"If you need confirmation that you're hilarious," said Peter. "Just ask yourself."

It felt good to have a friend.

* * *

After clearing the air and returning from lunch, Peter checked the schedule software from the morning Rhea got fired. She had an Emergency Response Team meeting with Rosen and the directors from campus safety, student housing, the health center, and HR, as well as Collins, who was listed as secretary. *He must have played a role in Rhea's firing.*

All the uncertainty in his life was becoming paralyzing. Tessa seemed to be slowly walking toward divorce. Six directors had been fired in eight years. If the sale of their home in Juneau didn't go through, his family would be in financial ruin. Knowing why Rhea got fired and avoiding her mistakes had to be Peter's top priority.

There must be truth to the lawsuit, or why would Parker be so quick to settle? Rhea must have said something in that meeting to get herself fired. Rosen doesn't seem to know what happened, but I don't think I can trust him. Did Tessa bring me here to divorce me so she wouldn't feel stuck in Juneau? Angela's so weird, but I really like her. Maybe I should just run off with Angela. Come back to the moment; focus; observe your thoughts; no judgment. Start with one piece of solid evidence. For now, the only thing that matters is that I'm able to provide for my kids. I need to work my plan to prepare Rosen for the interview. I need to talk with Rhea.

Find Rhea. Find out what she meant by stumbling into a rat's nest. Start there.

15

THE INTERVIEW

David Noon's lawsuit did not settle, which meant the interview was moving forward with the *STD* reporter with the porn star name. Vince Craven arrived early, Peter sized him up, as he wandered the office, waiting for someone to greet him. He was older than anticipated and had neatly combed hair that was saturated with so much product it looked calcified—not very reporter-like. Additionally, his baggy dress slacks and black open collar shirt with silver stripes oozed the vibe of door-to-door vacuum salesmen. Peter called Rosen to let him know they were on their way. He wanted to be sure Rosen's head was in the game. Rosen was smart but inexperienced with the press; he had no last-minute questions, which made Peter wonder if he was well prepared or overconfident. The *STD* was not

Portland's paper of record, but tanking the interview could attract the attention of other media outlets. Rosen needed to be careful. The lawsuit had enough chum to entice every sharklike reporter in the higher ed ecosystem. If this story went national, jobs would be lost. Peter's last-minute unsolicited advice was that if the interview went sideways, Rosen should remain calm and quiet, and let Peter take over.

Craven cleared his throat a few times before Angela finally greeted him. He introduced himself by handing her a business card, which she promptly brought to Peter, mocking Craven's title as she handed it over. "There's an invest-ta-ma-ga-tory reporter here to see you," she said making an ironically impressed look. Peter thanked her with a face that read "all-business" and a heart that wanted nothing more than to goof around with her. But there was serious work to do.

On the walk to Rosen's office, Peter plied Craven with friendly banter, hoping to glean details about his story. Attempts at chit chat all fell flat. Craven was too old to be jumping into a dying industry but too self-assured to have only three bylines to his credit. *Maybe he flamed out of his last career*, Peter speculated. *Or maybe he'd been disbarred as a lawyer, or he was a comptroller that absconded with company funds, or maybe he's just a trust-fund baby.* Peter gave up playing detective and went back to trying to build rapport by pulling out the Alaska Card. It was a hit, everyone loved to talk about Alaska. There was even an impressed raised eyebrow at Peter's mention of his job as editor of the *Juneau Daily*. But Craven remained cold and distant. Peter offered to buy him a beverage as they walked past the coffeeshop, but unlike movie hit men, reporters don't accept petty bribes of hospitality when they've come to kill you. Of the dozens of greenhorn reporters Peter had encountered throughout his newspaper career, Craven didn't look like any of them. He was unapologetically determined. The only valuable information Craven shared during their walk was that he had not contacted Reed College, Lewis & Clark, or University of Portland for interviews one day before the *STW* press deadline, tipping Peter that Craven was coming for the lawsuit story. *Guard up.*

Regret washed over Peter as they walked into Rosen's office. *This was dumb. Craven thinks he's here for a career-making story. We should have just sent a statement,* he thought before introducing the competitors entering the arena. Rosen and Craven took their seats on opposite sides of the conference table. Peter pulled up a chair close to Craven. "Staying to manage the message?" he sniped. Peter returned a sharp grin. Rosen showed signs of worry. "So, does Parker College have drug enforcement procedures? The last time I spoke with John McMahon in the DA's office, he wasn't sure you did." Craven mimicked Peter's grin.

As coached, Rosen calmly and succinctly recited his talking points: the assistant district attorney shared no concerns regarding Parker College's drug policy or its enforcement when they last spoke. Parker College's alcohol and other drug policy was the blueprint for many other colleges. The college has no problem calling law enforcement when needed, which is very rarely.

Craven kept bringing the conversation back to Rosen's call with McMahon. Rosen found different ways to say that the conversation had nothing to do with the topic at hand. Each question confirmed the mistake they had made by inviting Craven to campus. As Peter's regret grew, it made his spine more rigid until he looked like a lion ready to pounce on its prey. Limiting the damage became his only goal.

"So, Vince, are you here to talk about our drug and alcohol policy or are you here to waste our time? If it's the latter, then we should probably end the interview," snapped Peter as he leaned in Craven's direction.

"I thought Alaskans were jolly?" joked Craven.

"You're thinking of Santa Claus. Alaskans don't suffer fools. Vice President Rosen is a very busy man, and he made time to accommodate your request for an interview about our drug and alcohol policy and how that policy gets enforced. If that's not why you're here, let's stop wasting his time." Peter looked more intimidating than intended.

Insisting he wanted to know how the policy was enforced, Craven opened his notebook for the first time then reached into his pants pocket and pulled out a digital audio recorder. Rosen flashed a curious look, and Peter shrugged his approval. The interview began in earnest.

Rosen started with a history lesson that began in the '80s with President Reagan's drug czar mandating that all colleges have drug and alcohol policies. He highlighted the revisions to their policy that included its heavy emphasis on prevention and therapeutic intervention, in addition to a continuum of adjudicative solutions. They talked about which infractions warranted therapeutic measures and which would trigger punitive actions. Craven expressed doubt that a policy relying so heavily on administrative discretion could ever be administered fairly. Rosen redirected the conversation to emphasize that Parker's policy had a much lower bar for action than the law, which gave Craven an opening to talk more specifically about policy enforcement. Peter's butt puckered as Rosen explain the rules of engagement. "The caveat is that the situations must be hypothetical. I'm forbidden by FERPA to talk directly about disciplinary actions taken against current or former students."

Craven's face contorted slightly. "FERPA is the privacy act, can't share information about students and whatnot?"

"The Family Education Rights and Privacy Act," Rosen elaborated. "It protects the privacy of a student's educational record, *and whatnot*. Much like how HIPAA, the Health Insurance Portability and Accountability Act, protects the sharing of medical information. These pieces of federal legislation are intended to protect the privacy of students, and in the case of HIPAA, everyone."

Peter was confused and slightly panicked as to why Rosen brought up FERPA—*We're calling the lawsuit fiction. All the situations we're talking about are supposed to be hypothetical! This is a major fuck up*, thought Peter. *Is he bringing up FERPA, because there really is someone's privacy to be protected? But why did he include HIPAA?* Peter remained quiet and held his breath, hoping Craven wouldn't pick up on the gaff.

"And along with it, the reputation of the college," Craven smirked and sunk back into his chair like a pouty teenager. "You know, guys, so far, you've told me nothing. And now you're essentially telling me, well... You're essentially hiding behind these codes."

"These *codes* are also called federal laws, Vince, and they're not preventing us from telling you about our policies, which is why you said you came here," Peter grinned and waited for Craven to look at him. Feeling like they needed distance from Rosen's gaff, Peter went on the offensive. "You'd think someone who was sent fishing by the DA would have a better understanding of the law."

That got Craven's attention. There's no bigger insult to

an investigative reporter than being called the establishment's lapdog. It's not unheard of for the district attorney's office to encourage a reporter to poke around alleged criminal activity where there's no actionable evidence. It's like bird hunters sending flushing spaniels into the dense brush to rustle out game fowl. "Are you upset because there's no scandal here? Is that how you think this works? The DA hands you a lead and we hand you a story?"

Rosen was not comfortable with the escalation of emotions. He was a Parker College graduate after all; logic, reason, and knowledge were his three pillars. He wanted no part of this knuckle dragging. Peter paused and regrouped; his emotions were raw and regressing toward primal. He was a wolf defending its kill—*six directors in eight years. Must defend the pack. No meat for Craven.* "Why are you here, Vince?" Peter concentrated to make his voice steady.

"I want to know about your policies," said Craven.

"We're telling you about our policies." His eyes fixed on Craven's. "You don't seem happy with our answers. Are you here looking for a different story?"

"Is there another story?"

"Are you a reporter or the DA's bitch?" Peter moved his chair back from the table. "Have the balls to tell me why you're here."

Craven trembled with anger. If Rosen was wearing salmon-skin pajamas, bathed in honey, and thrown into a bear den, he would not have been less comfortable. Peter stood. Rosen waved his hand and talked nervously. "If we're not giving the answers you want, it's not because we're being evasive. I'm responding to the best of my ability," interjected Rosen. "If you still have questions, please go on. I'm here to answer them."

Peter was furious that Rosen intervened; it was his second gaff. Craven was on a very short leash. Peter was prepared to drag him out by his cheap open collar at the next smarmy comment or cross look. Composed and dignified, Rosen responded to inquiries about how often they called police to campus. Not often. And what kinds of policy infractions would warrant police intervention. Peter was happy with the direction of the conversation, until he wasn't.

"Can I give you a hypothetical situation, and you can tell me if you'd call the police in that situation?" asked Craven. "So, let's say that you find the body of a homeless man on campus, and you suspect that a student sold him the drugs that killed him." Craven looked to Peter waiting for him to interrupt. He didn't.

"Go on," said Peter, wanting to know how Craven was connecting William James' death to the lawsuit allegations that took place in the apartments.

"So, you suspect a student sold him the drugs that caused his death. You go to the kid's dorm room and find a thousand hypodermic needles spread around, stacks of cash, weapons, and all kinds of drugs packed for distribution. What would you do?"

"The lawsuit didn't say anything about stacks of cash, weapons, or drugs packed for distribution, and it didn't connect those accusations with the death of the houseless man," said Peter.

"What lawsuit?" Craven asked unconvincingly.

"Make-believe time is over, Vince. Where are these other accusations coming from? Did the DA feed them to you, or are you just a shill for Noon's lawyer?"

"The DA's office doesn't think you call the police when you should," said Craven.

Walking to Rosen's desk, Peter grabbed a copy of the lawsuit and dropped it on the table in front of Craven. "That's the lawsuit," said Peter. "Now we can all stop pretending."

"Okay, so I've seen it," said Craven. "That doesn't change the fact that Parker College doesn't call the cops when they should."

"Is your story about the lawsuit?" Peter put both hands on the table, leaned toward Craven, and waited.

"It's about the allegations in the lawsuit, yes," said Craven.

"Then let's talk about the lawsuit," Peter had worked himself into a lather. He didn't like being on the wrong side of the story, and he definitely didn't like being badgered by a smarmy greenhorn. Rosen sat upright, nervous, and ready to stop the interview. Peter held up one finger to Rosen. Craven's eyes widened. A career-making story was about to unfold.

"Alright." Craven was tentative. He wanted to choose his words carefully. "Who ordered Noon to cover up the crime scene?"

"The allegations in the lawsuit are baseless, and the college has no further comment," said Peter as he picked up Craven's recorder, turned it off, and handed it to him. "I'll see you to your car."

"I can see myself out," said Craven.

"This is private property, Vince, and you're here as my guest. It's one of the college's many strictly enforced policies that guests must be escorted by their sponsors while they're on campus."

* * *

Staring at his feet as they stomped toward the East Lot, Craven reminded Peter of his children when they were toddlers and mad about being told no. He wanted to mock him; *you were supposed to help me scandalize the college so my editors would like me! Wah!* But Craven was engaged in his own fantasies about writing brutally damaging stories about the college. Goading Craven had crossed a line, but Peter had no idea how far. In his mind, he'd won a schoolyard skirmish, but to Craven, it was the latest in a series of crushing psychic blows. Growing up in the shadow of Parker College, Craven and his friends would ride their bikes to campus to play frisbee and fly kites in the fields. During the crazy end-of-year party, Bacchanalia, they'd sneak onto campus in hope of confirming the lore of its Sodom and Gomorrah–like debauchery. One of those friends later enrolled at Parker and claimed to have found academic paradise, but Craven was denied admission as a freshman and then again as a transfer student. He came to despise the place. Peter didn't know about Craven's personal wounds, but he did know the lawsuit story was likely to run. It was in the college's best interest to keep the lines of communication open. As much as it killed him, he needed to extend a *mea culpa*.

Peter confided that he'd been told the lawsuit was groundless and that he had no evidence suggesting otherwise. Although, Rosen's gaff introduced considerable doubt. He went on to explain how difficult fact finding is within the higher ed bureaucracy because its management is so fractured. It's called the silo effect. Each department has its own mission that doesn't necessarily overlap that much with other departments. It can be frustrating when trying to get at the big picture, because there's not only one view. There are a dozen views that don't always fit neatly together. Additionally, there are regulations about who can know what, when, and why. Craven didn't care about any of it—all he saw was Peter blocking him from a story.

"Fuck off. You know what happened and you're stonewalling

me," snarked Craven. They were getting close to the East Lot. Peter checked to make sure no one was within earshot.

"Seriously, what do you know for sure? If they're hanging me out to dry, I'd like to know," pleaded Peter.

"Tell me everything you know, first. Then I'll tell you," Craven returned sharply.

"I'm telling the truth. As far as I know it's a baseless lawsuit. For real," said Peter to a stone-faced Craven. "I have no reason, yet, to believe otherwise."

Craven didn't believe Peter.

"The DA's office doesn't think the suit is baseless," said Craven.

"Have you talked to Noon?" asked Peter.

"Not yet," said Craven.

"Can you trust the DA?" Peter craned his neck around, being careful not be overheard.

"I've got a choice between trusting the DA or Parker College," said Craven.

"You have a choice between trusting me or the most politically motivated headline-snatching people on the planet," Peter said sternly. "Don't be a fucking tool."

"You don't believe the suit is bullshit," sniped Craven. "Parker earned its reputation."

"*Parker College* has no independent will, Vince," said Peter, although privately he was starting to agree with Craven, but he couldn't admit it. "Don't be too quick to fall for the myths the lawyer's playing on." Peter couldn't figure out if Craven trusted him or if he had completely written him off as a useless flack.

Craven's car was parked in the fire lane and had a ticket. "Can you take care of this?" asked Craven sheepishly.

"There are consequences for breaking the rules at Parker College, Vince," said Peter as he took the ticket. "You owe me one," Peter joked as he was trying to sort through all the new information. Who was lying? Everyone had something to gain: Noon had money, the assistant DA wanted to remove the word *assistant* from his title, and Parker College had its reputation to protect. Peter looked to the skies in despair. He wasn't sure what he hoped to see, but Goodwin staring down from his office window was at the bottom of the list. Goodwin waited to be seen before turning slowly from the window.

* * *

Collins was lurking in his office door. As soon as the doorknob rattled, he rushed toward Peter. Angela looked worried. Peter smiled at her, trying to hide his fear—*six directors in eight years*. In preparation of being number seven, he went to his desk and grabbed his car keys and wallet. Angela looked at Peter with a sense of loss and hoped it wouldn't be the last time she'd see him.

16

THE RAVEN

When Peter was a sophomore in high school, he lost his job as a busboy at the Red Rambler diner after three days of slow service and dropped dishes. He'd worn the same stained Dave Cowens number-eighteen Celtics tee-shirt all three days. The owner handed him some cash, patted him on the back, and said, "Peter, you're a nice boy, but it's time to retire your number." That was that. It was the only time he had ever been fired. He'd recovered quickly from the Red Rambler debacle, but the prospect of losing his job while the economy was plummeting toward a second Great Depression, was making him wonder if jumping over the side of the *Columbia* was a missed opportunity.

Do what it takes. Say whatever you need to say, Peter thought as he and Collins walked to Goodwin's office. If he made it through the day without being fired, he would trust no one until he found another job. *Why did I leave Juneau?* Peter thought as he entered the president's suite. A raven cawed from just outside the window. It wasn't the normal elongated caw, but a noise that combined a loud gulp with the plop of a stone as it hit the bottom of a well. It was a sound he'd only heard in Southeast Alaska. *Maybe it's a sign*, Peter thought. *Be the Raven!* The Raven is a trickster. In Northwest Coast mythology, Raven is a powerful figure who can transform the world. Raven is clever, deceitful, and almost always succeeds in his quests by exploiting people's insecurities and discomfort with uncertainty. The lesson of the Raven, for Peter, was to never believe without questioning.

Peter's fascination with the mythology of the Raven began with the real birds during his first week in Alaska. One kept taking the lid off Peter's trashcans to play with the Styrofoam packing peanuts, which got scattered throughout the neighborhood. After his third, not very thorough, attempt at cleaning the Corvus's mess, Peter stood at the end of his driveway looking at the raven perched in a treetop. An older Native Alaskan woman, walking her dog, asked if the raven had been up to mischief. Peter told her the story and asked for advice. Get some food for the raven and scatter it near the trash can, the woman said. "When the raven comes to eat, tell him in a firm but gentle voice, 'I have given you food to make you strong,' and then ask him politely to stop scattering your trash." Bemused but leaning into the mysticism, Peter nodded, desperately wanting to believe. "And if that doesn't work," the woman said with a glint in her eye, "go to Fred Meyer and buy some bungee cords to tie down your trash lids." She chuckled and left.

Peter had become the subject of a Cheechako story. He was

too eager to believe in the magical qualities of both the teller and the subject of the story. His desire to believe in something magical made him miss the obvious and practical truth: he needed to tie down his trash lids. The Raven is there to take advantage of the seeker, the dreamer, and the fool—the Cheechako. The tides rose and fell before the Raven, but if you look past that fact, he'll convince you he controls the ocean for the harvest of oysters and clams. Peter needed to become like the trickster if he was going to survive at Parker College. He needed to show he could control the space between the known threats to the college and Goodwin's worst fears.

* * *

Goodwin was standing by the windows where Peter last saw him. Dark rain clouds were sweeping in, muting the colors outside. Goodwin's gray suit almost made him disappear in the flat light. Gusting wind swayed the naked cherry tree branches against the darkening sky and caused the windows to chatter in their loosely fitting frames. The damp late autumn draft carried the unmistakable smell of an imminent storm. Peter felt like he'd walked into a black-and-white movie. *If we were in a noir, my problems could all be solved with a bottle of bourbon and the leverage of a snub-nosed .38 revolver.*

Goodwin's privilege had sheltered him from the kind of desperation Peter was feeling. He felt familial pressure to marry well and not disgrace the Goodwin name, but his trust fund sheltered him from the kind of panic that Peter was trying to suppress. Losing one paycheck could mean total ruin for Peter and his family—no health insurance, food, or shelter. Peter needed to introduce Goodwin to a world where his privilege and money held no value. It was time to shine a light into the dark box that held Goodwin's worst fears.

"If this is a bad time, Mr. Goodwin, I'll come back." Peter spoke with the confidence he'd been lacking. Goodwin wanted to know why he had been so friendly with Craven. Goodwin turned from the window, attempting to be dramatic. His face was so lacking in pigmentation that it continued the black-and-white–movie effect. "I don't think he would have described me as friendly," said Peter with little inflection. "He knew a lot more about our situation than what was in the lawsuit. I was trying to find out who was feeding him information."

The locked door handle rattled, followed by a knock—only Loch would try to open Goodwin's door without knocking first. Peter and Goodwin's eyes were fixed on each other's as if they were in a duel. There was no trust. Collins started to the door but stopped when Goodwin diverted his stare, then waited until he was invited to continue. Goodwin turned his back on his guests, returning his gaze toward the forbidden East Lot.

Loch apologized for interrupting, as well-heeled people do, but his apology was not sincere, as he had asked Sally to tip him anytime Peter entered Goodwin's office. He put his hand on Peter's shoulder. "I heard things got a little—*exciting*."

"The DA shopped the story to Craven," said Peter. Goodwin took his lip balm tin from his pocket and held it between his thumbs and index fingers as he turned to the others. "He was boasting about it. McMahon seems to be feeding him information," said Peter noticing the loaded exchange between Goodwin and Loch. "He mentioned McMahon by name several times and shared allegations that weren't in the lawsuit."

"Matthew also mentioned the new allegations," said Loch.

"He said you were pretty tough on the reporter—that you called him the DA's bitch."

Goodwin's eyes bulged, and Collins gasped. Loch chuckled, and Peter smiled. "I expect you to comport yourself in a way that's fitting with the reputation of the college," said Goodwin.

"A second ago you told me I was being too nice," said Peter with a grin, looking at Goodwin in a way that none of his subordinates had ever survived. "All due respect, but McMahon wants to paint Parker as a heroin den, and he's using the *STW* as his brush. The reporter's getting what he believes is credible information from a source who's probably running for office in the fall— *information* that would hand him a career-making story and give McMahon plenty of name recognition. I don't think either man is going to be dissuaded by good manners."

"Assuming the DA is behind this seems like a lot to infer," said Goodwin.

"I disagree," said Loch. "I couldn't understand why McMahon called us after William James' death. If he thinks Noon's allegations are true—and they're somehow connected to James—he could be trying to scare us into coming forward. But what I don't understand is why he wouldn't just pick up the phone and talk with us."

"It makes sense if he thinks we're hiding something. He said McMahon believes the accusations, and thinks the same student from the lawsuit supplied the drugs that killed William James," Peter confirmed, explaining Craven's timeline couldn't align with the events as they allegedly happened—being careful not to give much credence to the lawsuit—and then shared the new allegations of stacked cash, weapons, and drugs packed for distribution. The conversation paused. There were loud sighs and hanging heads, and a clear divide in the room. Peter and Loch were trying to find a path forward. Goodwin and Collins were trying to keep up. Collins felt the need to say something in support of Goodwin.

"Why would the assistant district attorney work with someone from *Stumptown*, rather than someone from a legitimate paper?" asked Collins.

"I'll fill you in on the basics later, Steven," Peter said curtly.

"Answer his question!" snapped Goodwin.

Peter explained that reporters are supposed to value fairness and objectivity. The DA went looking for a reporter who did not possess those traits. Further, Peter explained that the reporter had additional information about the night of the alleged cover-up in the apartments. The most obvious party who would benefit from feeding the reporter that information was former security guard David Noon—to expedite the settlement of his lawsuit. But the reporter revealed McMahon as his source of information. If the reporter was telling the truth—that meant the DA believed the allegations in the lawsuit. If the reporter was being honest about his source, then the college had more to worry about than bad press.

Collins was still clearly confused.

"We have a few possible scenarios. Deciding which to believe is complicated by the fact that all our information is coming from unreliable or unknown sources," Loch attempted to simplify Peter's explanation. "Either A, the reporter is lying about working with the DA and is getting his information from Noon's lawyer; B, he's making it all up; or C, he's telling the truth and John McMahon believes the allegations in the lawsuit are true. I suppose D, would be that McMahon sent him here to try to uncover if *we* believe the allegations in the lawsuit are true."

"There is a lot I don't know, and I'm not asking questions," he looked at Goodwin, *six directors in eight years.* "But I *do* know somebody is feeding the reporter information that is damaging to us and intriguing to him. No matter who's telling the truth, all scenarios benefit from settling the lawsuit and putting a gag on Noon."

"You don't think he's bluffing?" countered Loch.

"Who? Craven? The reporter?" asked Peter.

"Yes. Who do you think I meant?" asked Loch.

"I mean, somebody's obviously lying," said Peter while glancing in Goodwin's direction. "Someone's playing a high-stakes game of chicken, but I don't know who."

"Right," Loch nodded in agreement. "I'm going to check with our lawyer to see if Noon is any closer to accepting our offer."

"Everything we're talking about is speculation," said a horrified Collins. "Right? I mean, nothing can happen to us *because nothing happened.* So, I'm not sure what we're even talking about." He looked to Goodwin for approval which he did not get. Goodwin's worry and lack of engagement did not go unnoticed by Peter, or Loch.

"You're right, Steven. There's a lot of speculation, but what we know for sure is that DAs are whip-smart and hyperpolitical, and some of them can be ruthless, especially during election years. So, if they're comin' fishing, we'd be wise to drain the pond," warned Peter with a confident folksy Alaska earnestness. Nobody in the room, including Peter, completely understood his fishing metaphor, but it caused Goodwin to put his hands in his pockets and stare at the empty space in the middle of his office. The muffled popping of his beeswax tin sounded like a nervous heartbeat. Peter was hoping he had sufficiently scared Goodwin into keeping him around a while longer.

"Alright, I'm going to go call the lawyers," said Loch. "Peter, why don't you come with me just in case he has questions about something that came up during your conversation."

If I can make it through that door, I will have survived for another day, thought Peter. *Please, please, please let me make it.* Walking through the door felt like winning the lottery.

17

RHEA SMITH, GENERAL MANAGER OF MORTON PARK

Portland is a foodie heaven and the *crème fraiche de la crème fraiche* of the region is the Pearl District. The *New York Times* covered the goings-on in the Pearl so frequently that Portland's mayor quipped he was governing the sixth borough. The most illustrative story when trying to understand Portland's food scene is the incident where Portland chefs threw punches during a cooking show while arguing how far outside the district one could slaughter a pig and still call the meat locally sourced pork. Peter lived closer to the Pearl than the pig, but his non-ironic normcore wardrobe kept him out of the bougie district before he went looking for Rhea Smith at Morton Park. The restaurant was nationally known for its eccentric, perhaps ostentatious menu, which featured items like the $75 Parthenon cheese steak sandwich. "The Parthy" was made of dry-aged American Wagyu tenderloin and Pule—$700 per pound Serbian donkey milk cheese. Peter considered Morton Park more of a curiosity than a place to eat, though others disagreed: reservations were required months in advance. Peter arrived at 4:15 p.m. on a Tuesday. Pretty people dressed in jeans and black tee-shirts emblazoned with the Morton Park logo were folding napkins, polishing utensils, and laying them carefully on place settings of butcher block paper that spread across communal tables. A server broke from her side work to greet Peter with a look that suggested Applebee's was around the corner. She likely assumed he was a vendor looking to sell his wares and directed him to the bar, where Rhea was staring at a clipboard.

Peter admired the detail and workmanship that went into every aspect of the décor. The old brick building had once housed a furniture manufacturer. Machine parts and old tools were turned into artwork that decorated the walls. Theater lighting hung from the thirty-foot-high ceiling, and the cocktail area was entirely reclaimed from a legit frontier saloon. Beyond the bar were semi-circular private booths on risers, where people could order the *table d'hôte*, which priced out at $150 per person before drinks.

Rhea didn't immediately recognize Peter as he approached the bar, which caused him to feel even more like an interloper. He'd come unannounced, assuming the college paid her to keep quiet. He didn't want her to dodge him. When she finally recognized him, she jumped from her seat with open arms. Peter promised to leave before the fancy clientele arrived, as not to bring down her Q-rating. They hugged long enough for it to be slightly awkward. They felt a bond that neither could perfectly articulate, like soldiers who'd served in the same military unit during different deployments. Rhea was tall and slender, with chestnut eyes and a smile that was felt directly in your heart. Peter was both intimidated by her intelligence and accomplishments and totally put at ease by her manner. Everything seemed to come naturally to her. Her words flowed effortlessly to form witty, pithy, and sometimes bawdy observations. She didn't seem to notice or care that she was attractive, and Peter assumed she fell out of bed looking as she did. He was in awe of her.

"I assume your first question is 'What the fucked happened?'" She asked with a grin.

"Well, since it's out there..." Peter told her everything he knew about her departure: Goodwin had followed her into her office after an emergency team meeting; she'd left and never came back. Then Peter speculated that she had discovered the events detailed in the lawsuit, and that Goodwin was afraid she'd tell the *Times* or try to make them do the right thing.

"I bet you always win at Clue," Rhea said tossing out a mischievous smile. "I didn't know about the lawsuit."

"A former security guard, said the college fired him for refusing to cover up a crime in the Parker College Apartments."

"What did Goodwin and Loch tell you?"

"Nothing," said Peter. "A hack from *Stumptown* came chasing down the story and they sent me flying into the fog totally blind."

"Assholes!" Rhea was getting drawn in. She waved for the bartender. "Do you want a drink? Of course, you do," she said with a devil-may-care grin. She ordered two Beefeater gimlets, with real lime. "I'm afraid all this day drinking is going to become a habit. I fucking love it," Rhea said with a laugh. "You'll come here ten years from now, and I'll be all sloshy, closing the bar, talking about how I once had a promising career as a reporter. By then, I'll probably have to explain what a reporter was. My hair will be dyed all brassy, and I'll have pointy silicone tits like those horrible plastic hags from Lake Oswego who are always telling me they don't need reservations because of how important their husbands are."

"I think you'll be fine," said Peter.

"None of us are going to be fine. Have you not been reading the news?" said Rhea becoming animated. She started with the death of daily newspapers, before transitioning to Treasury Secretary Henry Paulson saying everything is fine before scaring everyone with predictions of an international financial collapse. She moved on to failing banks and plummeting stock markets and home prices. "It's a fucking mess, but at least my tits are still real and perky," she quipped.

"You're awfully fond of your tits," said Peter with an animated chuckle.

"Aren't you?" she joked. The bartender placed the drinks on the bar. "To you," said Rhea as she held out her drink for Peter to toast. "Welcome to Portland, the damp suburb of Nikeville!" They clinked glasses and drank. "As much as the *Times* fawned over this place, I thought I was moving to Nirvana, but I'll be damned if it didn't turn out to be Courtney Love."

"Oh, that's too real," said Peter with a subdued laugh. "I thought you loved Portland."

"Yeah, I'm feeling right at home. I saw another Black person like two or three days ago. So, you know—" she said wryly and waited for Peter to stop laughing. "I think I'm just hating on it because it's not New York. And of course, I'm just slightly more than bitter about what happened at Parker. Goodwin is such a tool. Have you ever met anyone over twenty-five who talks as much about where he went to college?" Rhea scooted closer and became even more animated. "Whenever we'd meet, he'd start every third sentence with *when I was at Harvard . . .* as he molested his Burt's Beeswax." She pretended to fumble with a tin. "I was always like, should I be paying attention to your anal fixation, your phallic fixation, or trying to actually decipher the cryptic fucking Morse code beeping from your mouth?"

Peter laughed so hard the waitstaff stopped to look at him. Rhea was good medicine. Peter hadn't laughed that much since the night he'd left Juneau. "Seriously," Rhea continued. "If I'm in my fifties and still talking about my days at the *Times*, or Columbia, and my only friend is an obsequious manservant—which, I'm pretty sure they're fucking by the way—I'm giving you permission—actually, I'm begging you—to put me out of my misery. Loch just needs to throw a tent over that whole department and admit it's a fucking circus."

"Are Collins and Goodwin really fucking? That would explain so much," said Peter. "You know he's doing your job now?"

"Um, he's not doing my job. He's doing Goodwin," she joked. "The actual job is not getting done." They joked a bit more about Parker, Goodwin, and Collins. She asked about Angela. Then came the loaded pause. Time was running out before the post-work crowds would start to arrive. Rhea stood, gesturing with her drink for Peter to follow her to a luminary table.

"You know, I feel guilty for having hired you. I thought we'd make a good team. I felt like if I had just one ally in that place, we could have made a difference," Rhea grimaced. "They've forgotten why the college exists. They're so entrenched in the aristocracy; all they care about is defending the status quo. They don't give a fuck about anything except keeping their jobs."

"Even Loch?" asked Peter.

Rhea was sipping her drink and had to catch herself from spitting it out. She wiped her mouth and chuckled. "Yeah, I forgot you had a crush on Doc Loch."

"He was the last of the liberal lions of Boston politics!" Peter laughed at his defense of Loch. "The guy's a legend."

"Sorry to kill your fantasy, my dear, but he's an also-ran... *for the fucking mayor of Boston.* He's irrelevant. The man is the answer to a trivia question that nobody's asking," said Rhea with a chuckle, "and you're the only one who'd know the answer anyway."

"You're brutal," Peter joked. "The Need-Blind op-ed was a gamechanger."

She smiled at his naïveté and took a deep breath before jabbing another pin in Peter's Loch bubble. She gave him the inside scoop as to why need-blind admissions became a top priority for the college. The Board of Regents hired Loch with the directive of moving the college's reputation from a drug-friendly safe haven where rich kids came to cosplay at counter-culture shenanigans, to something near the mainstream. Loch had the institutional research department see which students were committing the acts that were deemed reputational threats. The study found that over 90 percent of the disciplinary actions, medical leaves, and suspensions came from rich kids who had been accepted off the waitlist. It was determined they needed to broaden the applicant pool—need-blind admissions and eliminating the application fee were the ways to do that. Since Peter was in his first job in higher ed, she gave him an overview of the admission process.

Super-simplified college admissions: to enroll a class of 300 freshmen, the college needs to accept 1,500 applicants, knowing that roughly 1,200 of those students will enroll at other colleges. That's the easy math. There is not enough financial aid for all 300 students. Some get a free ride, and everyone else pays somewhere between a little bit and full price. This is where the calculus gets more complex, but it's easy to see how the process favors the rich. The kids who can pay full price, have good grades, and have clean records all get in—all of them. A dozen or so of the poorest kids with perfect GPAs, no blips or blemishes on their records, and outstanding extracurriculars also get in—and everybody feels good about that. The poor kids with hiccups on their records, like a B-plus in calculus, get put on the waitlist with all the dumb, rich troublemakers. At the end of the process, when all the financial aid has been distributed but there are still seats to fill, the college starts choosing students off the waitlist, based almost solely on their ability to pay full tuition. For those last ten-to-fifteen spots, money trumps piss-poor GPAs, trumps lethargy in extracurricular life, and, for a few very wealthy applicants—money even trumps criminal behavior or failed attempts at rehab, or both.

"That last cohort of kids makes up about five percent of the entire student body, but it comprises over ninety percent of disciplinary actions, medical leaves, and suspensions," Rhea explained. "From a marketing standpoint, schools with need-blind admissions attract a lot more applicants. Bigger pools mean more choice of students across the socioeconomic spectrum, which means you can stretch your financial aid further, which means having to admit fewer rich delinquents. Loch saw need-blind admissions as the best way to eradicate the troublemaker waitlist, full-pay students who were causing all the reputational issues. In Parker College admission jargon, they're WFPs, Waitlist Full-Pays, or as some call them WTFPs—What the Fuck, Parker?"

"You said medical leaves? I assume that's code for rehab?" asked Peter.

"What's the *Stumptown* angle?" she asked, ignoring Peter's question.

"He seems to be talking to an assistant DA who doesn't think we call the police when we should," said Peter.

"You should start looking for another job, now. Seriously," said Rhea as she took a long pull from her gin. "I'm not sure how much more I should say."

"Just tell me about medical leave," said Peter.

"You heard none of this from me. Right?" Peter nodded. "Okay, so you know about HIPAA, right? It's intended to prevent the sharing, or selling, of medical information for its use against patients, blah, blah, blah. It makes it illegal for an institution to talk about people's medical issues. So, the richest, most well-connected kids who are, let's say, selling drugs on campus, mysteriously take ill and go on medical leave. Sometimes it's forced by the administration, and sometimes it happens after a talk with Mommy and Daddy or their lawyer."

"But always before the police are called." A light came on that dimmed Peter's idealism.

"No comment," said Rhea.

"So, a disciplinary issue, or, as they call them in some circles, a felony, becomes a confidential medical issue, and then the student transfers to Hampshire College?" intuited Peter.

"It all depends on how well connected or rich Mommy and Daddy are," said Rhea.

"I though FERPA protected all that information, anyway."

"It does, and it doesn't," explained Rhea. "FERPA allows Rosen, or Rosen's successor, to tell an employer, or another college, anything they deem important for them to know; under HIPAA, nothing can be legally disclosed, ever, by anyone."

Rosen did not slip when mentioning HIPAA during the interview, thought Peter.

"Do students ever come back to Parker after a medical leave?" asked Peter, knowing he might be treading into muddy waters.

"Sometimes," said Rhea. "And of course, sometimes it's legit. Kids really do get sick, or, as you pointed out, go to rehab in earnest, or whatever, but it's hard for the rest of us to know the real cases from the privileged ones."

"Hypothetically speaking, of course," said Peter with an insightful and pained expression, "could you imagine a situation where a student who was caught operating a heroin shooting gallery on campus would be allowed back into Parker College after taking a medical leave?"

"If something like that happened, I'm not sure I would want to know about it, because suggesting a course of action is the type of thing that might get you fired. Hypothetically speaking, of course." Rhea finished her drink and said a rushed goodbye. She opened her arms as she stood. Peter couldn't tell if she was wearing a look of concern or regret. His was regret. Rhea was young and had a sparkling resume. He had no worries for her future. His outlook, on the other hand, was open for debate.

18

LIFE OF THE MIND

Several days of rainfall cleared the skies in the Willamette Valley, and the southerly winds kept the haze from resettling. Peter arrived at the North Lot to a brilliant morning. The green peaks of the enormous sequoias and hemlocks punctured the spotless blue skyline. There were no birds, planes, vapor trails, clouds, or traffic helicopters. Colors were so vivid, it was surreal; Peter felt like he could be standing in timeless space. For those few moments, Parker College was a tranquil urban oasis. As encouraged by Dr. Redmon, he took a moment to appreciate the pure air before gathering his sack lunch and laptop from his car. He closed his eyes and imagined he had no future and no past—he had only this moment. After his first session with Redmon, Peter had begun meditating daily and made mindfulness a regular part of his routine. It was paying off, but he was still a long way from getting over the hump. His triggered episode on the ferry was still raw in his memory.

"Hey, jackass!" shouted Angela as she hurried toward him. Peter's contented smile stretched wider as he began to laugh. "What the hell?" she continued. "I thought you had an aneurism or something. There's nothing to even look at!"

"Exactly," said Peter. "I was just noticing there was nothing in the sky right now, absolutely nothing. I don't think I've ever seen that before."

"End Times!" said Angela. "It's a sign of the apocalypse."

"So, moving on," said Peter in his announcer voice. "Do you know the WOD?"

"Da what?"

"The Word of the Day! *Our thing.* Did you even look it up? Because I did. I know what the word is for *our special thing.*"

"Do you do this to your wife?" asked Angela. "Is that why she hates you? Actually, let me tell you. This is why your wife hates you, and if you didn't know she hates you… she does, because you do shit like this to the wonderful women in your life."

"She doesn't hate me. Well, she might. We don't talk enough for me to know how she feels about me," Peter chuckled.

"Oh, I struck a vein. Are you one of those couples I read about in the *New Yorker* who don't have sex?" Angela watched Peter turn beet red.

"Demotic," Peter said as they approached their building.

"What did you call me?"

"If you cared about *our thing*, you'd know."

"I see. You are. No sex. Are we talking like weeks or months? God, longer?"

"It means everyday language, commonplace vernacular." He was clearly enjoying the banter. "Of the common people."

"I hate to see a perfectly good man go to waste like that. It's a sin," she quipped, enjoying how red she was making Peter. "Okay, okay, so us rabble are demotic?" asked Angela.

"I think, more like the language we use is demotic, like as opposed to the Queen's English."

"I might not live the *life of the mind*, but at least I'm getting a little life of the booty," Angela said with a laugh, but also a little chip on her shoulder.

Peter's phone was ringing as he and Angela entered the office. He jogged to catch the call. Angela followed out of curiosity, which drew Collins from his office. It was Sally, asking him to come see Loch. Peter put on a concerned look when turning to his audience. "Steve, have you spoken with President Loch today?"

Collins seemed concerned but also excited that Peter was asking him about anything. "No. Why?"

"I don't know. He sounded odd just now," Peter rubbed his chin and snuck a wink to Angela. Collins also rubbed his chin, as that's what the how-to-advance-in-business book had told him he should do, in the chapter on matching and mirroring. *If you subtly match the gestures of the person you want to impress, then their subconscious will pick up on the similarities and it will immediately put them at ease. Their inner self says, "Hey, he's just like me."*

"Angry?" asked Collins. "Worried? What?"

"Nothing alarming. It just seemed slightly out of character, is all," said Peter mugging at Angela as Collins turned his head. "I just don't have the word for it. A more colloquial fashion. Not folksy, but . . ."

"Demotic?" interjected Angela.

"Yes! That's exactly the word I was looking for: demotic," said Peter patting Collins on the shoulder as he walked past. "Anyway, probably nothing. Well, I'll be back."

Collins looked like someone who'd suddenly found their fly open in public and retreated to his office.

* * *

Loch was standing behind his desk, looking like he had good news to share. David Noon had sued the college for $300,000 and settled for $20,000. He'd also signed a non-disclosure agreement, which likely meant the college was out of the woods as far as the *Stumptown* story was concerned. Loch and Peter breathed a collective sigh of relief.

"Were you surprised we were able to buy him off for twenty grand?" asked Peter.

"Buy him off?" Loch objected to the demotic phrase. "He was trying to extort the college. We weren't looking for any favors from Mr. Noon." Loch motioned for Peter to join him at the conference table. Loch's ability to disagree in a way that felt affirming put Peter at ease. His gibes were playful. Conversations with those he liked were collegial games of one-upmanship, but he tensed as they sat. "Peter, look, there's something else. There was more substance to the suit than I was originally made to believe."

The events outlined in the lawsuit were starting to take shape for Peter. He didn't want Loch to lie to him. Donning a poker face, he bit his lip and waited for the "official story." Loch admitted there had been drugs found in the Parker College Apartments that night. "It wasn't heroin packaged for distribution, and there was no blood, weapons, and scales and whatever else that was asserted by Noon and the reporter," Loch explained to Peter. "The night in question consisted of a small amount of cocaine, which the now-former head of security flushed down the toilet."

It was clearly a convenient story concocted by someone who knew the law. Possessing any amount of heroin is a felony, but there are misdemeanor amounts of cocaine, which come in the form and amounts preferred by white-collar users. The cocaine story was an attempt to write off the incident as poor judgment. If Loch believed what he was telling Peter, it was out of convenience. "So, like a personal-use amount of powder—like a misdemeanor amount?" Asked Peter with a dubious look, trying to insinuate it was unlikely to hold muster with the press.

"That's what I'm told. Yes." Loch was sticking to his story and knew he was going to have to work harder to convince his audience. "Peter, I came here because I believed Parker is a special place—filling a need in higher ed for truly inspired scholars and mentors to live the life of the mind."

There's that phrase again, thought Peter, feeling like he was being baptized into a cult.

"I came here because I believed Parker is a place for those who are motivated by the spirit of pure inquiry. I still believe that, and I think you do too," Loch's voice became more earnest as he spoke. "In fact, I believe in the mission of Parker College more than any place I've ever worked. I believe it's that special, while also recognizing that those who responded to what happened that night in the apartments exercised extraordinarily poor judgment. But there is nothing we can do about that now. It's over, that student was removed, and the employees who mishandled the situation are all gone. As president, I don't feel as if I can publicly chastise people for following orders that, frankly, I should have known about."

"Sir, I know that I'm new, and I certainly don't want to speak out of turn, but from what you're telling me, it might benefit you if that story did get out," said Peter. "A story that you discovered what happened and corrected our course could actually help you."

"I'm not throwing anyone under the bus," said Loch.

Peter moved the conversation forward. He was still curious about Craven trying to link the death of William James to the dealer from the lawsuit. There was still a potential story for the *Stumptown* reporter to chase. Loch was convincing in his belief that the two incidences could not be connected—there was significant time between them—but Peter expressed his concern about the remaining narrative. Loch dismissed it whole cloth. "It doesn't matter. They've all been silenced."

Peter was confused by the statement and kept talking while his brain caught up with his ears. "Maybe I'm over-thinking this. Noon settled, but the stakes still seem pretty high. I just don't want to leave any threads for Craven to pull. He could still identify others from the suit by their job descriptions."

"That's what I'm telling you. They've all signed confidentiality statements," said Loch. "There are no threads left to pull."

Holy shit, they gagged everyone involved with that night. He knows this was about more than an ounce of coke. Play dumb, thought Peter. *Be clever like the Raven.* "Good. Good," said Peter as he knocked on the wooden table. "Nothing else to worry about."

19

MONDAY, MARCH 10, 2008

March arrived disguised as February, which was indistinguishable from January, and almost exactly like December, which had been eerily similar to November. It was always 45 degrees and rainy, except when it was 35 degrees and rainy and everyone lived in fear of the snow that never fell. Peter remained desperate to find a new job, but the economy was still in a free fall and the bottom was not yet visible. Private- and public-sector jobs were being eliminated in droves. College endowments were contracting. Many institutions were eliminating entire academic programs, and most were implementing hiring freezes. Portland was second only to Detroit in its percentage of unemployed. TV newscasts were dominated by stories of bankruptcies and foreclosures, while being sponsored by ads for gold-buying services that would pay top dollar for grandmother's earrings and gold fillings. The houseless population exploded, and tent cities were popping up all over the city.

Portland's winter was long and gray, but on the bright side for Peter, he was still employed, still married, and still supporting his family. The college slowed to a lazy pace over winter break before returning for the spring semester and the cyclical intensity of academic life. The outlook was bleak for finding another position in higher education or any comparable job, but Peter's improving mental health was helping him balance the emotions that had previously flipped and flopped from fear to gloom. Meeting more faculty and staff had helped him understand that Parker's reputation for excellence was earned, outside of a few notable exceptions.

Sessions with Dr. Redmon continued to be helpful but were also often painful. Some sessions were slogs through the dense undergrowth of rationalization, while others felt like hiking through the pure air above the tree line. He was learning about himself and growing more self-aware with each visit. Redmon had diagnosed Peter with posttraumatic stress disorder and was teaching him to manage his triggered states with mindfulness and other tactics that kept him grounded. His meditation practice was helping him to be present in his interactions at work and to identify the onset of his triggering episodes. Their current therapeutic work was to identify the trauma that had resulted in Peter's PTSD.

Peter mostly enjoyed his sessions with Redmon. It was an *Odd Couple* relationship, with Redmon meticulously focused on a clean Felix-like approach in contrast to Peter's Oscar-like desire to tromp sloppily toward whatever shiny object that popped into his mind—which often had him talking about work issues. Redmon was always redirecting him back to his childhood to get him comfortable in the space where he was sure they would find Peter's trauma. Therapy was giving Peter tools to manage through his days, but he was frustrated that it was not quickly revealing the deeper issues the pair was seeking to heal.

"Even Zen masters get frustrated, so don't worry about that," said Redmon. "In here, we talk about being honest with ourselves and others—living an authentic life—being accepting of people where they are in their journeys. Unfortunately, you're in a work situation where being honest might get you fired, ergo, there's little room for authenticity in that environment. In a different economic climate, this kind of sacrifice may not be necessary, but for now it's part of your journey. So look for ways to learn from it."

"Yeah, I don't know. I do like when you say *ergo*. But besides that, though, I feel like I've been thinking down a slippery slope. There's an inside and an outside to life at the college. They talk about the *life of the mind* like Catholics talk about the Holy Trinity—part of this mystical force that only certain people can access. I know it's not a phrase used uniquely at Parker, but there is this inner circle of Parkies who really own it and give it an almost religious connotation, like a quest they believe excuses them from other societal conventions, like common courtesy, personal hygiene—and, at times, the law. It's bizarre. Everyone seems to be trying to convince me that no one outside the Parker bubble could possibly understand what happens inside the bubble, but that's my whole job—explaining things to outsiders. This indefinable thing must always be defended. It feels like a cult."

Redmon agreed those were attributes of cults: creating distrust of outsiders, an inner sanctum where greater status could be achieved, adherence to a unique ideology, creating an environment of self-governance. But Redmon observed that those attributes can also be identified within the Greek system, sports teams, and military units. He warned Peter to be concerned if the rationalizations were used to normalize what otherwise would be considered dangerous actions.

Parker College was an extreme place. Intense. Rigorous. Peter conceded and admitted he was afraid he'd started drinking the Kool-Aid. Many of the students he met were exceptional people, admirable, even inspiring. But there were others whose extreme behavior went unchecked and often rationalized as part of the unique exploration that is *the Parker College experience*. He wondered if his thinking was just too conventional. Peter desperately wanted help sorting through his moral dilemma. Redmon, however, desperately wanted Peter to focus on addressing the issues that were going to lead to deeper healing.

"When I was a reporter, I understood my responsibility to society. I have a lot of respect for—" Peter couldn't finish the sentence. He felt like a hypocrite. He'd left journalism because he believed in the power of education to expand minds. He'd hoped to foster the next generation of leaders, but he'd never thought the reality of his job would mostly consist of trying to normalize aberrant behavior. "The other day, Ben overheard Tess and me talking about Bacchanalia, the end of the year party. We were talking about increased security to watch for drug dealers. Anyway, Ben comes into my room in the middle of the night. He was crying, afraid I might be killed by drug dealers while I'm at work. How do you tell a nine-year-old that the dealers on a college campus are different than the ones under a railroad bridge? Every rationalization I would have used on a reporter fell to pieces while looking into Ben's eyes. This isn't the type of role model I want to be. If I believed in karma, I'd be asking myself what I did to deserve this."

Redmon's eyes lit up like he had been waiting for Peter to say the magic word. "Karma is something to be liberated from, not accumulated!" he exclaimed. He compared karma to the memories we hold in our subconscious that control our perception and sense of identity. It is a force that informs our self-worth and quietly influences what we believe we deserve in our relationships and our lives. Karma, he explained, is not left behind when you change jobs; it's something you bring with you. "Your karma is your karma. No judgment. It is what it is. In the same way that your past is your past. Regardless of how you got to *this moment*, now is always the time to take control of your life. *To live in this moment.*" Their job in therapy, he reaffirmed, was to make Peter aware of the forces keeping him from living consciously—to understand the emotions compelling his decisions. "We can control those forces by accepting their origins and by living consciously to identify their influence in our lives."

It all sounded reasonable, at the same time, overwhelming, and oddly mystical coming from Redmon. "So, like, we choose our karma and it filters our perception?"

"Not quite. We're speaking in metaphors, understand, but karma is what shades our perception. Living consciously is understanding how your reality is being filtered so you're able to see it without the filter. For instance, if you are afraid to see a snake while walking through a field, then every stick will look a snake. Your mind will treat them the same. If you free your mind from your fear of snakes, then you'll see a stick as a stick," said Redmon to Peter's obvious confusion. Redmon became more sharply focused. "You've felt stalled in your progress. I thought it would be a good time for us to really start looking at why our progress feels stalled."

"So, are you suggesting that, what? That I am somehow not—" Peter struggled for the right word, "being forthcoming?"

"Maybe. I don't know," said Redmon with a lack of emotion.

Peter's face turned red hot. His ears rang with a throbbing electric whir. He perceived a threat but was disoriented by its source. *Has Redmon turned on me? Where is this coming from? I completely trusted him with everything—every secret, every fear, and now he's doubting me? Is he attacking me? This is the one place I feel safe.* Peter was becoming triggered. A chill spread across his body, leaving a wake of goose bumps. Peter felt anxious and confused. He wished he wasn't there.

"How are you feeling right now, Peter?" Redmon's voice was once again soothing and friendly. Peter was not receptive. He was hunched over. His eyes focused on the empty space in the center of the room. "Peter, I need you to bring yourself into the present with me." His voice was filled with patience and concern. "I think you've come to an important place, and I need you to engage. Ask yourself why you're feeling this way." Peter was in a vulnerable state. He felt totally exposed, lost in the wilderness. He could see no reasonable alternative to trusting Redmon. He turned his head and raised his eyes like a scolded child, not knowing what was coming, not believing it could be anything but painful. "Just say the first thing that comes into your mind," said Redmon.

"It feels like you're blaming the victim." The words surprised

Peter as they left his grasp. He didn't know where they came from, and he wanted to take them back. Redmon nodded in what seemed to be relief, which confused Peter even more.

"Good," said Redmon. He cupped his hands in a clap and looked at his watch.

"That's it?" asked Peter, disappointed.

"You've taken a huge step today," said Redmon. "Continue to meditate. You're getting there. You should feel good about the progress you've made."

"This was progress?" asked Peter.

"The choice I've been asking you to make, Peter, is to examine the cause of your pain, to realize how it's making you feel in your current circumstance, so that you can understand it dispassionately, accept it, and let it go. Move past it. I want you to understand that you don't have to be defined by it—this is where non-judgment comes in—but first we have to know what *it* is," continued Redmon. "Parker College might not be the right place for you in the long term, but don't just be stuck there. Don't just do your time. Learn the lessons that are in front of you. Do the hard work of following your pain back to the place where you first grabbed hold of it—because it's not Parker College. I'm asking you to find its source so you can heal it and let it go. So you can live the life you're capable of living. Part of you is still seeing, interpreting, the world through the eyes of a traumatized little boy—*a victim*. We need to find that little boy so we can help him."

20

VOTING REFORM

CONFERENCE

In the spirit of Sir Thomas Malory, Marquis de Sade, and Paul Crewe from *The Longest Yard*, Peter was determined to embody Redmon's advice to make the most of his time at Parker College. Each morning, on their way to the campus coffee shop, Peter and Angela greeted everyone, faculty, staff, and students, on what they called their goodwill tours. Parkies lived in their heads and very few acknowledged those with whom they shared the world; this was especially true along the college's walking paths. Some of the greeted looked at them with scorn, others bemusement, but on average only one in thirteen would say hello back. If the pair could get their response ratio under one-in-ten by the end of the semester, they agreed to have the Latin translation of "We made Parker suck less" tattooed on their *pygae* (Latin for buttocks). He held onto these moments as if Rick Blaine had handed him the last exit visas out of Casablanca.

The work-related highlight of Peter's job since the start of the spring semester, however, was helping a group of political science students with the promotion of a voting reform conference. He was inspired by their excitement for the project and astonished by their intelligence. It felt like he was finally doing the work that drew him to Parker. Befriending students also gave Peter an unvarnished, unfiltered, but often unreliable porthole view into the goings on at the college. Having a broader perspective was helpful for his job, and his sanity.

Peter left the library meeting room with Glenn Nurse, a junior from rural Colorado and one of the conference's student coordinators. Glenn was a magnificently odd fit for Parker. He and Peter bonded over their love of the outdoors, or more accurately, their love of telling stories about outdoor adventures. Glenn's family had worked in resource extraction industries since the 1870s. He was an intellectual, born into a family of miners, tie hacks, and sawmill operators. Glenn embraced the entirety of his personality, which made Peter's embrace him and treat him like an old friend. Years of sun beaming though thin mountain air etched Glenn's face with impressive, crisscrossed contours. Deep crow's feet combined with the bend of his cheekbones to create the deception of a permanent smile, which belied his lonesome spirit. Glenn was reserved except when sharing his Paul Bunyan– like stories about his father. Peter's favorite was when the elder Nurse went mule deer hunting in Wyoming and startled a grizzly that swiped at him, taking a groove out of his arm. He made a tourniquet from his belt and started the three-hour hike back to his truck, but the bleeding persisted. Lightheaded, he stopped and made a fire to heat the blade of his Bowie knife. He used the glowing hot metal to cauterize his wound before pressing on. With almost an hour left to hike, he spotted a deer in a clearing, shot it, dressed it, and hiked it out. When Glenn's mom asked what the hell he was thinking, he smiled, winked at Glenn, and said, "we still had room in the freezer." Glenn had dozens of similar stories, but on this day, he was interested in knowing a story of Peter's.

As they walked past stacks of books in the architectural marvel of a building, Glenn whispered something that ran chills down Peter's spine. Glenn spoke so quietly that Peter only heard the words "Noon," "lawsuit," and something about keeping busy. Peter's eyes bulged and his heart skipped a beat. Glenn's knowing smile turned cold from concern.

"How do you know about that?" whispered Peter.

Glenn shared he had been a security guard and was on duty the night the incident took place. He'd worked with David Noon before they "professionalized" campus security, which meant they stopped hiring students to police other students. The administration figured out that after you fire a student worker, they remain a student and tended to stick around. It's harder to erase institutional memory when there are tuition-paying witness roaming the campus. Peter was face-to-face with firsthand knowledge that he wasn't sure he wanted to know, but still he cleared his schedule to make lunch plans with Glenn. They chose Pok Pok because Peter was as excited to try their world-famous chicken wings as he was nervous to learn what Glenn had to tell him.

* * *

Food & Wine Magazine called Pok Pok's fish-sauce chicken wings one of the ten best dishes in America. The recipe was a specialty of the lunch chef who'd brought it from Vietnam. The wings were marinated in fish sauce and palm sugar, deep-fried in peanut oil, and tossed in a garlic and caramelized Phú Quốc fish sauce. They were sweet and spicy, crispy and succulent, and often caused the lunch line to stretch around the block. As the two got close, Peter could have floated to the entrance like a cartoon character being enticed by the smokey come-hither aroma of the charcoal grills. The only things distinguishing Pok Pok from the residential houses on the block were the small line of people waiting by the door and a plastic tarp covering the outdoor grills. They were seated quickly. Peter ordered the wings, and then they talked about the conference as Peter tried to casually scan the small dining room for anyone he might recognize from the college.

"Parkies don't come here since it got all the good press," said Glenn with a smirk. "It's not even the crowds. It feels too much like conformity."

"Did they pay you to keep quiet?" Peter blurted, before realizing he was getting ahead of himself. "I don't want to get you in trouble for talking to me."

"I didn't take the settlement the others took. I couldn't have come here if they didn't give me full financial aid. So I already felt indebted," Glenn fidgeted and cracked his knuckles one at a time as he spoke. "I really do love this school. I don't think I would be who I am if it wasn't for Parker. Where I grew up, the word 'intellectual' is a euphemism for Bible-burning Devil-fucker. Parker was the only place willing to give me a chance.

I think a lot of students feel like I do. I didn't want some rich jerkoff creating a national myth that Parker's just a drug college."

Peter asked why he assumed it would be national news, and Glenn's demeanor took a 180-degree turn. He became distant and cautious. Tense. The waiter filled their water glasses while Peter and Glenn watched each other in silence. Peter shared that, except for the lawsuit, all he knew about that night was Loch's story about a small amount of cocaine. Glenn laughed in disgust. "Well, that's bullshit, but you really don't know who was involved that night?" Glenn fidgeted, and his eyes darted around the room. Glenn didn't spook easily, which caused Peter to contemplate whether he should brace himself for the bomb that was spiraling toward him or just turn and run. "It was Carson Billings Jr.," Glenn said carefully. Peter showed no sign of recognition. "Carson Billings Sr. is the founder and CEO of Billings Clean Energy, which owns the rights to half the natural gas in Pennsylvania, which is second only to Texas in new wells since, like 1990." Glenn seemed annoyed for having to educate Peter. "They're also into renewable energy... Anyway, Billings is a billionaire, or close enough to round up."

The waiter brought Peter's wings and coconut rice and Glenn's Tam Kai Yaang—roasted game hen—and left quickly after his pleasantries went mostly ignored.

"I'm going to guess that after that night, Billings went on medical leave," said Peter.

Glenn confirmed this and said Carson should never have been admitted in the first place. Billings leapfrogged half the waitlist after Goodwin got a personal call from Carson Billings Sr., according to Glenn's roommate, who was a student worker in the admissions department. The head of admission was furious and threatened to quit. *Billings was a waitlist full-pay who went on medical leave*, thought Peter. The details of Rhea's story were becoming clear.

Carson Billings Sr. wasn't psyched about his namesake attending Parker until they toured the health center. He had wanted him to go to an Ivy, but that changed after seeing how well-equipped Parker was for dealing with recovering addicts. In telling the story of how he enrolled at Parker, the junior Billings had joked that a relapse might kill him, but it would absolutely kill his father's political aspirations.

"Billings told you all this?" asked Peter.

"Yeah. We were friends until I found out he was using," said Glenn. "He told me he was clean, that he only used during high school, but he never stopped—still hasn't, as far as I know. Pretty soon after we met, campus security got a medical transport call to the apartments. Billings had overdosed on heroin."

"Was he just using? Did anyone suspect him of selling at that time?"

Glenn laughed in a burst. "So you really don't know any of this? He got amnesty that night. Calling campus security for help is like a get-out-of-jail-free card when somebody is so effed-up they might die."

"Makes sense; you don't want someone to die because their friends are afraid of getting in trouble."

"It's good. For sure. I know a lot of colleges do it, but there should be a limit—" Glenn veered the conversation back to the night Billings OD'd. "The apartment looked pretty much like it was described in the lawsuit. Except for the blood, it might have been worse. There were needles, scales, baggies, and the place was filled with trash: bare mattresses, beer cans, charred tinfoil everywhere. Later, much later, Noon told me he saw someone hide a gun. I didn't believe him until I saw it the night we went back."

"Billings had a gun?" Glenn nodded. He described the night like he was explaining a Peckinpah movie. Their food was getting cold. "So, you were there when he got transported to the hospital. It was clear to everyone he was dealing," Peter waited for Glenn's affirmative nod before continuing. "But he got amnesty because he'd called it in?"

"He got amnesty, but someone else called it in." Glenn was uneasy.

"So, was that person still with him when you got there?" asked Peter.

"The relevant detail is that he got amnesty," said Glenn before moving on to explain the night from the lawsuit. The director called him and Noon to rush to the Parker College Apartments. When someone dials 911 on campus, it's automatically routed into the campus dispatch. Campus Security and Portland Police simultaneously got a call about screaming and cars screeching out of the parking lot. Knowing it was Billings, the security director wanted Glenn to be there. He met them out front and told Glenn to warn Billings to hide anything incriminating. "His exact words were, 'Billings is a friend of yours. Go inside and be a friend. Make sure the cops don't find anything. You hide it if you have to.'"

Glenn's eyes were glassy, and his mind seemed stuck in the past; Peter's were popping out of his head. He glanced down for a moment at the tantalizing sight of one of the ten best dishes in America taunting him as he lost his appetite. *I might have one of the worst ten jobs in America*, he thought. Glenn's description of the night from the lawsuit was beyond Peter's ability to comprehend. Billings' girlfriend was naked, high out of her mind, barely coherent, and probably in shock. She had been drenched with blood. It was caked on her face, arms, and hair, but it stopped sharply around the outline of the clothes she was no longer wearing. Glenn covered her in a blanket while she shuffed her feet in circles through the sea of hypodermic needles. He tried to get her to sit, but it was like she was in a trance. Blood was splattered on the kitchen floor and walls; bloody footprints were tracked all over the apartment. Another woman, who seemed too old to be a student, had curled herself in a ball, holding her knees as she rocked on the floor in the hall by the bathroom. She kept repeating, 'just go away now, you need to make it go away now.' When Glenn opened Billings bedroom door, he saw a gun on the bed and a hand reaching for it. "He grabbed the gun and pointed it at me," Glenn's voice trembled momentarily. "But he, um, he stopped when he recognized me."

"Holy shit!"

"Yeah. Holy shit. The only thought going through my mind was *eight bucks an hour*. I'm going to die on my work-study job, making eight fucking dollars an hour. My roommate was giving tours and making coffee in the admission office, and I'm going to take a fucking bullet. Anyway, Billings asked me if I was there to score. There were bricks of heroin on the bed, four or five of them—kilos tightly wrapped with cellophane, like you see on the news. I told him the cops were on their way—he didn't care. He thanked me and said, 'Parker's got me covered.'"

"Was he just so fucked up that he didn't know what you were saying?" asked Peter.

"He was using, for sure, but he knew there would be no

consequence for him," said Glenn. Two police cruisers showed up, and Billings watched from his bathroom window as the director told them they weren't needed. As the cops drove off, Glenn noticed clothes and a knife soaking in a chemical solution in the bathtub. "So, right after the cops pulled off, Billings asked me how I was doing in my research methodologies class. He knew I hated that class. I was speechless. Billings went on medical leave, and a few days later, everyone who helped clean the apartment was called into a meeting with college's lawyer. He never told us we didn't cover up a crime; he just said that what the college did was not illegal." The quote Glenn remembered was, *there is no legal obligation to report a crime that happens on your own property.* A few months later, most of the people who helped clean the apartment had quit or were fired. The director retired and moved to a cabin somewhere up by the Molalla River.

"What was the blood? What happened?" Peter asked.

"Billings was in way over his head. There were cartels involved. Everything that went down that night was gang related," said Glenn. "It sounds like Billings funded some big shipment. All I really know is that it had to do with a lot of money and someone not getting their cut. I don't know any of the details, and I don't want to know them. Look, um, I've got to get back for a two o'clock class, but I really wanted to talk about Willy. I thought you knew all this."

"William James? How does he play into this?" Peter shifted around in his chair. It was clear how little he knew.

Glenn was worried whether he was doing the right thing or not by sharing his secrets. He'd assumed Peter had been brought in to help with the cover-up. He didn't think he was involving

Peter beyond the terms of his employment. Glenn sat upright, leaned forward, and spoke in a low forceful voice. "You do know that Billings is back on campus, right? He's living in the same fucking apartment—next to the community gardens."

"Jesus—" Peter was so tense that it looked like his skin might split apart.

"I assumed you knew all of this," Glenn conceded.

"These motherfuckers," said Peter. "I can't believe they didn't call the cops."

"Well, everyone who suggested that is gone—including David Noon. It was never an option, not after Billings paid his way in, and his way out," said Glenn. "Do you still want to know what happened, or is it better you don't know?"

"At this point, I have no idea what's best, but yes, please, I do want to know," said Peter with a frustrated grimace. "That way, at least I'll have the real story for my jailhouse memoir."

David Noon knew through the grapevine that Billings hooked up Willy with the drugs that killed him. Billings got a very pure shipment—the purer it is, the faster people get addicted, and the easier it is to OD if someone relapses. Noon sued the college to force Parker's hand. It wasn't about the money; he assumed the lawsuit would go public, and they'd be forced to expel Billings. Upon hearing this, Peter became overwhelmed with guilt for his role in killing the *STW* story.

"If this place had a heart, it was Willy," Glenn was on the verge of tears. Willy went to Vietnam at eighteen and saw atrocities that made him question every assumption he'd held about humanity. When he rotated out, he went to the seminary on the G.I. Bill, hoping to find answers. He quickly knew the seminary wasn't for him and went looking for God in other places. He ended up in a cult in Northern California taking peyote to induce visions, and speed to conquer sleep, thinking it would make him see God. He'd told Glenn, "I never found God, but I sure as fuck found out that I loved getting high." He was in and out of trouble and treatment for twenty years before ending up in Portland. He'd said he found in ideas what he was looking for in God: peace, strength, and direction.

"Billings hooked up Willy, that's all I really wanted to tell you. It's been eating me alive. I needed to tell someone. I thought you knew everything else. I didn't mean to get you mixed up in all this shit," said Glenn. "What happens now? Can you even still work here?"

"People did this," said Peter.

"But they're the people who are running the place,"

"They need to be exposed."

"I don't want to hurt Parker. This place means too much to me," Glenn seemed worried he'd set off a catastrophic chain reaction.

"This is bigger than the college, Glenn. You didn't do this," assured Peter. "What these fuckers did is evil. That's not your fault."

But is it mine? Peter worried, as he became engulfed with guilt. *What do I do now?*

21

BACK-UP PLAN

It was Peter's turn to choose the restaurant for date night. After Glenn connected the dots between Carson Billings, William James, and the lawsuit allegations, Peter needed comfort food in a quiet spot to talk with Tessa about a Plan B for their "new life." He picked O'Malley's, which Tessa disliked because it hadn't been painted since people could still smoke indoors and the ceiling was the color of rotting teeth. Peter blamed the brownish-yellow hue on poor lighting and chose not to look up while eating. After being nearly paralyzed with anxiety, he hoped their New England décor plus a few Sam Adams would work like Xanax to bring the calm and courage he needed to suggest the verboten idea of moving back to Juneau. It took a couple extra Boston Lagers and some bread pudding to get him over the hump. Tessa met the idea with fury and tumult. They fought for the rest of the evening. All Tessa wanted to hear was that Peter would work though his issues at Parker, and she wasn't terribly interested in knowing what they were. Ultimately, she wanted Peter to choose her over Juneau. If the choice was Alaska, however, Tessa made it clear that he would be returning on his own. It was Peter's second ruined restaurant meal of the day.

Since the couch hadn't made it into the trailer of useful things, Peter made peace with sleeping on the reclining chair. Grabbing a Bridgetown IPA—his favorite Portland thing—and a stack of unread magazines, he set up camp for the night. He fell asleep one beer and half a *New Yorker* later.

He was completely disoriented when his iPhone woke him at 2:15 a.m. to the sound of a marimba. In his roused grogginess, he thought it might be his alarm, until he saw the name of the campus safety director, Mike Marino, appear on the screen. Peter cleared his throat and braced for bad news. "You should probably get here A-SAP," said Marino. "A student OD'd in the dorms and the medical examiner is on the way." Adrenaline worked faster than coffee to bring Peter fully awake. Marino gave him a quick debrief of all the known facts: the student had a history of opioid use and fresh track marks on his arm. They assumed it was heroin, though there was no needle. He was found alone in his room at Munk Hall by his roommate. Peter told Marino to send any reporters to the North Lot and he would be there to meet them in twenty minutes.

Peter went into the bedroom and shook Tessa awake. She was resistant. "Tess, it was my work," Peter's serious tone made Tessa turn to him. "A student died in the dorms. They think it was a heroin overdose."

Peter was hoping, at least, for a conciliatory gesture from Tessa before he left. She just said, "fuck," rolled over, and let out a defeated sigh.

* * *

Peter was conflicted over the absence of TV news vans upon arriving at the North Lot. A well-done brief on the morning news could help dampen interest in the story. Breaking news reporters only have time to do superficial formulaic reporting: something happened near where I'm standing. A quote from someone with information, an additional fact or two, attach an ironic, sentimental, or sober hook when sending it back to the studio where the talking heads would reflect awkwardly on the hook before moving on to goofy banter with the sports desk or meteorologist. In this scenario, Peter would be the *someone with information*. He would be concise, contrite, and earnest while responding to questions. He would explain the devastation the college community would feel over the loss of the student and why legal protocol prevented him from sharing any details of the death until they knew the wishes of the parents. If Peter did his job well, the story would be boring enough to air after the first commercial break when most viewers had already changed the channel or started making breakfast. His interview would leave no dangling threads for additional reporters to tug on. In the absence of a morning TV brief, the print reporters would see the death in the police blotter and start looking for evidence that matched their suspicions. They could spend a day or two digging for information before he even knew they were on the story. If it broke in print, it was much more likely to break badly. Peter's task was to find the most sympathetic story arc and direct the news coverage into that narrative—his job was to make the college look good, or at minimum, competent. If there were a hundred story angles for the night's events, maybe two were reasonable, seventy-five were awful, and the other twenty-three were devastating. *The DA is three months closer to elections than when he was busting our balls over the lawsuit. Why couldn't I be a reporter? There's a career-making story for anyone with half a brain and a pencil.*

Peter's mind spun ahead, anticipating variations on reporters' questions. His ears were ringing, and his eyes struggled to maintain focus. The grounding tactics he'd learned in therapy were proving ineffective against counteracting images of his family living in the tent city by the Ross Island Bridge. He hadn't felt this scared since disembarking the *Columbia*. Trying to stave off a total loss of control, he sat in the car and practiced box breathing. He filed his lungs with air to the count of four. Then held it for a count of four, before exhaling at the same pace. Then he kept his lungs empty for the same count, one, two, three, four before repeating the pattern several times until he was calm enough to function. The stakes were too high. Failure would mean disaster. Exiting his car into the night fog, he took one last deep breath while trying to recall which path led to the dorms. The farther along the path he went, the thicker the fog became, making Peter question if he'd gone the wrong way. *I miss the briny smell of Juneau fog*, he thought, before seeing the lights of the coroner's van parked at the entrance of Munk Hall.

A student died. The reality hit him like a gut punch. A heart stopped beating. Peter hadn't paused long enough to see the human tragedy, but as he did, it made him lurch forward and vomit on the path. He doubled over, spat in the grass, and remained there until he was sure nothing else was coming up. Someone's child was never coming home. Parents were about to know the pain of losing a child; the very feeling that haunted Peter so deeply it tempted him to jump from the *Columbia*. Such a loss was unbearable to fathom, *but what kind of a monster am I for having overlooked it*. His thoughts rushed to his own children sleeping in their beds. *I want to hold them. I didn't even get to tell them I loved them before they went off to sleep tonight*.

His focus turned from concerns of bad press for the college, to worries the media would try to make an example of the student. God forbid his death was somehow tied up with Billings, he'd become a footnote in the scandal that rocked Parker College. *His death will not be his own*, thought Peter. He swore to preserve the student's humanity while at the same time cursing the conviction that he'd lost his own.

The moisture in the dense fog clung in beads on the pile of Peter's fleece jacket and glistened like diamonds as he walked under the lampposts that lined the entrance to the dorm. Peter saw the silhouette of a large man waiting in the glass foyer of Munk Hall. The harsh lamp light refracting off fog made it hard to see who it was. Peter hoped it wasn't Vince Craven waiting to pounce on the story. After brushing beads of dew from his jacket, he cupped his cold hands to his mouth to warm them with a gust. Smelling his breath, provoked a *whoa face* and made Peter check his pockets for a mint or gum to cover the sour acidic taste of bile polluting his mouth. The silhouette moved to open the door. It was Mike Marino. Peter shook Mike's massive hand. "Hey, thanks for meeting me. You doin' okay?"

"Me? Oh yeah," said Marino as they walked into the dorm. "I'm sure it will hit me as soon my head hits the pillow, and I'm trying to fall asleep. The ME is here. They should be wrapping up any minute—Jesus. Sorry. I really didn't mean that."

Peter smiled uncomfortably. Marino updated Peter: no signs of press. The medical examiner was still in the dorm room with the deceased. The police in Chevy Chase, Maryland, had been dispatched to inform the parents of their son's death. The roommate was in the study hall with a counselor. Lots of students were inquiring about the emergency vehicles, so Rosen was writing an email to inform the students who live in the dorm about the death. "He knows we can't name the student until the parents have been notified, right?" interrupted Peter.

"I don't think he does," said Marino. "He was asking for his laptop when I left him. We should probably catch him to be sure."

Peter followed Marino as he rushed through the foyer and down the narrow corridor. A uniformed Portland police officer came around the corner and instructed them to stand against the wall. After poking his head into the study room by where the hallways met, the cop gave an okay gesture to someone around the blind corner. Peter and Marino pressed their backs against the wall as the squeaking gurney wheels swiveled to find a unified path. As the medical examiner walked faster, the repetitive squeaking escalated in pitch. Peter heard the noise as if it were entering his body through his spine; each squeak was like the jab of a needle climbing up his vertebrae. The dreadful anticipation of seeing the body, Peter's guilt, and his visceral reaction to the squeaking wheels combined to create a warzone of emotions within his body and mind. He was focusing on the diffuse shadow moving along the back wall when from around the corner came the flash of blue plastic, white sheets, and stainless steel. The hallway was dense with the smell of off-gassing plastic. Breathing the intense chemical smell made Peter dizzy. The blue bag snuggly hugged the student's head, feet, and shoulders. Peter and Marino had to turn their feet parallel with the wall to allow the gurney to pass. *I don't even know his name*, thought Peter, as the body got close enough to touch. More accurately, he hadn't cared who it was before seeing the ME's van. While driving to campus, the death only represented a problem to be solved—bad press, a threat to his job. *How did I get here?* Peter wondered. The uneasy rustling in the pit of his stomach became a tempest of guilt and anguish. *Am I complicit in this kid's death? Could I have done something to prevent this? What should I do now?*

The seam of the body bag dug into Peter's jacket causing his knees to buckle. He pressed his palms against the wall to steady himself. Then came a flash of horror. For an instant, it was as if Peter's mind had traveled back in time to his childhood home in Brighton, Massachusetts. He was experiencing the memory, like he was in his eight-year-old body. Standing by the living room window of his parent's rented home, he could smell the musty wooden window frames. Young Peter was dressed in denim painter's pants, Converse All-Stars, and a blue tee-shirt with a white Adidas logo. Alone, afraid, and confused, he was trying to open a window that overlooked the driveway, but humidity had swelled it shut. Outside, near the garage, his aunt was standing with a Boston cop on a strip of grass they called their yard. He wanted to be with her. It was hard to tell if the cop was keeping her from falling or restraining her. His aunt reached her hands to her mouth as a gurney rolled from the garage. Men in dark slacks and white short-sleeved shirts were wheeling out a body covered by a white sheet.

A second pair of uniformed men came from the garage wheeling a smaller body. Peter's aunt shrieked in anguish, struggled away from the cop, and ran toward the gurney. The cop only feigned to stop her, shrugging off the angry comments from one of the EMTs who moved to block her from reaching the body. While fighting to get past the EMT, she grabbed a fistful of sheet. As the cop helped the EMT pull her away, the sheet came with them. Peter saw his lifeless mother lying on the gurney. He screamed, "Ma! Ma!" Pounding to loosen the window frame, he couldn't get it to budge. He ran through the kitchen, past cops and gossiping neighbors, and out the back door. By the time he got around to the driveway, her body was in the ambulance, and the doors were closed. His aunt was hysterical. She grabbed the horrified young boy and continued to sob uncontrollably. Peter felt lost and alone.

This was the moment Peter had been working toward in therapy. The memory of his parents' death came back to him but chose the worst possible moment to reveal itself. The body bag was still brushing against the fleece of Peter's jacket as his mind drifted back into the present. The sight of the student on the gurney had loosened the memory he'd been trying to dislodge. Now that it was free, he felt the full weight of its burden. There was too much to process, too many levels of complexity stacked atop one another to make sense of any of it. He had to compartmentalize his personal trauma from the current crisis. It was like a leak in a submarine. Peter had to contain it by sealing off the flooding compartment, adjust the ballast, and concentrate on saving the whole ship. The water was ankle deep and rising quickly. Marino helped steady Peter.

"You gonna make it?" asked Marino with a friendly wink.

Peter forced a smile and took a breath to steady his nerves. He conjured a triumphant memory, so his smile wouldn't seem fake. The captain of the submarine had to exude confidence even as the water was rising. He forced a chuckle. "I'm fine. It's just, uh, as a dad, it's just hard to see. You know?"

"If this becomes normal for us," said Marino dryly. "I want you to promise me that we'll go open a hotdog stand or something."

"Deal," said Peter with a grin, hoping Marino couldn't sense the shockwave of panic surging though him. For a few seconds, Peter allowed himself to wonder about the context of his memory. Clearly his parents hadn't died in a car crash as he'd always assumed. But what did happen? Then Peter closed and sealed the hatch to the memory and continued with the tasks at hand. He had no choice but to keep going. Parker College did not accept weakness—especially not in a time of crisis—*six directors in eight years*. Rosen followed behind the corpse. He had been in the room when the ME zipped the student into the bag. Rosen knew of students who'd died after being expelled, but this was the first time he had seen a body being prepared for the morgue. His eyes were hollow. Marino put his hand on Rosen's shoulder.

"You alright, boss?" he asked.

"Well, Mike, I'm not certain any of us is alright," said Rosen. "But thank you."

Peter checked; the email had not been sent. The police told Rosen the college could not share the student's name before his parents had been notified. If they did send an email without naming the student, warned the police public information officer, they should be prepared to get overwhelmed with calls.

News travels quickly, and everyone will want to know the deceased was not their friend or child or whomever they care about most. Rosen let them know the student's name was Josh Leonard. Peter didn't know him but hearing his name for the first time made him feel like he might vomit again. "I can help you write the email, if you'd like."

"Will you call the parents for me too?" joked Rosen, immediately regretting his light tone. None of them spoke. Nobody knew what came next. The break in conversation made the rhythmic squeaking of the gurney wheels agonizingly loud even as it faded down the hallway. Rosen made plans to meet with Peter in his office for help writing the email, then excused himself to check on Josh's roommate.

"In the interim, I'm just going to walk around a little bit and make sure there aren't any reporters snooping around," said Peter.

"Would they really do that?" asked Marino.

"Only the ones I'm worried about," Peter replied.

"I'm going to check in with dispatch to see if there's anything else going on before I head out," said Marino. "It is Friday night after all; there must be something else going wrong."

Peter wasn't really worried about finding reporters. He was afraid he was losing his mind and needed a minute to ground himself. His most formative childhood experience and possibly the key to mitigating his PTSD, was drastically different than anything he'd imagined. *What did happen?* Peter wondered. He'd lost touch with the conscious world for two seconds, maybe less, but it seemed like a lifetime. *That can't happen again. I need to be flawless.* There would be no safe place for him moving forward. He couldn't show any signs of cracking under pressure.

How did my parents die? Their bodies were recovered at our house. They obviously didn't die in a car accident. What happened? Did I witness it? God, was I involved somehow; was it my fault? Is that why my aunt never talked about it? Peter felt raw and exposed. *I have no choice but to disregard my fears,* he decided. *It's the only hope I have at keeping my shit together. Don't be reckless, but don't fear the outcome. Stay in this moment. It's all I have.*

Peter indulged himself a moment of yearning for his mother's caring voice to wrap him like a warm blanket, tell him she loved him, and that everything would be alright. He wondered what advice his father would have offered. Then Peter hardened his façade into the seasoned professional Parker College demanded; but raging just beneath the surface were the emotions of a frightened eight-year-old boy. *It's all uphill from here,* thought Peter, *and the path to the summit is obscured by clouds. I don't know how far I have left to travel, but I need to keep moving.*

Peter wandered through mist and fog toward the North Lot, focusing hard to stay in the moment and to feel of the ground beneath his feet. He got a text, asking him to meet in Rosen's office sooner than planned.

* * *

Peter needed to stay focused on his job. *I need a work ally,* he realized. He needed information that was not being filtered through the college's hierarchy. Mike Marino was the only other person embroiled in the current situation who was not entangled in the events from the lawsuit debacle. *If Billings is involved in Josh's death, we'll be asked to comply with the cover-up, and I can't do that. Either way we'll both be dispensed the second we're not needed.* Peter decided he'd go looking for Marino when he saw his giant frame cutting a path through the fog on his way to the North Lot. "On your way home?" Peter asked as Marino approached.

"I think it's time to call it a night," said Marino.

"Did Rosen ask you to check on Billings first?" Marino's eyes bulged and he leaned aggressively toward Peter.

"That's not something you need to worry about, my friend. I ain't the last guy," said Marino with a glint in his eye to do harm to anyone who continued along that line of questioning. Peter laid his cards on the table. He told Marino he thought they were in the same situation—covering for sins they did not commit—and that they would be the next ones fired unless they helped protect Billings. Marino was not in the mood to hear anything Peter was saying.

"Look Mike, I'm going to do everything this side of legal to support my family. I'm a big boy and understand how the world works. All I'm asking is that you tell me if they ask you to lie about what happened here tonight. I'm not covering for some fucking deplorable billionaire."

"What went down with Billings was nuts, but that was on the last guy. Not me," reiterated Marino.

"I'm only asking for a heads up," pleaded Peter. "If they ask you to lie, we both eventually lose our jobs, you first, probably." He had Marino's attention. "The only ones left who had a hand in the first Billings fiasco are Loch, Goodwin, and Rosen. Everybody else is gone. Everyone. There's only room in the lifeboat for guys like us while we're rowing them to safety."

"Jesus Christ," said Marino. "I didn't want to believe that's how things work around here."

"Me either. I hope I'm wrong. I hope they don't ask us to

lie," said Peter. "But if they do, we'll know it's broken beyond repair. I'll keep you in the loop. Will you do the same for me?"

"I'll let you know what I can. There's no evidence, that I know of right now, that links Billings to Josh," said Marino as he slowly swung his hand in for a shake. "For what it's worth, Rosen tells me that Loch puts a lot of trust in you. I'm certainly glad you're on my side."

"Thanks, Mike."

"That wasn't a compliment," said Marino with half a grin.

* * *

Massaging the bridge of his nose with his thumb and index finger, Rosen arched over his keyboard with his elbows on the desk. The only light in the office was the green glow of his computer screen. Rosen's silhouette made it hard to judge whether he was exhausted, crying, or angry. As Peter got close, Rosen pulled the chain of his banker's lamp. The increased light illuminated no additional clues about Rosen's disposition. Rolling his chair from the desk to make way for Peter to read the draft, Rosen said he was aspiring to be concise, non-alarmist, and congenial. Peter smiled because he wasn't sure if Rosen was joking or having a nervous breakdown. Peter's only edit was to the speculation at the cause of death.

"He had fresh track marks on his arm and a history of use," Rosen was on the calmer end of the annoyance continuum but edging toward exasperation.

"It's not our job to call it. It's speculation until the coroner determines it officially," said Peter. "Until the coroner makes the call, we have to wait and see if the parents are willing to publicly share the cause of death. If you want to send something sooner, we just have to be more careful. We can't get ahead of the parents. And, yes, we should assume your email will find its way into the press, and if it does, and we're wrong, that would really suck."

They were interrupted by the ringing of Rosen's phone. Peter thought it might be the parents which caused a pang of dread. When Rosen heard the voice on the other end, it drained the limited remaining blood from his face. He squirmed in his chair as he looked to Peter. *How much worse could it get?* Peter wondered. Rosen shook his head as he put the phone on the desk, covering it with his hand. "Well, it appears the shitstorm has hit landfall."

"What?"

"That was John McMahon, the assistant district attorney, letting us know he'll be watching closely as we respond to our *current situation.*"

"Fu-uh-uh-ck, are you kidding me?" Peter covered his eyes with the palms of his hands. "Yeah, getting a threatening call from the DA at four in the morning, is um… a category–we're-fucked hurricane."

"Insightful," said Rosen with the smallest hint of a smile. Rosen agreed to change the wording of his email to reflect Peter's suggestions. He also let Peter know Loch had called a meeting with him and the VPs for the morning. "There was an agenda attached, which he predicted had just changed with that phone call. Go get some sleep, and we'll see you in a few hours. And if I'm not at the meeting, please ask them not to come looking for me."

Peter wondered if the DA's call was the impetus for Rosen's increased sense of comradery or if he had begun grooming him to take part in the cover-up. Peter hated that he had to wonder.

22

RAIN FROM A BLUE SKY

Peter managed a few hours of sleep, a shower, and hugs with his kids before getting back to campus. It was one of those odd Pacific Northwest days when rain was falling from the only cloud in an otherwise clear blue sky. The revelation surrounding his parents' death, and the single rain cloud that seemed to be following him, made Peter feel like the well-meaning Joe Btfsplk from the Li'l Abner comic, who had a dark cloud perpetually hanging over his head. Like Joe, Peter chose to ignore the dark cloud, at least until he could process it with the help of Redmon. When Peter got to the president's office, Rosen, Goodwin, and Loch were already meeting, and Collins was waiting in the outer office. Peter was unable to muster the energy to hide the disappointment of seeing Collins. Sigh. He wanted to press his ear against the door to see if they were talking about Billings, but he knew Collins would snitch. Peter wasn't proud of treating him like a dishrag, but it was hard to respect someone who chose to master the art of kissing ass over mastering the skills to do his job. Death, however, has a way of stimulating altruistic impulses.

"Steve, can I talk to you like a friend?" Peter asked Collins, sincerely. He nodded indecisively. "You're in way over your head." Collins rolled his eyes. "Steve, I'm trying to help you. I really am. It's likely that any road we choose here is going to lead to disaster. We've got to be really good and really lucky to get out of this with our heads still attached. The best thing for you to do is to stay out of the way, survive this, and learn how to do your job because you might end up as last man standing."

"What did I ever do to you?" asked Collins. "You've been irascible with me from the second you learned I was in this position. You owe me respect."

"I'm not sure I owe you anything, Steven, but I'll give you an explanation," Peter continued earnestly. "You got Rhea fired because she wanted to do the right thing. That's why I don't respect you." Steven looked away. "And *irascible* was yesterday's Dictionary.com Word of the Day," Peter continued. Collins slumped and shook his head in disgust. "Stop focusing on mastering the bullshit and learn how to do your fucking job. We should be working together right now, but I can't trust you. Nobody trusts you. That's why your staff treats you like a toddler with a handgun. They're only afraid of the damage you can do. I'm telling you this because I respect your staff, Steven. Now, I'm being completely serious: for your own good, stay out of the way."

They sat in uncomfortable silence. Peter was feeling as if he'd done his good deed for the day. Collins was plotting his revenge. Loch poked his head around the door and signaled for them to enter. Rosen was in the same clothes as the night before, unshaven, with matted hair. Loch clearly hadn't slept. Goodwin looked clean and fresh, wearing dress slacks, a sports jacket, and a tie.

Loch brought Peter and Collins up to speed. The parents knew about Josh's drug problem. His father said he went to bed every night fearing, dreading, anticipating the night when the police would come knocking with tragic news. After the parents learned of the uptick in overdoses near campus, they agreed to share the cause of death to spare another family from going through the same pain. They were unwilling, however, to publicly share Josh's history of use. Not disclosing that Josh died while relapsing, they understood, would make everyone assume his heroin habit was acquired at Parker. Putting on his clinician's hat, Rosen shared that Josh's parents believed he had been clean, which fits with the profile. Overdoses are common during relapse. Addicts default to their previous dose, but their tolerance is diminished. Rosen looked like he was trying to read the room. "I think that could also be a lifesaving message that would be very useful to share."

There was an awkward balance while walking the tight-rope between the institution's reputation and the legacy of a nineteen-year-old. The knee-jerk impulse of the top brass was always to protect the college—to defend the *status quo*. At the most basic level, the group was about to choose between acting in accordance with the credo professed in their founding documents or acting to protect their brand and their position in the college-ranking magazines. During times of crisis, people show their true nature, Peter believed, and he yearned for Loch to make the right choice. It felt like watching the wheel of fate.

"I don't see why we can't just share whatever we think is in the best interest of the college," said Goodwin. There was a weighty pause.

Loch pondered aloud if HIPPA and FERPA were still enforceable after a student dies, before suggesting it was probably in the college's best interest to observe the parents' wishes. Peter agreed it was wise to follow the parents' desire. He didn't care how they got to the right decision, he just wanted to be on the right path. To reinforce Loch's direction, Peter moved the conversation to the next decision.

"My experience as a reporter, when covering untimely deaths... Well, let me just say, there is a marked difference before and after family members see the deceased. First comes denial and then comes anger and bargaining. It would be good if the parents spoke with reporters before they got to Portland, or at least before they got to the morgue, if possible."

"Why do the parents need to talk with the press at all?" asked Goodwin. "God knows what they might speculate, or who they might try to implicate?"

"We can't appear to be discouraging the parents from talking with the press," Loch quickly cut off that line of conversation. "Peter, what's next?"

"We need to know what we *are* going to say publicly about the death," said Peter. "And who's going to say it. Keeping in mind whatever we say internally is likely to find its way into the press. My thoughts are that we should send a statement to faculty, staff, and students from the president, expressing what a terrible loss Josh's death is to our community. I think we should include the cause of death, and of course include the parents' statement as to why they thought it was important we share it as a warning. Then detail whatever additional heath center and counseling support we'll provide. Does that sound about right?"

Everyone remained silent, which Peter took as acceptance.

"Who talks to the press?" asked Loch.

"Different institutions handle it differently. One school of thought says the president only delivers good news."

"And bad news preceding his resignation, I assume?" Loch asked wryly.

"To date, you've been the face of the institution—" Peter paused as his brain caught up to his mouth. He had to check himself to make sure he was not about to reveal more than he was supposed to know about Billings. "But I don't want to put you in a situation where you may contradict information that might come out later."

"Such as—" Goodwin snapped, sitting upright in his chair.

"Look, we need to be able to speak honestly in this room. We are all aware of the allegations from the lawsuit," said Loch in a passionate and lecturing tone. "A student is dead of a heroin overdose. There are accusations, of which some reporters are aware, that we had a heroin den operating on campus. *There*—I said it. Peter is rightfully concerned that some ambitious reporter may try to connect one with the other, and that I might be trapped in what may appear to be a contradiction. As I see it, the stakes are the same regardless of who speaks with the press. If I'm not willing to do it myself, I'm not willing to send one of you out there to do it either."

Peter wasn't sure Loch would fall on his sword so valiantly. *He must be protecting me*, thought Peter. Protective or not, it was likely that both of their jobs hung in the balance.

"I respectfully disagree," said Peter, testing Loch's sincerity. "You're the president of the college. That carries more weight than if *I* 'misspoke.' A spokesman is expendable. That's why we exist. No one measures institutions by the reign of their spokesperson."

"Well, then I'll be careful not to misspeak," said Loch. "I've been pretty vocal to this point. I think it would be conspicuous if I suddenly became shy of the media."

"I agree," chimed Goodwin.

"I'm sure you do, Alistair. I'm sure you do," said Loch. "Sounds like we have our plan."

"I'll take first crack at writing the email," said Loch. "Heartfelt messages should probably come from the heart of the signer."

23

MANAGING THE PRESS

Two were dead of heroin overdoses on campus, and if Peter's intel was right, the college was protecting the drug dealer. Peter didn't know the whole truth, but choosing between the *official story* and the *credible story* was testing his veracity. Lying to a reporter felt like a life-or-death ultimatum—a red line he had never contemplated crossing. As he arrived at work on the Monday after Josh's death, however, the fear of becoming destitute as the economy continued its freefall had Peter testing the strength of his convictions. *What I know about Billings is more like a rumor. If I stick with what Loch told me, rather than what Glenn told me, then I'm not really lying, because I'm just sharing the official version of what happened.* The rationalization caused an icy shiver to run down his spine. He waited to see if the chill would warm as it settled in his gut—it did not. Desperation invited fatalistic thinking. If he was going to be fired anyway, he hoped it would come before saying something he regretted to the press. There was nothing enviable about the tasks that lay before him. *This is how it happens,* he thought as he turned off his car. *No one decides to become evil. You make one concession to your principles, then the next comes easier, then it starts to feel normal, and then you start to defend the corruption of your soul as being pragmatic. Then it's just who you are. You give away little bits of yourself until someone else owns you.* Peter took a deep breath. *At 12:15, I meet with Redmon. I can make it until then. Stay focused and in the present.*

Angela shouted, "hey, jackass," as she jogged across the parking lot. Peter struggled to manage a smile, but it didn't hide the pain in his eyes. Angela knew that look. She'd seen it before, just before Rhea was fired and in the two directors before that. She slowed her pace as the joy left her body. Having predicted this moment in a joke made her hate it more as she witnessed it in reality. "Be careful about falling in love with the college," an old Parkie once told her. "It will take everything you have to give, but it can never love you back." She'd shaken it off as a bitter trope, but now she was starting to understand.

Peter told her about Josh's death. "When they wheeled his body past me on the gurney... I have no words for what that felt like," Peter admitted. "Now I'm going to have to figure out a way to talk about him to the press, as they likely blame us for his death."

"What the fuck were you even doing there?"

"There's no playbook for this," he said. "Nobody knew what they were doing."

Angela stopped on the path and put her hand on Peter's arm. He could feel the compassion in her touch. Intense emotion shone in her eyes, sending chills to Peter's core. Trying to look away, Angela stepped into the path of his gaze. "Are you okay?" She was the first to ask how he was managing; everyone else just wanted to know if the circumstances could be managed. She didn't know the depths of his challenges, but the warmth of her eyes penetrated so deeply that it touched the emotionally abandoned eight-year-old boy who needed to know he'd be okay. For one moment, Peter found a place where he was seen and felt safe. He wanted to tell her everything. He wanted to lose himself in her kindness. But he could not trust his feelings for her. He didn't know if they were real, and to make it through the day, he needed to cling to the protection and familiarity of his armor. Tears welled in the corner of his eye. He dabbed them before they fell.

"I'm okay," he lied.

"I don't believe you," she said. "You can trust me, you know."

Peter nodded, knowing his voice would belie any reassuring words that he could get to slide past his lips. They walked in silence for a while. Angela was frustrated; Peter was hoping his brittle façade would hold.

"Did you know the student?"

"No," said Peter. "I was on campus Saturday to meet with Loch and the VPs. Afterward, I went to a dorm meeting where they talked about him. Josh Leonard was his name. I learned a lot about him, though. He seemed like a pretty amazing kid."

"Nobody says shitty things about the dead," said Angela. "Was he rich?"

"Probably. He was from Chevy Chase," said Peter. "Why do you ask?"

"Was it heroin?"

"They think so," Peter was worried by the ease with which she was able to diagnose the scenario. "Did *you* know him?"

"I know the stereotype. Suburban white kid pays $60 a pill for Oxy until they get caught, their money gets cutoff, and then they turn to heroin because it's cheaper and more accessible. It's common with rich kids, but also working-class people who lose their health insurance and still need pain meds."

"How common is this?" Peter asked.

"I don't know," she said, "common enough for me to have read about it in the *Times* or wherever. We don't hear about it as much because it's mostly a white suburban problem, so Congress hasn't declared war on it yet."

"I knew about Oxy, but heroin! Jesus?!?"

"It's the same high, evidently," she said. "And, you know, I knew he was rich because the poor kids get kicked out and die in the privacy of their own homes."

"Good lord. Okay, well, thanks for filling me in. I'll include our conversation in my talking points for the VPs." Peter said with a defeated smile as they reached the stairs.

* * *

It was 9:45 a.m. and Peter's phone had not rung. He fought the temptation to feel like the college had dodged a PR bullet. He continually checked the *Portland Daily*, the *STW*, and TV news websites for mentions of Josh's death. He Googled "Parker + College + Death," "Parker + College + heroin," "Portland + college + student + dies" and it returned nothing, nothing, and nothing. Peter wandered upstairs to the president's suite to ask Sally if she had received any press calls. "Not yet, but we will," she said. It had been more than twenty years since they'd lost an enrolled student—that had been to suicide. Sally kept a handwritten list of all the kids who died after they left. She wanted to know they wouldn't be forgotten. Sally got to know the students on both extremes: the kids on their way up and the kids on their way out. Top students looking for grad school and grant recommendations, and the financial aid students appealing their suspensions to the president on their way out.

Peter nodded warmly. Sally was the rock of Parker College, a quiet plodder who never openly questioned the decisions of her superiors or showed her cards to anyone—until now. Peter held out his hand for Sally to hold. She grabbed it quickly and squeezed hard. A tear welled in her eye. She released his hand as quickly as she took it and then reached for a tissue.

"We'll get through this, Sally," Peter said confidently. "And we'll fix the rest later."

Her smile was hard to read, Peter wasn't sure if it was acceptance, or defeat, or appreciation she had someone to help her bear the weight. "And soon we'll have world peace," she said with a small brave smile, knowing the work is never done. Sally and Peter shared a bond. They knew things above their paygrade. Holding those secrets came with an emotional cost. The burden of watching the few students who fell through the cracks each year was multiplied by the length of her career. It had become a burden too heavy for Sally to carry alone. In her own way, she was asking Peter to help shoulder the load. Presidents stay at Parker for five or six years before moving on, presumably forgetting, but Sally was left to remember all the fallen students.

At roughly the same time Sally had begun her job at the

college, Peter had watched Loch on the WCVB-TV Five O' Clock news in Boston with Chet Curtis and Natalie Jacobson. Loch had made a campaign stop at a picket line in the neighboring city of Lynn to show support for striking shoe factory workers. He opened by saying, "I know that no one here can cast a vote for me, but I came to say that I stand with any man, and any woman, who is willing to demand fair pay, decent working conditions, and the right to organize. And I stand in opposition to anyone willing to deny these basic human rights. I'm proud to stand with you today. A right that is taken for granted is a right that will be taken away. Every generation must reestablish the equality its forbearers earned, just as you are doing here now. I would assert that anyone who stands against your cause stands against the American way of life."

That's the guy Peter had left Juneau to work for. He wasn't sure Loch was still that guy.

* * *

Angela swiveled around in her chair as the doorknob rattled. "Hey, the guy with the sausage fingers was here looking for you," said Angela. "It seemed important. He left a note on your chair."

Peter reached for the note as he checked his voicemail light. No blinking. The note was written on copier paper, folded into thirds, and placed on Peter's chair. It was from Mike Marino: "They asked me to lie. I'll be gone by the time you read this. Get out!"

This must be a joke, thought Peter as the phone rang. *Surely, I was a Nazi in my last life. I was just following orders.* It was Debbie Samuelson of the *Portland Daily.* Everyone *in the know* called her Sam. Peter had not yet earned that privilege.

Samuelson had started at the *Daily* as a news clerk when she was in high school. She simultaneously worked her way through Portland State University and up the ladder of the *Daily*'s newsroom. A call from Sam increased the likelihood of seeing your name on the front page above the fold by about 40 percent. She was sharp, confident, and affable. She engaged in the requisite small talk with Peter, knowing he would become one of her regular contacts. They mostly chatted about Peter's background as a reporter and editor in Alaska. As their get-to-know-you chat wound to its conclusion, she told Peter she was having coffee on Sunday morning with a friend who worked in the medical examiner's office. She said Josh's death came up as part of their casual conversation, which seemed to be an obvious lie. It puzzled Peter. *What's her motive to lie?* he wondered.

Peter wanted her to trust him and immediately told her everything he knew. Josh's name, age, hometown, dorm, and suspected cause of death. "Of course, that's not something I would normally be able to tell you, but the family was aware of his circumstances, and they agreed we could share it. They really wanted to share the cause of death to help prevent this from happening to anyone else in case the drugs were tainted or something."

"You said his family was aware of his problem. So, he had a history of drug use?"

"I said they were aware of the circumstances. I meant the ME let them know it was a suspected heroin overdose. If I insinuated anything else, I apologize. As far as a history of use, that's not something I would be able to share without the family's approval."

"So, his family won't let you share his history of use?"

"I didn't say that," Peter replied as evenly as he could.

"But you wanted to," said Sam with more empathy in her voice than Peter expected. "People will assume he was introduced to the drug at Parker. I mean, that is the reputation."

"Well, that's unfortunate because there's no evidence that he developed his habit here, but if people want to believe it, there's not much I can do." Implied at the end of that statement was, *or about a reporter who is willing to perpetuate that reputation.*

"I have to say, this is not the conversation I anticipated," said Sam. "Parker has never been known for its transparency."

"I think folks here are realizing the college's reputation has probably suffered as a result. The truth is usually more boring than people's imaginations." *Except in this instance,* Peter hoped was not implied. Their conversation wandered like strangers on a bus. She seemed intrigued by the new direction taken by the college, and Peter was happy with their exchange, though he wondered if he was lulling her or if she was lulling him.

Peter shared personal tidbits about Josh. That he was leaning toward majoring in philosophy and excelled at software coding but wasn't sure that's what he wanted to do with his life. When Josh was in high school, Word kept crashing while he was writing a paper. Out of frustration, he created his own word-processing program that he called Not Word. He was interested in European soccer leagues, but from a sociological lens, not as a sports fan. He studied astronomy as a hobby. He was one of the few people at Parker who said hello to strangers on pathways and in hallways.

Sam asked if she could speak with the parents. Peter let her know they were on a plane heading to PDX and that he'd connect her with them if they were willing. As their conversation wound down, Peter got choked up while remembering the promise he'd made to himself to maintain Josh's humanity. "I've had a chance to talk with his some of his friends. He sounded like a great kid. I hope that doesn't get lost in all of this. I hope your story will be about how he lived and not just how he died. Do you know when and where the story is going to run?"

"Right now, it's a brief in Metro, but it's going to depend," said Sam. "I'm waiting to hear back from the narcotics unit; they're looking through Josh's cell phone to see if they can find out who sold him the drugs. With the recent influx of heroin into Portland, the DA's office is looking to use the Len Bias law as a deterrent for dealers. Whoever sold Josh his drugs could be facing twenty to life for his death." Sam unwittingly admitted the DA had tipped her to Josh's death. Peter's phone wasn't ringing because the DA was working reporters from the other end. McMahon was feeding the media storylines to hang Parker College in the public square.

"So that must have been John McMahon saying he was going to use Bias?" asked Peter. "He's the drug guy in the prosecutor's office, isn't he?" Five seconds of dead air confirmed Peter's hunch. He could almost hear her mouthing, *oh fuck!*

"Yeah, he's on ROCN." Sam got tense and distant.

"What's roncon?"

"R-O-C-N, it's the regional organized crime narcotics task force. It's the local, state, and feds who work on drug trafficking—big stuff—as the name indicates, organized crime."

"Jesus. Do they suspect Josh's death is connected to some major drug ring?"

"All drugs are tangled up in some major drug ring somewhere along the pipeline," Sam said and rushed Peter off the phone.

Any story by Craven in the *STW* would be sensational and easily dismissed, but the *Portland Daily* was Oregon's paper of record. The DA wanted to make an example of Parker College, but all he had to go on was its reputation and accusations in a lawsuit that settled out of court. His other tool was working the media to build public pressure for some sort of intervention or investigation. McMahon was holding all the cards. He was about to drop a steel trashcan around Parker College and start pounding it with a broom handle until something crawled out.

Threatening the use of the Len Bias law was either desperate or brilliant, depending on McMahon's next move. It made no sense if he wanted to advance his career in liberal Multnomah County, but it was a cynical stroke of genius if he was looking for name recognition. Invoking the use of that law was an invitation to the national press.

The federal law was the polar opposite of Oregon's soft laws regarding the sale and possession of heroin. Len Bias had been a basketball phenom out of the University of Maryland. The Boston Celtics drafted him with the second overall pick in the 1986 NBA draft. Bias died two days later of a cocaine overdose. His death was used to gain public support for federally mandated guidelines for people convicted of drug offenses. The suite of laws was controversial from the start, and many saw them for what they were—flat-out racist. The law targeted drugs that were distributed in low-income urban centers and was used to send Blacks to prison in disproportionate numbers. The section of the law that Sam referenced authorized the DA to charge dealers with reckless homicide if the drugs they sold could be traced to a user's death. The mention of this law would spark an ideological debate that would be hugely unpopular in

Multnomah County. Whether it was desperate or calculated didn't really matter, this case was on a path to attract national headlines. Peter went upstairs to alert Loch of the escalation by McMahon.

24

FIFTY-MINUTE MAN

Peter's fifty-minute sessions with Dr. Redmon were a refuge from the pressures and fears that had been dominating every other fifty-minute segment of his life. It was a place where he could lay to rest his emotional armor and stand bare to the truth. Redmon had been guiding Peter toward confrontation with the unaddressed trauma surrounding his parents' death. Since that time, a terrified and confused eight-year-old boy had been sharing control of Peter's perception, turning normal concerns into threats of mortal danger. Living in fear and a state of hyper-vigilance had worn Peter down, but the revelation that came as Josh Leonard rolled past on the gurney promised a start to the next leg in his recovery.

The taut leather chair brayed as Peter fidgeted in vain to

find a comfortable position. Waiting to confront the events he had been avoiding for decades had his heart racing and his breathing thin. There was so much tension in his shoulders and neck that it caused him to hunch forward. His jaw was flexed, his teeth were clenched and grinding. His body vibrated with the intensity of a street fighter about to brawl. Sensing that Peter was ready, Redmon wasted no time. Peter searched in vain for the best jumping off point. He looked to Redmon for a prompt. "Just say the first thing that comes into your mind," he said.

"Bicycle." The word surprised Peter. He let out an uneasy laugh.

Redmon prodded him to explain the significance of the word, as he sat forward in his chair, remaining intensely focused. Peter's eyes moistened as he let out a small laugh and flinched with irritation. He was there to talk about the emergence of a traumatic memory that accosted him on the night of Josh's death, and Redmon wanted to talk about bicycles. Redmon continued prodding gently as he slid to the edge of his seat. Peter hunched over and drew his shoulders inward. Feeling like a lost child with no one to comfort him, Peter wanted the session to be over before it began. What he had to say felt too powerful to be freed into the world. It had been held in secret for too long, and he feared the damage it could do if he called it by name. Shaking with terror, Peter wished Redmon could simply replace the fuse in his brain that would make him feel normal.

"Stay with me, Peter," Redmon edged closer with every exchange. "Focus. Tell me what happened this week." Peter told him Glenn's story about Billings, his fight with Tessa, being woken in the middle of the night and called to campus, Josh Leonard's death, and the memory. Then he diverged into a tangent, speculating how his call with Debbie Samuelson that morning was going to spinout into national press coverage. Redmon let him wander a bit before gently reeling him back. Peter was in a deeply triggered state; Redmon told him to put his feet firmly on the ground and identify five blue things in the room to bring him back into the moment before redirecting him to the night in the dorms.

"When they were taking out the body . . . the student's body . . . when they were wheeling him on the stretcher—" Peter's lower lip quivered. His eyes scurried. He crossed his legs and pulled his knees toward his chest and rocked in place. He could find no comfort. "I was standing in the hall as the gurney rolled past. The body bag brushed against me. It had that plastic smell that will haunt me forever. The seam of the bag dug into the pile of my fleece as he rolled by. I got lightheaded and then flashed back to my childhood. It was like I blacked out for half a second, and this memory became my reality. I was in my childhood home in Brighton, and I was standing by a window, looking down on my aunt who was in the driveway. It was the day my parents died. I was wearing my favorite shirt, watching them take my parents' bodies out of the garage. They were draped with sheets, but I knew it was them. I was all alone. My aunt was standing with the police in the grass near the driveway. There were other people around—neighbors, gawkers."

"How does the bicycle fit into this?" asked Redmon.

"It doesn't," Peter snapped. "For fuck sake!"

"Think about it, Peter." Redmon' voice was soothing and reassuring. "Think about the bicycle. Think about what it means to you. What it might symbolize? What role does it play in what we're talking about?"

Peter was frustrated with the bicycle talk. It had been chosen randomly, the first word to pop into his mind. "I just told you that I was essentially assaulted by a repressed memory while I was on the job, and all you want to talk about are fucking bicycles?"

"I don't want to talk about bicycles, Peter. I want *you* to understand why you chose the word *bicycle* in that moment."

"Well, I'm sorry, but it seems ridiculous to me."

"Indulge me."

"Okay, I was brutally beaten by a bicycle when I was eight and it left deep emotional scars." Peter was as tense as he was defiant.

"Feel what's going on, Peter. Why are you so angry? I've never seen you this angry. Be in this moment and tell me about the bicycle. Ask yourself what is bringing all this emotion to the foreground."

Peter tried to compose himself. He turned his head away from Redmon sharply. The leather of the couch squealed again under his fidgeting. He thought back to his bike and how free it had made him feel. It was blue. The paint had flecks of silver that sparkled when the sun hit them just right; they gave the paint depth. He'd gotten it just before Huffy came out with their first BMX bikes and sort of changed everything. Peter's bike had a banana seat and swooping handlebars, called sissy bars. After the Huffys came out, his bike looked old-fashioned and silly. His family couldn't afford a new one, but his dad bought him a cool BMX seat and handlebars to make it look more like the other kids' bikes.

Riding through the neighborhood gave Peter a sense of freedom. He'd take it to the corner store and ride it to friends' houses. It was thrilling to coast down the steep streets near his house. The wind would make his eyes tear. He'd ride it to his rich friend's house in Brookline, by where Loch lived, and not far from JFK's childhood home. Living close enough to ride his bike to the wealthy neighborhood made him feel less poor.

"Tell me about that day now, Peter. Tell me about the day your parents died." Vibrations started in the pit of his stomach, and he lurched forward. Chills swept across his skin like he was doused with cold water. He straightened his body and opened his eyes; they were distant, still searching for clues in the past. They closed again suddenly as if he had seen something awful. He bent forward putting his face in his hands and sobbing uncontrollably. "It's okay, Peter, no one can hurt you here. Nothing can happen to you here," Redmon continued in a kind and comforting voice. It was a few seconds before Peter could speak, but for him, it felt like much longer.

"I came home from school, and my mother wasn't in the house, so I went to the garage to get my bike. I kept a key to the padlock on a hockey lace around my neck so I could always get my bike whenever I wanted it. The padlock was on the regular door, which had wire mesh so no one could break in through the window. My father's car was in the garage. It was strange for it to be there on a school day—it was strange for his car to be there and for nobody to be in the house. I was focused on fitting the key into the padlock, but it wouldn't go in. Somebody had broken something off in the lock. All at once, I noticed the sound of an engine idling and saw movement in the garage. The inside of the car was totally filled with smoke. There was a hose running from the tailpipe into the rear window." Peter was reduced to a crying mess. His hands and face were covered in mucus and tears. He sniffed and gasped for air. It sounded like he was drowning. Redmon handed him a box of tissues and comforted him.

Peter took several tissues to dry his hands and face as he tried to compose himself; it took several more to get the job done. He focused on his breathing and took one last deep breath before beginning again. "I watched my mother die," he said. His father was unconscious in the driver's seat as he watched his mother try to climb over him to see Peter in the window. The car was thick with smoke and the windows were fogged with condensation. Her hand wiped against the glass and her eyes searched for the sound of her son pounding on the wire mesh. Peter screamed to her and ran around to the car entrance, but that door was also locked. Neighbors ran to the sound of his screaming, but they couldn't break through the doors. Someone brought him in the house, and he watched from the living room until they wheeled his parents out of the garage.

"Peter, you're okay here. You're safe now. I'm so sorry you had to see that," said Redmon. "What you just did takes tremendous courage. Take a minute to be with that boy. Console him. Let him know it's not his fault. Let him know you made it this far and that he's okay."

They sat in silence as Peter imagined he could travel back in time to be with himself as a boy. Together, they looked through the garage window. *What would I say to Ben or Blythe?* He cried thinking about the pain he would have caused his children by jumping off the *Columbia. Eight-year-old me kept this secret hidden until I was strong enough to see it, until I had the ability to deal with it*, he thought. Like every parent who's ever wished they could take away their child's pain and feel it for them, Peter released his younger self from having to hold the memory. *This is mine now. You get to be a child again,* Peter imagined saying to his younger self while staring into the smoke-filled car. He imagined hugging the boy and was overcome by empathy as the burden of holding the secret faded away. Doctor and patient continued to sit in silent acknowledgment of Peter's breakthrough.

"There's more work to be done, for sure, but this is a major breakthrough," said Redmon before recommending that he take the rest of the day off from work.

Peter chuckled. "That's not an option. I have to respond to the *Daily* reporter, and the rest of the week will just get worse as other outlets pick up the story."

"Peter, your condition is covered under the ADA; you have legal protection."

"In this economy, my only option is to get Parker to the other side of this situation or win the lottery." Redmon wasn't sure what else to say. "I'm barely making it as it is. Look, it doesn't matter what else I have to carry, because I have to carry it. No disrespect, but the only thing I want to hear from you right now is how to make my back stronger and my shoulders wider." For the first time since Peter started seeing him, Redmon was at a loss for words. He sat back in his chair and sized up Peter.

"It's hard to know what to tell you," Redmon spoke more like a friend than a therapist. "Frankly, I don't know what else to say, other than I feel confident that, somehow, you'll get through this."

"These motherfuckers can't break me," Peter said with a sparkle in his eyes.

"You need to be with that little boy," said Redmon. "He needs to know that he's made it through safely. The child who experienced that trauma is still very much a part of you, and he needs to know he can handle whatever else comes his way. He needs to know that he grows up to be one badass motherfucker."

Peter and Redmon basked in the glow of their awkward badass motherfuckery, then made plans for Peter to check in later in the week.

25

THE 100-YEAR STORM

Juneau was hit by a pair of Hundred-Year Storms during the same spring. Many Juneauites wondered how one hundred years had passed in the weeks between storms (because 2020 hadn't happened yet). The term isn't a measure of time, Peter had written in a story for the *Juneau Daily*, but rather an estimate of how often all the atmospheric conditions needed to create such an epic storm would coalesce. It is meteorological terminology used when forecasting how often a storm of a certain magnitude might happen, not to catalogue how often they actually do happen. Peter thought about that column as he stood over the kitchen counter, eating a bowl of oatmeal while reading Sam's epic hundred-year hatchet job of an article on the frontpage of the *Portland Daily*. It was unimaginable. It was John McMahon's first salvo in his war against the college, and it exploded on Peter's doorstep with the headline "Parker's Drug Culture Takes a Promising Life" with the subhead "The Cost of Tolerance." The lede photo was of the picturesque, ivy-covered, brick classroom building, and not the brutalist '70s glass-and-steel dorm where Josh died.

Both the headline and its placement on the front page above the fold were shocking to Peter. He felt certain it marked the end of his misery at Parker College. The story exclusively and extensively quoted Assistant District Attorney John McMahon. "We've had our eye on Parker College for a long time," said McMahon. "This death is as tragic as it was predictable. This is what happens when institutions believe they are above the law." McMahon was also quoted as saying, "I hope this death does not go in vain. Maybe now they'll start paying as much attention to what's going on in the dorm rooms as they do in the classrooms."

Oh good, something positive about academics, thought Peter. *I'll probably get a bonus for that.* His peers on other campuses were sending out calendar listings for choral performances and press releases about professors winning science grants, while Peter was dispatched to the frontline of the war on drugs.

"Good morning," said Tessa, barely awake, as she came from the bedroom in sweatpants and a tee-shirt. It was odd for Tessa to be out of bed before Peter left for work. She leaned into his side and hugged him.

"What are you doing up?"

"We didn't get a chance to talk about how your therapy went yesterday." She looked for the right words. "You, seemed, um . . ."

"Unhinged?"

"No," Tessa laughed. "You just seemed, I don't know, you just seemed different. I wanted to make sure you were alright. That's all." Tessa was not being very direct and was quick to finish. "I just wanted to see if you wanted to talk about it."

Peter hugged Tessa tight. He held her long and close, kissing her neck as he let her go.

"I'm good. It was good. I don't really have time to get into it before I head off to work, but thanks for asking." Peter changed gears before his emotions got away from him. Thinking about his last session made him want to crumble. "This is what I'll be dealing with at work today."

Peter turned the paper so Tessa could read the headline. Her shoulders drooped and her head fell to one side. She picked up the paper and let out a sharp breath.

"Seriously?"

"Yup. Today's gonna suck!" Peter said as Tessa simmered to a boil. "Or this week, or month. Anyway, I'll give you a call when I can. Hug the kids for me, tell them I love them, and that I hope to see them again before they go off to college."

"This pisses me off." Tessa grew angrier with each word she read. "*You saw this coming?* Well, what did you do to stop it, Mr. Fucking Law Man! Can't he see that statement is an indictment of his own incompetence?"

Peter smiled. "I'm glad you're on my side," he said. "The whole story was a blindside. Samuelson never even asked me to comment on any of the DA's quotes. She's in the DA's pocket. Whatever; I'm on the outside looking in, and it's about to get a lot worse."

"So, what, the drugs came from the poppy fields behind the dorms?" Tessa mocked. "What's his responsibility in keeping the drugs off the streets? They're everywhere in this town!"

Peter hugged Tessa again, gently.

"You're going to wake the kids," said Peter as he kissed her one more time. "I'm going to be fine. We're going to be fine. Okay?"

Tessa forced a supportive smile, but it didn't hide her concern. Peter didn't feel like he could tell her about the memories until he had a better grasp on them. They were still new and raw to the touch. Tessa needed tidy answers, and Peter didn't have them. He needed to deal with one thing at a time. Before giving Tessa more to worry about, he needed to know he'd make it through the media blitz and still have a job. He needed to make it through this day.

* * *

Peter's drive to work was a master class in rationalization. He needed to find a true, compelling narrative about Josh's death that would be palatable to Goodwin and believable to the press. A story that allowed him to maintain his credibility would be a bonus, but at this point, dignity was a distant second to keeping his job. It wasn't easy. *It might be an impossible task*, he thought, and his mind wandered for relief. Seeing Angela would be his one chance at a normal interaction before either getting fired or entering the rhetorical tennis match with the press. He was disappointed when he didn't see her in the parking lot, and he slowed, hoping to hear her morning greeting. *Funny*, he thought, *they didn't include in the job description that being called 'jackass' would be the highlight of my day.*

Marimba music chimed from his pocket, making Peter wonder if he'd ever get used to answering the call of a xylophone.

It was Jim Galvin with News Talk Radio *Eight-Eighty* hoping to get a few words on air about Sam's *Daily* article. He didn't give Peter a chance to say no, plowing forward with "tape is rolling." Galvin was kinder than he needed to be and didn't cherry pick the worst allegations from the story. He focused on McMahon's quotes about hoping "the incident causes Parker to reevaluate its drug policy and start treating drug crimes as crimes." Peter stopped on the path and made sure he was not within earshot of anyone who might interrupt him.

"Jim, the incident mentioned by the DA was the tragic death of a student, Josh Leonard. The college is mourning the loss of a friend, a student, and a brilliant young man. There will be time to reevaluate the college's drug enforcement procedures after we've had an opportunity to pay tribute to Josh." The second he stopped talking, Peter realized he had left a huge opening for a decent reporter to exploit.

"Wouldn't it be a fitting tribute to Mr. Leonard to make sure no other students die from a drug overdose?" This was precisely how Peter would have responded when he was a reporter and got a deflective answer. It was the first time he had been on the receiving end, and he didn't like it.

"Absolutely, Jim," said Peter, calmly. "That's why Josh's parents wanted to share the cause of death with the community to help accomplish exactly that. It was a hard decision for them to make, but they believed it was the right thing to do to help prevent another family from having to feel the same pain they are in right now. The college is working closely with the police to help bring his dealer to justice." Angela came up the path moving quickly. Peter motioned for her to not interrupt. She made a snooty face and waited for him to get off the phone.

Galvin had gathered enough audio to cover the requisite *Portland Daily*-reported-this-morning story and wrapped it up. Angela was appropriately sullen as she approached. But Peter was hoping for one normal interaction. She was trying to gauge Peter's demeanor. "Was that a reporter?" Peter nodded. "Why aren't you freaking out? I would totally be freaking out right now."

"That's not really an option for me when talking on the radio."

"You were just on the radio talking about a dead student and now you're . . ."

"Not on the radio," Peter deflected, trying to cajole Angela off the topic.

"You're just acting like this is all normal. It's not normal! That you're treating it like it's normal is weirding me out."

"Dying is an unavoidable part of living," said Peter, trying to nudge Angela into his denial. He only saw his cruel indifference as it was reflected in Angela's expression.

"The kid was nineteen and died of a heroin overdose. That is one hundred percent avoidable."

"You know what? The truth is probably much more disturbing than that. Possibly much worse than you can imagine, but it's not healthy for me to walk down that path with you," Peter was becoming more animated. "I have to fill my brain with the good things that Parker College is doing and will continue to do in this area *that we take very seriously*. I have to focus on the progress being made, not the mistakes. If I don't, I'm not going to get through this."

"God, Peter, calm down."

"I didn't mean to bite your head off," said Peter.

Angela smiled, then pouted. "Love means never having to say you're sorry."

"Thanks, Tipper."

"This whole thing makes me want to burn the place to the ground," said Angela. "But I guess it is kind of your job to make it all seem normal."

"I hadn't really thought of it that way, but I guess you're right." Peter changed gears quickly as they approached their office building. "Are we still friends?"

"Yes, but you're still a jackass," muttered Angela with a smile as she walked past.

And for one more moment, Peter's life felt normal.

26

THE FIRST DRAFT OF HISTORY

Rosen, Goodwin, Collins, and Peter met with Loch in his office to discuss Sam's story and set a messaging strategy for moving forward. A well-worn copy of the *Daily* sat on the table with the headline visible. It was 9 a.m., and the group waited for Loch to fill his mug with the pungent coffee in the glass decanter before starting the meeting. Goodwin was wearing the type of sneer that generally preceded his subordinates boxing their personal items on their way to spend more time with their families. He lifted his gaze from the headline to Peter, reached his fingers under his glasses, massaged his eyelids, and inhaled to speak. Cutting short Goodwin's ritual, Loch asked, "Was there any indication as to how bad this story was going to turn out?"

All eyes went to Peter.

"None. It was a complete hatchet job. I don't know what changed after telling you she'd been tipped by McMahon, and her telling me it was going to be a brief in the Metro section. It was shockingly unprofessional for her to have run this without giving us a chance to respond to his comments. I've never experienced anything like it."

"Full disclosure," said Loch. Sam had left a message for Loch the night before, which he did not receive until arriving at his office for the debrief that morning. Loch's update didn't make Peter feel better. Samuelson should have called Peter's cell when she didn't reach Loch.

Dragging the paper slowly across the table, Goodwin picked it up and dramatically tossed it in Peter's direction. "How is it possible that we didn't know the college was going to be the subject of such a scandalous front-page article?"

Frustration took hold of Peter as he repeated the response he'd given to Loch. With all previous directors, a show of exasperation would have been cause for termination. Peter stopped caring; he was tired of Goodwin's bullying and wasn't going to hide it any further. If he was going to be the seventh director fired in eight years, he was not going meekly. The college needed Peter to get through the media storm, but the second he became dispensable, he certainly would be dispensed. His days were numbered, and he had chits to call. It was time to collect.

"That is not an answer," scolded Goodwin.

"Two reporters have implied or directly stated to me that Portland's drug czar is coming after Parker because he thinks we don't follow the law," Peter said, looking Goodwin directly in the eye. "He seems to be utilizing all the tools he has at his disposal."

"That still doesn't answer my question," Goodwin was indignant.

Peter looked to see if Loch would intervene. There was no sign of it. "The DA's office thinks the college is complicit in two deaths on campus. If you're asking for my opinion, McMahon is using his influence with the press to scare someone into coming forward with information, maybe in exchange for a plea deal," Peter leaned slightly forward as he spoke. "Knowing why McMahon thinks the college is complicit in these deaths is the key to answering your question. Are you suggesting I should call and ask him why he believes that?"

"Would you like Peter to call him, Alistair?" Loch asked wryly. Goodwin looked sideways at Loch. "Good. Then I suggest we move on. We can't put the genie back in the bottle," Loch continued. "Have there been any other press queries?"

"I spoke with *News Talk Eight-Eighty* this morning. They were doing a follow-up on the *Daily* story. He picked up on the DA's quotes. 'Is the college doing enough to keep students safe?' That sort of thing," said Peter.

"This is ridiculous," said Rosen. "Josh's therapeutic intervention was far beyond anything he would have received at our peer institutions."

"Privacy laws, and the parents' wishes, prevent us from sharing medical or disciplinary information." Loch's patience was wearing thin. "A student died on our watch. We have to get over the fact that people are going to question our approach!"

"But why? At this point, Charles, whose privacy are we protecting?" asked Rosen.

"At some point we need to start protecting the reputation of the college," added Goodwin.

"Again, Alistair, what action are you suggesting?" Loch snapped. "We do have a drug problem! Shall we throw out every kid who has a drug offense? Every one of them? How many is that—half of our full-pays? What does the baseline survey show? The percentage is staggering."

"Most of that is pot," said Rosen. "This is something very different."

Goodwin took off his glasses and rubbed his eyes before responding. "We need to protect the reputation of the college if we want to have any hope of reaching our fundraising goals. Your fundraising goals!"

"I'm still waiting for your suggestion," Loch fired back, accompanied by a cold stare.

"Tell the truth." Goodwin did not hesitate.

"*Which* truth, Alistair?"

"We are risking the reputation of the institution for a drug addict!" Goodwin proclaimed.

Loch was furious. His silence felt like the cocking of a gun. The tension grew thick as smoke, making it difficult to breathe. "We can sit around this table crying 'poor us,' but the DA was right!" Loch sat tall in his chair and slapped his open palm on the table, startling everyone. "This *was* predictable. In fact, Matthew, you predicted it. You were sitting right there when you asked, 'What happens when one of these medical transports doesn't make it to the hospital on time?' Well, here we are answering that question a year later. And the answer is that we don't scapegoat the kid! He had an addiction! He sought help, our help! He was a good kid trying to do the right thing." Everyone waited for the others to speak. It had the feeling of an intervention. Somebody finally talked about the problem as it was seen outside of Parker's ivory tower. No one was sure how to react. Peter was certainly confused by Loch's admission. It didn't seem consistent with the actions of someone who was covering up a crime.

"Frankly, revealing that his problem predates Parker wouldn't be helpful," Peter chimed in. "We're being accused of turning a blind eye to drug activity. I'm not sure it would be helpful to say we provided Josh with world class addiction treatment while the DA is claiming the treatment center is inside a drug den."

"We did everything right with Josh," said Rosen.

"Maybe that's true, but it's a pretty tough sell," said Peter. "We're not talking to a seminar of college healthcare professionals. We can't isolate and highlight his treatment as if the other accusations don't exist. The DA is saying we do everything wrong when it comes to drugs on campus. We have a student in the morgue and only one of us gets to sound credible. Right now, I'm afraid the DA has the upper hand."

Rosen was shocked. "The truth is not credible?"

"No. *The opinion* of Parker College is not a credible source in this matter. Besides, if you're the parent of a student, do you want to hear that when Parker College does everything right, our students die?" Peter asked incredulously. "We are dealing with perceptions, and we need to be honest with ourselves about what those perceptions are. You may have done everything by the book, best practices, or whatever, but the perception is that Parker College ignores the dangers of drugs. Josh is dead, and the drug czar is out there telling everyone that his death is our fault. Does anyone disagree that these are the facts? Given that context, it seems to me that saying, 'We did everything right' comes off as deaf, dumb, blind, foolhardy, and possibly negligent." Loch had punched a truthiness hole through the wall of denial, but Peter brought down the tower. In that moment, it felt good to speak truth to power, but in the next moment, he imagined himself in the unemployment line.

"Peter's right," Loch broke the silence. "But how do we not sound deaf, dumb, and blind, and especially not foolhardy and negligent?"

"We need to find a narrative that's both true *and credible*," said Peter.

Sally knocked to let them know campus safety called; the Channel 8 News truck just pulled into the East Lot and students were gathering nearby. They wanted to know what to do. Peter was dispatched into action. The timing felt like divine intervention. "I'm sure they're trying to get student reactions," said Peter. "Well, that's a bad idea," said Rosen. Goodwin nodded in agreement. Peter looked puzzled. "I'm already hearing from students who are concerned we're going to use Josh's death as an opportunity to crack down on drugs."

"Aren't we?" asked Peter.

"I don't think that's something our students should be hearing through the press," continued Rosen, "unless we're also willing to find some *true and credible* response for why there are protests on campus ten days before Bacchanalia."

Against Peter's advice, the group decided that Loch should be the one to talk with the press. Peter wanted to make sure the lawsuit wasn't the main storyline before committing Loch to speak on camera. Since taking over as president, Loch had been outspoken on matters large and small. Silence on Josh's death, Loch accurately presumed, would look conspicuous and cowardly. But if the DA was, in fact, sharing details about the cover-up with the press and Loch was caught in a lie, it would be the largest scandal in the scandalous history of the college. Peter reiterated that the DA was feeding information to reporters, and he just wanted to minimize the greatest potential threats.

"I appreciate your concern Peter, but this isn't Watergate, and Woodward and Bernstein didn't just pull up in the Channel 8 News van," said Loch. "I think I'll be able to hold my own."

Loch's protecting me, thought Peter. *He's got my back.*

There were too many thoughts bouncing around in Peter's head to process in real time. It felt good to believe that Loch was protecting him. He held tightly to that feeling. He needed that. *Stay focused on the task at hand. Deal with the reporters. Keep Goodwin at arm's length. Don't think about the memories. Don't trust Collins, Goodwin, or Rosen. Just stay focused!*

27

BOMBSHELL

The Channel 8 reporter and cameraman stood by the open panel-door of their news van, ogling the growing crowd of unhappy students. Conflict makes good news content. Peter wanted to gauge the temperature of the students, not wanting to hand the news crew an easy shot for their tease: "What are these Parker College students rioting about? Tune in at five to find out!"

His worries that students might get confrontational with the news crew were quickly assuaged. They simply didn't want their classmate being used as a prop in the war on drugs. Assuring them their goals were aligned with those of the administration, Peter listened to several students make intelligent and nuanced arguments as to why the college should not engage with the news media. Their opinions were compelling but not altogether practical. Then they listened to Peter's less compelling and more expedient reasons as to why engaging with the media was the right tactic. Neither party totally agreed with the other's position. Peter admitted he didn't completely agree with his own arguments, but it seemed like the least bad choice before them. Promising he would work hard to keep the press from dehumanizing Josh, Peter left wishing all his interactions were as civil and thoughtful.

Knowing students were approaching this rationally gave Peter confidence as he walked toward the news van. The crew waved as they saw him coming. Nodding politely, Peter remained unexpressive. The crew had arrived on private property without permission, and Peter wanted to establish the rules of engagement. The reporter was tall with sculpted jet-black hair. His thick foundation makeup stopped abruptly before reaching his hairline making him look like he was wearing a poorly fitting mask. He thrust his hand toward Peter and boomed, "Justin Warfield, News Channel 8." Peter shook his hand, ignored the introduction, and asked why they came to campus without calling first. Justin told him they were there to cover Josh's death.

"He died last week, so I think you missed that one," Peter quipped, which made the cameraman laugh under his breath. The reporter had assumed cooperation. Peter wanted to take it away and make him earn it back. Peter smiled and looked to the camera operator before introducing himself. Camera operators on local news crews are often the brains of the operation. They don't ask the questions, but in many cases, they edit the package and have control over the final product. It's good to have them on your side.

"Ray Rodriguez," he smiled modestly. "I'm just along for the ride."

"I know better than that. Well, it's good to meet you both," said Peter switching to a friendlier tone. "I'm a one-man operation, so when reporters show up unannounced, it doesn't give me time to do my hair or make tea. Anyway, what's the story?"

They were honest about having talked with John McMahon that morning and having plans to interview him later in the day. Sam's piece on Josh was the paper's top story. An interview with Loch, in newsroom parlance, would be "a good get." They talked through their package, explaining the kinds of interviews they hoped to conduct. Their desire for student reaction interviews was a non-starter. Peter used the student's request to ban news crews as an entree into expressing their mutual concern that journalists would dehumanize Josh. The more they talked, and the more doors and windows Peter closed, the bigger the Loch interview loomed. Peter frowned and shrugged, like he was hoping they wouldn't ask. "Gosh, I don't know. I could probably get you a dorm advisor or someone from the health and counseling center," said Peter hesitantly. He paused. "He's obviously pretty busy right now."

"I think the public would really like to know what he has to say," said Justin. "He's been very, um, vocal on other topics."

"I think the word you were looking for is *provocative*," joked Peter.

"Your word, not mine," laughed Justin. "But it is sweeps week."

"You know, we didn't get a chance to respond to the DA's quotes in the *Daily*—it sounds like Sam talked with McMahon late and we weren't able to connect after that," said Peter. "It would be good to correct the impression that we don't take drug enforcement seriously."

"We'd give him that opportunity," said Justin.

"I don't know. Like I said, he's taking it really hard, and I don't want to put him in a situation where people are, well, blaming him for this," said Peter. "He is well aware of the college's reputation in this area, and he's been doing a lot of substantive things to improve how the college handles these issues."

"What the college is doing to move forward is exactly what we're after," said Justin. "If you're doing things to lessen the impact of this problem, that's what our viewers want to know."

"Let me see what I can do," said Peter, and they exchanged cell numbers. He directed them to a nearby convenience store that Parkies frequent to get student reactions, but also to gain himself a little more time to prep Loch for the interview. "If I get you Loch, you need to promise me that you'll ask McMahon what he's doing to keep the drugs off the streets. He's acting like it's our job to mitigate the flood of drugs pouring into Portland. Someone needs to remind him that's his job. Okay?"

By playing it this way, Peter hoped to ingratiate himself to the reporter. It's harder to screw someone if they're doing you a favor. Good reporters, however, are ruthless in their pursuit of the truth, and bad reporters are just ruthless. It can be difficult in advance to know the difference. This was the part of the job that brought Peter the most satisfaction. He knew he could not control the outcome of the story, but he felt a modicum of control while setting it in motion. He'd bought the college some time to strategize, while making the reporter feel as if he'd won the golden ticket by negotiating for an interview that Loch had already granted.

* * *

Students cheered as the crew climbed back into the news van. The crowd had quadrupled in size while Peter was talking with Ray and Justin. A hulking figure broke from the throng and lumbered toward Peter like a zombie hunting for brains. It took a second for Peter to recognize it was Glenn Nurse. His eyes were dull and unfocused, and his face was pale and drawn. Hunched like an old man, Glenn was so depleted of vitality, Peter thought he might be looking for a ride to the hospital. Glenn tried to start a sentence five different ways before giving up. Reassuring him that he was there to help, Peter took Glenn's arm and led him away from the crowd. "Just say it, Glenn. Whatever it is, I'll help you get through it."

"I was with Josh the night he died," said Glenn.

Fuck. Unless you tell me that. Peter tried not to react too strongly but feared Glenn's confession made him a suspect in what was effectively being perused as a murder case. "Did you supply Josh the drugs?" Glenn shook his head no. Peter stepped in his way, blocking his path. He needed to hear Glenn say the words. When they stopped, Peter grabbed Glenn's shoulders and asked again.

"No!" he insisted, and they walked a few more minutes before Glenn spoke again. "I wouldn't lie to you about that, but I wasn't completely honest about how I knew Billings. I'm the one who called for amnesty," Glenn admitted. "That first night I told you about, when Billings OD'd. I was with him. I was also using. I didn't want you to know I'm an addict."

"It's okay, Glenn," said Peter. "I'm glad you told me. It doesn't change my opinion of you. It's okay." Glenn looked like he might cry, but quickly gained composure and forged ahead.

"We both got amnesty. We had to attend Narcotics Anonymous. It was part of the agreement to stay enrolled. That's why they sent me into his apartment that second night— the night from the lawsuit. It would be weird to say that we were friends, but there's a bond when you're using, and then when you try to stop. NA is where I met Willy and Josh. Willy OD'd after a meeting, and so did Josh; they both left the meetings with Billings." Glenn painfully laughed at the irony. "It's probably the best place for him to find new business: a bunch of addicts sitting around talking about how hard it is to stay sober and old bastards talking about how their cravings never go away."

"Glenn, are you using now?" Peter was filled with compassion as he spoke. "I'm really worried about you."

"I'm clean, but I feel like I can't go back to the meetings since Josh died. It's been really hard since Billings came back in the fall because everyone knew he was a source. God, I have so much work to do. And things are so fucked up," Glenn was growing tense, paranoid. "I'm just not sure what to do."

"About what, exactly, Glenn?"

Glenn tensed up and stopped walking. "There's too much to deal with."

"You're starting to freak me out a little bit, Glenn," said Peter. "I feel like we maybe need to get you some help."

"I just need to get through a few more weeks, and then school will be over. And I can get the fuck out of here for a while. I have a lot of work to do, and then I just need to get away from this place. I'll be fine then." Glenn seemed on the verge of a mental breakdown. Peter desperately wanted to help, but he also had to talk with Loch about the interview and get back to the news crew. He couldn't go missing for this long when the

press was converging on campus. Peter offered to bring Glenn
to the counseling center. "They'll know how to best help you.
And everything you tell them is confidential."

"I left the meeting with Josh and Billings that night." It
was like the floodgates of Glenn's conscience broke open. "We
went to Josh's dorm room after the meeting. We said we were
just going to hang out and watch a movie or something, but we
both knew, we both hoped, I hoped, that Billings was holding.
I wanted to jack-up so bad."

"Glenn, were you there when Josh died?" Peter asked firmly.

"No! I told you that already."

"Tell me what else happened. Tell me everything and tell
me right now!"

"We were hanging around the dorms and Josh started asking
Billings why he was gone from campus, if he got suspended or
whatever. He didn't say anything about the lawsuit night. He
just said the college let him back after his dad worked some
deal—he made a deal for the college to keep him out of trouble.
If they did, his dad would make a huge contribution to the
Need Blind campaign after graduation. It sounded legit. He
explained the whole thing: money in escrow with a *friend of
the college*. Anyway, this led Billings to say he was not staying
out of trouble. He told us to wait, that he was going back to
his apartment. We both knew what was about to happen. All I
could think of was Willy. I'd been clean for over nine months,
and as much as I wanted to stay, I couldn't throw that away. I
left before Billings got back."

"Did you tell anyone else?"

"Who am I going to tell?"

"Did you go to the police?" asked Peter.

"No. That's not the right thing to do." Glenn's voice trailed off, and he shut down again.

"Glenn, it's the only thing to do. It's your only way out of this," Peter was becoming impassioned. "Go to the police and tell them everything you know about what happened at the apartments. The DA is crawling up Parker's ass right now. They know that the night from Noon's lawsuit and Willy's death are connected, but they haven't linked it to Billings. They'll believe you, and then you can tell them what happened to Josh. You might be the only one alive who can connect all the dots for them."

"But what about you?" asked Glenn. "What will happen to Parker? It will be a cluster. I don't want that. Billings' money is going help Parker become need-blind. It's going to help other kids like me."

"Don't worry about that. That's not your problem, Glenn," said Peter. "Other people created this mess. Not you. In no way is this your problem."

"I can't go to the police," Glenn said abruptly.

"Why?" asked Peter.

"Just stop talking about the police."

"Are you afraid of the cover-up? You have no responsibility for that," said Peter. "That's . . . you were a student worker. You were just there."

"Parker let me stay as long as I never talked about it," said Glenn. "They let me keep my financial aid—they pay for everything! I don't pay a dime, but I have to stay clean, and I can never talk about what happened."

A wave of paranoia crashed over Peter. His arms started to tingle. He got that feeling in the back of his neck and his chest started to constrict. *Why had Glenn sought me out? Why is he telling this to me and not a student? I want to help him, but I also just want to run away. If he's lying to me, he could go to jail for life. What's my responsibility here?*

"Billings came to my dorm the next morning and asked me to help him," Glenn continued.

"Glenn." Peter was trigged and edging toward losing control. He wasn't sure he wanted to hear the rest, but he desperately wanted to help. "What did he ask you to do?"

"He told me that he got a tip that they'd be searching his room." Glenn was shaky.

"Who tipped him?" asked Peter.

"Think about it." Glenn was frustrated at Peter's naïveté. "Someone who had a lot to lose if Billings got caught—*a lot*—like twenty-five million dollars."

"Holy motherfucking shit!" Peter was realizing how deep in over his head he really was. "Tell me you didn't do anything. Tell me you didn't help him."

"I didn't know." Glenn grew distant again. "No, I didn't help him. I didn't know Josh was dead when Billings came to my room. I didn't know until later that day when we got the email from Loch."

"Glenn, you need to tell me the whole truth. Okay? No more half-truths. No more lies," Peter didn't know how to get through to him. "The DA is going to use the Len Bias law. That means they are treating this like a murder. Okay? Murder! Do you see how fucking serious this is?" The fear was radiating though Peter's chest and starting to cloud his thoughts. His ears rang like the crashing of cymbals. Fear and betrayal, empathy and doubt exploded like fireworks in Peter's mind. "You have to go to the police, Glenn." Pain shone through Peter's eyes. "I don't know what else to tell you. But I need you to tell me that you'll go to the police, okay? Because I don't know how else to help you. They will believe you, and I'll corroborate everything. You'll come out of this alright, but you must do as I say."

Glenn nodded reluctantly. Peter couldn't shake the feeling that he had failed Glenn. He grabbed Glenn's enormous shoulders one more time and pleaded. "Go to the police. Right. Fucking. Now!

28

DISCO PANTS AND HAIRCUTS

There's a car chase scene in the *Blues Brothers* movie where Jake and Elwood Blues, John Belushi and Dan Aykroyd, are being pursued by every unit of every branch of Illinois law enforcement in addition to the National Guard. The brothers smash into a shopping mall, destroying every kiosk, storefront, and decoration in their path while evading the police on their "Mission from God." At the height of the destruction and chaos, Jake nonchalantly points out the car window to admire a purveyor of disco pants and haircuts. That's what it felt like for Peter to go back to work after having a $25 million conspiracy bombshell dropped at his feet. Ridiculous. The world around him was being smashed to pieces, but he needed to keep his focus on the mundanity of his job.

He called Justin Warfield from News Channel 8 to say he was on his way to Loch's office; he'd let them know in twenty minutes if the interview was a go. Then his mind wandered into darkness. What could he believe, and what should he do about it? He created a list of places his mind should not wander. *Don't trust my emotions. Don't trust most humans. Concentrate on what's known and on accomplishing my immediate task. Be vigilant about watching for Collins and Goodwin. Only rely on what I can verify. Stay in the moment. Be fearless.* He took a few confident steps before his mind exploded into a mushroom cloud of doom. *Glenn must be using, or he's had a nervous breakdown. What if everything he told me was a lie? What if none of this is real? What if I'm making all this up? Maybe I've already lost my mind. Maybe this is like one of those movies where at the end, you find out that I'm strapped to a gurney in a mental institution, and all of this is a drug-induced hallucination.*

He took one more deep breath and concentrated on each step, feeling the pressure on the bottoms of his feet as they touched the ground. Becoming aware of the tension between his shoulders and the bottom of his neck, he couldn't believe he hadn't noticed the pain. *Stay here. Stay in the moment.*

* * *

"I saw the van drive off," said Loch as Peter entered his office. "Did you send them away?"

"They'll be back," said Peter. "I was trying to buy us some time. You know these aren't going to be friendly interviews, right?" Loch did not need to be told the obvious, and he waited for advice. "On top of the growing disdain for elitism and privilege, for which Parker surpasses even Reed College as Oregon's poster child, you came from out of state and immediately threw shade at some beloved Oregon institutions." Peter waited for an affirmative nod from Loch.

Loch smiled and nodded. "And the press is going to treat me like a rented mule."

"The redheaded stepchild of rented mules, yes, to combine some metaphors," said Peter. "They're interviewing McMahon after they leave here, so they'll ask him to respond to your quotes. They're at the Plaid Pantry now, looking for students to interview, so God only knows what they'll get someone to say—"

"Why aren't they interviewing students on campus?"

"Because there was a group of eager students standing by the van," said Peter. "I didn't want to risk that they were the ones lobbying Rosen to let them keep their drugs flowing—and we needed this time. Alright, I won't ask you again, but you don't have to do this. I didn't promise the news crew anything. I said I'd do my best to get you to agree to an interview."

"So, again, just say what you're poorly trying to insinuate."

"I'm saying it's my job to protect you. There's a lot I don't know, and it's making my job impossible."

"It's not your job to protect me. It's your job to help shape the narrative of the news coverage, to the extent that that's possible," said Loch.

"I don't mean to be disagreeable, but part of shaping the story is creating a wide berth around you and any potential controversy," said Peter. "It would be helpful to know exactly what I'm protecting you from and exactly what the stakes are."

"This conversation is over," Loch was emotionless. "What's your advice for the interview?"

"Don't say anything you'll regret," Peter said cynically. It was met with a blank stare that became an ironic smile. "They'll use your statements to get a reaction from the DA. Ultimately, the guy's a bully. I suggest we go after him; knock him on his heels. Question if law enforcement is doing enough—or better, say they're not doing enough to keep these dangerous drugs off the streets. Express outrage that heroin is so cheap and readily available, and demand that something be done."

"Do you really think it's sensible to pick a fight with the DA?" asked Loch with a smile.

"We're in a fight," quipped Peter. "He sucker punched us this morning! We just need to decide if we're going to punch back."

"I'm not ruling out a more aggressive approach, but I'm not sure our best option is to reach directly for the DA's jugular. We're not running a political campaign. The college is going to be here for a while. We need to manage this for the long term," Loch said calmly and flashed Peter an appreciative smile. He liked the way Peter thought.

"The more dignified approach might be to share all the ways we're cooperating with law enforcement, *whose job it is to curb the use and trafficking of drugs in Portland,*" Peter continued. "And something like, 'This is an enormous issue that touches every part of society. None of us can handle it alone.' This will help counter the accusations in the *Daily* that Parker doesn't take drug enforcement seriously, or that we don't cooperate with the cops, but it gently reminds people that the burden for policing drugs belongs with the police. He's getting away with making it our job."

"Good, but do we think that's credible?" asked Loch. "The truth is that for years Parker didn't take drug enforcement seriously," said Loch. "When I first got here, students regularly smoked bongs on the front lawn. Bongs, by the way, that were openly stored on a shelf in the pool hall. We'd walk past clouds of pot smoke, and I don't know, pretend the students were reading Chaucer."

"Yeah, and not to beat a dead horse, but since you just handed me the crop, this is exactly the situation I've been trying to keep you out of: 'Loch says Parker takes drug enforcement seriously,' declares the well-manicured reporter, 'but our News 8 cameras found fifty bongs on a library shelf,' or here's a random drug-addled student who said he came to Parker because *US News* ranked it as the best college to snort heroin. This isn't fair, reasonable, and responsible journalism. This is the DA pushing a story as TV stations are loading up for ratings week."

"Is it really ratings week?" asked Loch.

"Yes!" said Peter. "This is what I've been trying to get across without sounding like a conspiracy theorist. It's ratings week in an election year, and frankly, it feels like we're on the verge of a class war. To the rest of Portland, we represent the aloof Coastal Elites who are causing the economy to crash while suffering no consequence."

"Maybe everything you say is accurate." Loch's expression made it clear he did not think so. "But I have a hard time believing that an interview about Josh is going to turn into a story about class struggle."

"It already has," Peter talked quickly. "McMahon has already set the narrative. The assistant DA, who was supposed to keep the drugs out of Josh's hands, is blaming us for not doing *his* job, and nobody is even vaguely questioning it. He's tapping into the growing disdain for the arrogant elitists who think the rules don't apply to them, 'this is what happens when institutions believe they are above the law.' Does that quote sound familiar? Look, average people are seeing banks getting bailed out, while homeowners are losing their houses. People who are resisting eviction are going to jail, and not one banker has even been fined. They aren't going to ask you about class; it will be the undercurrent of the story—it's the silent assumption. It's the tone in the national press, and McMahon's quotes in the *Daily*. We're just the punching bag for people to take out their frustrations."

"So, what are you suggesting I do?" snapped Loch.

"You need to be the guy who ran for mayor of Boston," said Peter. A tear welled in his eye, which caught them both off guard. Peter felt a closeness to Loch that he couldn't exactly explain. "Look, there's no nuanced way to tiptoe our way out of this. If we're going down, I want us to go down swinging in a bloody, bare-knuckled Boston street-fight."

"I'm in, when we arrive at that point, but we're not there yet. Where are the landmines?"

"Don't make a statement that indicates some dramatic policy change. They'll use it to support McMahon's claims that we weren't doing enough," said Peter like he was reading off a list. "Lead with empathy. Commend Josh's parents for making the difficult choice to share the cause of death to help bring attention to this regional and national epidemic—broaden the problem as much as you can: *it's a national epidemic that touches every corner of the country, especially along the Interstate-5 corridor.* Remember to mention all the ways we are cooperating with the police investigation. Again, if you have a chance to knock McMahon back on his heels, please, for the love of God, take it. He has all the momentum right now. We really need people to question what the cops are doing to keep heroin off the streets; remind them it's not your job—it's his. And no matter how annoying the reporter may become, don't say anything that could come off as glib or unctuous. No matter where the interview goes, always remember it's about Josh. Right? *It's about Josh*—not *you*, not the *college*. If the camera's on, anything you say is fair game. They *will* use footage out of context."

"Unctuous," said Loch quizzically and partially amused. "Glib, I'll concede—with reluctance—but unctuous? Let's not worry about that, shall we."

"It was today's Word of the Day," admitted Peter with a chuckle.

"And so you felt compelled to use it to describe me—to me?" quipped Loch.

"It's kind of a *thing* in our office," said Peter with a mischievous grin. The lighter tone was a welcome break, but what should have felt like a moment of bonding under pressure only felt unsettling. The walls were closing in on Peter from every side: the memory of his parents, Glenn, Billings, who could he trust? Was he trustworthy? Should he tell Loch what Glenn told him? He focused on his breathing to keep his mind from starting to spiral. *Remember to breathe and focus.* His phone rang. *Focus!* He thought again before he spoke. He held up the phone, making Loch aware it was game time as he started to walk to the door. "Remember, they're not reporting so much as they're fishing for statements to plug into the *Daily* story. They'll be looking for evidence of Parker's flaws, no matter where they find them," he said before answering the phone. "Justin! Good news, President Loch agreed to the interview. He's eager to set record straight."

* * *

Upon being introduced to Justin and Ray, Loch made the obligatory offerings of coffee, tea, water, and small talk to let Justin know he was familiar with his work (thanks Google). As Ray wired Loch with the lavalier microphone, Peter wished they'd had more time to prepare. Nervousness. Loch, however, had an air of confidence that made him seem untouchable. Justin stood next to the camera as Ray framed the shot, and Peter situated himself where he could see Justin's reactions. Justin asked Loch to say and spell his name into the camera so Ray could check audio levels and spell his name correctly on the chyron. "Sound is good," said Ray. "Ready whenever you are."

There's an electric silence the moment before a recorded interview. It's a combination of energies. On one level, there is the anticipation like turning the ignition when jumpstarting a car—did I cross the wires? Is it the battery or a bigger problem? Or, will the engine start and get me where I need to go? On more of an esoteric plane, the air changes like during the approach of a thunderstorm. Ultimately, it's the moment when you learn if the rationalizations that have been smoothing the bumps in your conscience will hold up to scrutiny. The next words spoken will be the first draft of Parker College's history and the legacy of Charles Loch.

Justin began by summarizing the *Daily* story and then dove straight into the accusatory questions. What could Parker have done to prevent this death? Given Parker's reputation for drugs, shouldn't you have anticipated this? What is Parker College going to do to ensure another student doesn't die from drugs? Loch delivered. He was convincing and earnest. He resembled the mayoral candidate Peter admired. The man who'd promised that, when he became mayor, he'd look out for people like Peter and his family. As the camera rolled, Loch became the guy that Peter left Alaska to join.

But join in what? Peter wondered. He wanted to believe that Loch was doing the right thing, but he didn't know what to trust. He couldn't trust his own memories. What could he believe about a guy he met once in a Dunkin' Donuts parking lot? Peter struggled to focus on the substance of the interview. All he could see was a master politician deflecting and redirecting question after question so naturally it was barely detectable.

Peter's mind drifted back to the day they'd first met. He could smell the sugary dough caramelizing in hot grease and fresh coffee brewing into bubble-shaped decanters. Peter was eating a butternut donut that was half the size of his head. With each bite, "butternuts" shed the pastry and clung to the wool of his Patriots letterman jacket—a gift from his aunt and one of his favorite possessions. A tan Buick pulled up to the curb, and before Loch could open his door, a man with a thick Boston accent called out, "Hey, Loch! You got my vote," and a crowd started to gather.

"Early and often, boys! Early and often!" Loch called back through his open window as he climbed out of the Buick and walked directly to Peter's father. Loch smiled, winked, and patted the "Loch for Mayor" campaign button pinned on his dad's Pipefitters Union jacket. Loch pulled his open hand back toward his shoulder and snapped it forward in a grand greeting gesture. The Dunkin' mug that looked like a dixie cup in the elder's hand seemed giant as Peter took hold of it to free his dad to shake Loch's hand. Peter had never seen his father so impressed.

"So, are you going to play for the Patriots when you grow up?" Loch asked Peter as he shook his father's hand.

"The Sox need him mo'ah," shouted someone from the back of the circle that was forming around Loch. "They need pitch'ahs und'ah thirty."

The crowd laughed, and Loch leaned down to greet Peter on his level. When Loch stood back up, he left his hand resting on Peter's shoulder. "Maybe he'll play for the Patriots or pitch for the Sox, or maybe he'll be a cop or a schoolteacher. Maybe he'll be mayor of Boston—but hopefully something more useful, like his dad. But one thing I know for sure is that he is the future of our city. And if you make me the next mayor, I'll make sure he has the best schools and the safest streets of any city in America. I promise to keep unions strong and housing affordable. That's my promise to him and to all of you."

Loch smiled at Peter and looked him in the eyes. "I've got a good feeling about you," he said with a wink. "You'll do great things one day, son. I know you will."

Peter drifted back into the moment. Loch's delivery was so masterful that Justin didn't realize he was only collecting talking points. With each answer, Peter's confidence grew that he and Loch would get through this with their heads still attached.

"So, one last question," Justin said like TV sleuth Columbo before nabbing the guilty party. "Given that one student has died from drugs already this year, is the college going to cancel Bacchanalia?" Boom goes the dynamite. How did they miss that? Loch was in a standoff. If he said yes, the students would rebel. If he said no, McMahon would have his opportunity to build public and political pressure to launch a probe into Parker's drug culture.

Loch looked inward before delivering. "Josh's loss was a tremendous shock to this community," he said. "Right now, our focus is making the community whole, caring for those who need help, including Josh's parents, and getting through the most academically challenging time of the year."

As Justin pursed his lips to ask a follow-up question, Peter lunged into Ray's shot, pointing at his watch. "Alright," said Peter before quickly turning his attention to Loch. "You have a call with the board in about two minutes. Sorry guys, I promised Sally that we'd stay on schedule. We can't keep the board waiting."

"Or break our promises to Sally," quipped Loch. "She runs a tight ship."

Peter knew that after the story aired, Bacchanalia would become the dominant storyline. For every other college in the country, it would have been a nightmare; but for Parker, it was a lucky break. Bacchanalia amounts to an average Saturday on any college campus with a NCAA Division I football team, but because Parker closed and decorated campus, and the students dressed in themed costumes to celebrate academic achievement, the party took on a mythic air. Given the choice, Peter would take allegations of gluttony over the Billings story, which contained all seven of the Deadly Sins.

As Ray powered down the camera, Peter felt a bit of relief. The situation was heating up, but they had gotten through the first media wave without a mention of the lawsuit allegations. Peter continued to struggle to constrain his thoughts. *Am I really happy that I'm protecting a billionaire criminal to save my job?* Everybody wanted something. McMahon's intention was political. Loch wanted to make the college need-blind to solidify his legacy. The media wanted higher ratings, and Peter wanted to keep his job and care for his family. Peter thought of Josh and Willy. *How many lives had they touched?* Then he thought about the story of Billings with kilos of heroin lying on the bed and pointing a gun at Glenn. He wondered about all the lives he'd affected, which made him want to stop thinking altogether.

"Can I help you carry something?" Peter asked Ray.

Peter walked Ray and Justin back to the news van. TV cameras are a magnet for people with axes to grind, and Peter didn't want anyone with a dull ax intercut with Loch's keen performance. He watched the van drive off campus before going back to Loch's office to debrief.

29

PLANTING SEEDS

As Peter returned to Loch's office, after running interference for the news crew, Loch had his ear pressed to the phone and gestured for Peter to sit. Like an obedient dog, he sat and awaited the punishment he'd surely get for not predicting the Bacchanalia question. Loch cocked his head and smiled to Peter as he hung up. "The police have a few leads on Josh's dealer," Loch said. "They have his cell phone and are going through his contacts and call records for the numbers of known drug dealers. So, *here we are,* cooperating with the police. They've searched Josh's room, we've, obviously, turned over his cell phone, and we are doing everything they've asked of us, but I'm certain none of that will make its way into the press."

"Have they decided for sure if they're going prosecute

through Bias?"

"They are," said Loch.

"What if the dealer turns out to be a student?" asked Peter.

"Well. God," Loch had an uncharacteristic moment of doubt, which he shooed away like a fly. "I guess we'll jump off that bridge when we get to it."

There was a moment of heavy silence.

* * *

As Peter and Loch debriefed their interview, the cold body of a nineteen-year-old boy with a needle hole in his arm lay on a gurney in the Multnomah County coroner's office. Josh's parents took the redeye out of Dulles and drove straight to the morgue. His mother still clung to her denial that the news of Josh's death had been a horrible misunderstanding. She felt embarrassed by her wish to see a stranger's son revealed when the coroner pulled away the sheet. Having to identify her lifeless boy was a thought too dreadful to bear. Until she confirmed his death for herself, she would flame any spark that promised the smallest bit of hope. All his mother wanted was to see the light in her son's eyes that gleamed each time they reunited.

In a stark basement room with concrete floors, surrounded by the tools of his trade, the coroner stood next to a gurney draped with a sheet. He asked Josh's parents if they were ready to identify the body. Taking hold of each other, they nodded and braced. His mother hoped if it was him that he would look like he was sleeping peacefully. When the sheet was pulled back, it unquestionably revealed the body of their son, but he wasn't there. All the intangible traits, quirks, and imperfections—the spark that animated his personality—were gone. All that was left was the empty vessel that had once held their love.

Forced to abandon her denial felt like her own life escaping her body. She tried to push away the anguish by search for joyful memories. Rather than easing her pain, the memories brought the realization they would never create another. The sense of permanence was so devastating that she began to mourn the loss of every moment she could not remember, every ride to soccer practice, every scraped knee, and all the nights lost to sleepovers and boarding school. She wanted it all back. She wanted her son back. She pleaded with the universe for some sign that Josh was not scared and that he felt no pain. She wanted assurance that he could still feel her love.

* * *

"So how do you think it went?" Loch asked.

"I thought it went really well," was Peter's truncated response. "But—"

"But, sorry for not predicting the Bacchanalia question— that's a game changer," said Peter. "Now they'll go interview McMahon. They'll ask him about Bacchanalia, and the storyline moving forward will be some version of druggy school plans drug party after drug death."

"Hmm, well, we'll see," quipped Loch. "Depending on how this shakes out, that may actually become the most desirable storyline."

There was a change in Loch, but Peter couldn't put his finger on what it was, exactly. "Have you talked with the parents?"

"On the phone. They took the redeye and got to PDX this morning," said Loch. "They thanked us for getting them a car and putting them up in faculty housing. Again, they were aware of his problem before he came to Parker. They don't seem to be blaming us in any way."

"I guess I'm just a little concerned about what they might say if there's a reporter waiting for them outside the morgue," Peter continued.

Loch didn't like where the conversation was going. "The parents have no reason to turn on us," said Loch sharply.

"After denial comes anger," Peter reminded Loch of the stages of grief. "We should just be prepared if they do. That's all I'm saying. The parents might start looking for someone to blame. McMahon could use the investigation as an excuse to meet with them, and I don't trust him. All it would take is for him to plant one seed of doubt about Parker's culpability. I just want you to be careful—for us to be careful."

"You watch too many movies," said Loch and turned his attention to a stack of papers on his desk.

"The story is supposed to air at five and six and again at eleven," continued Peter. "We should probably meet in the morning to plan for whatever direction the story takes."

"Good," said Loch without looking up. "Set something up with Sally."

Peter's mind was spinning as he left the president's suite. Checking for Goodwin's watchful eye didn't even cross his mind. He was forgetting to do the small things. *Vigilance*, he thought, *I must remain vigilant*, as he descended the stairs toward his office.

* * *

Questions ran through Peter's mind on an endless loop. *What would McMahon's next move be? What was the change in Loch?*

What was the lie that caused Mike Marino's departure? Would Glenn be alright? Did he go to the police? How long would it be before Billings becomes the storyline? Peter was so deep in worry and speculation that he didn't notice Angela's attempt to catch his attention, and he barely noticed her following him into his office. The strings that held the Parker College universe together all stemmed from the hub of his mind. He was trying to follow every storyline to its logical conclusion, and his mind had no room for additional input, good or bad. He couldn't risk taking his eye off his tasks for a second.

Angela was the personification of disappointment. She had watched too many of her coworkers sacrifice the best parts of themselves to the cause of protecting, inflating, or proving themselves worthy of the institution's reputation. She and Peter were supposed to be above such vacuous endeavors; they were the ones who were supposed to mock the hungry ghosts who chased after empty promises and hollow rewards. "Are you going make it?"

"They probably won't fire me while we're in crisis mode, if that's what you mean," Peter smiled tersely. "Unless, of course, I'm quoted saying something really stupid." His desk phone rang. Peter watched for the caller ID. "It's Craven," he said with desperation in his voice. This was the call he dreaded most.

"Are you going to get it?" asked Angela, angry that Peter couldn't see he was losing the part of himself that she adored. The part that made them friends and made Parker suck less.

"It's better to let him leave a voicemail and then call back," said Peter, not looking at Angela as he spoke. "It gives me a chance to think of what to say."

"You know, I get that we're the keepers of the reputation

because that's what separates Parker from other schools, and
shit," she said. "But you also have a reputation, and hopefully
a conscience, and maybe even a soul. At some point soon, you
should probably figure out which of those things is worth
defending. Because, right now, I think you've chosen the
wrong one."

Craven's call went to voicemail. Angela waited for a response,
but Peter didn't have one. He was busy plucking shrapnel out of
his psyche from truth-grenade she had tossed at him. Peter was
expressing his friendship, he believed, by shielding Angela from
the horrible truth, while Angela expressed hers by destroying his
self-delusion. Peter was all the way down the rabbit hole before
he realized he'd even stepped inside. He didn't know how to
get out. He remained silent to avert the resentment stirring in
his soul from getting misdirected. He didn't have the energy to
be angry. He was numb. Angela moved her lips, but no words
came out; her body shifted as she searched for some way to
understand Peter's indifference. It looked like she was going to
say something else, but she just let out a sharp huff and left the
office. Peter listened to the recording.

"Please return the call," was the whole message. He'd given
Peter nothing to prep for. Peter suppressed all his personal
thoughts and emotions and went through his mental checklist
before calling back: *praise the parents, we take drug enforcement
seriously, we're working with the police, any investigation questions should be directed to the cops—including questions about the
Parker College Apartments. If pressed, reveal the lawsuit settled for
peanuts—use the word "frivolous."* Peter dialed the number as if
he was calling in his own obituary.

There were no fake pleasantries to begin the conversation.

All pretense of fairness was gone. Craven knew he had been stonewalled and was coming to this story with a machete and a basket large enough to collect as many heads as possible.

"The DA's office tells me there are suspects," Craven floated.

"I heard that," said Peter flatly.

"Who did you hear it from?"

"Parker College and the Portland Police Bureau have an excellent working relationship." Irony dripped from Peter's voice.

"What did you hear?" Craven asked with hopefulness.

"I wouldn't want to say anything that could compromise the investigation," said Peter. "But we were told they have leads to known drug dealers."

"You don't know shit," snapped Craven.

"Have you run out of questions, Vince? Because I've got other things I need to do."

"I know it's all connected," Craven blurted in frustration.

"What's connected?" Peter played dumb to give himself time to think of a plausible denial, *or maybe this would be a good place to redirect all my anger and resentment.*

"William James, Josh Leonard, the lawsuit, and the suspect are all connected, and I'm going to find out how," Craven shouted into the phone. "This is bullshit, Peter, and you know it. You can't hide the truth forever. You're on the wrong side of this!"

"Oh, good, I thought you figured out it was all connected to the UFO we're hiding in the library basement," he said, tossing the lunatic card. It was out of desperation, but it still felt good. "Vince, you sound like someone with a tinfoil hat and coat hangers wrapped around your head. Call back after you pull your shit together."

Not a textbook press call, thought Peter as he hung up the phone. Craven might have been guessing, but it's possible that he guessed correctly, and there was no requirement at *Stumptown* to show your work. McMahon had Sam from the *Portland Daily* in his pocket, and he was spoon-feeding Craven. *Jesus, Angela was right. What the fuck am I defending? Is this really better than being houseless?*

The Billings story was taking shape. If it ever hit the newsstands, Loch would be forced out, and the door handle would rattle as Goodwin came for Peter's head. Desperation was fomenting catastrophic thoughts. Suicide suddenly felt like a practical and expedient solution. If he could make it look like an accident, his life insurance policy would give Tessa and the kids enough money to start a new life. Two hundred thousand dollars would be enough to get Tess and the kids through the Great Recession. *My life is worth $200,000—less than the cost of a single Parker College diploma.* Peter thought, and it sent a bolt down his spine. *What emotions are driving these thoughts?* He struggled to find a moment of clarity. *Are these the thoughts of a father of two, or are these the emotions of an abandoned eight-year-old?* He closed his eyes and wiped the slate clean. *Step back,* he thought. *Separate everything out; be rational. Remember what Redmon said: I'm strong enough to get through this.* He became angry that he had allowed his mind to go such a dark place. He was angry at Loch and Goodwin. He was angry at himself for not taking better care of that scared eight-year-old boy. His emotions were not tethered to his current reality. *This must stop! No more wondering who's on my side, and who's lying, or why. I'm not burning for someone else's sins. My loyalty is with the truth.*

30

PEELING BACK THE ONION

Redmon used his time waiting for Peter in the foyer of the old four-square by searching for a squeaky floorboard near the good-juju-burning sage machine. He looked like he was stepping around napping cats that only he could see. Having reached a pivotal moment in Peter's treatment, Redmon wanted to optimize their time to build on the progress of their last session. Uncovering his traumatic memories was a spur to awaken Peter to more conscious life. It was a vital step, but Peter was still vulnerable to the dangers created by his coping mechanisms. Peter was easily susceptible to manipulation from anyone he viewed in a paternalistic way, especially if they appeared to be offering him a sense of belonging and security. Redmon wanted Peter to understand the potential dangers this created at Parker. When

Peter came through the door, he was eager to engage, but also curious why Redmon was standing in the middle of the foyer swaying back and forth. "Tai Chi?"

"Squeaky floorboard," he said as he gestured for Peter to follow him. They began their session before reaching the office. Redmon started with a check-in about the events of the past few days to make sure Peter was keeping himself together. They moved seamlessly between present and past—from Parker College to his apartment in Brighton, Massachusetts, from the dormitory hallway to the window of his childhood home that overlooked the garage, and back to his relationships with Tessa and the children. He felt unsupported in his current challenges, terrified about his future, and even more horrified by what he'd learned from Glenn. Finally, Peter expressed he felt overwhelmingly disappointed.

"Let's look at that," said Redmon.

Tears pooled, but Peter's expression remained unchanged. He was tired of crying. As he inhaled to speak, a single tear shook loose and wove a path through his thick stubble. "Having my own children now—understanding what that means, how that feels—what my parents did is inconceivable to me. I understand that type of desperation. I do. But being a grown-up, being a parent—being responsible, is about living with the consequence of our decisions."

"You said you understand that type of desperation they must have felt—" Redmon prodded carefully. "Are we talking about thoughts of ending your life?"

"Yeah. We are. It crossed my mind, today," admitted Peter. "I can't see a way out of this. I really can't. I'm feeling constant pain. Fear. Confusion. Panic. Uncertainty. I don't know what to do, honestly. It's exhausting always trying to tell if my emotions are warranted in the present or attached to something in the past. I have no idea how to get through this, but I'm not going to let it beat me. I know that. I'm not going to stop fighting for my family, or for that little boy who got me here. It's hard, but my whole fucking life has been hard. Quitting now would feel like giving up on a marathon in the twenty-fifth mile because I have a bloody nipple."

Redmon grinned, and they took a moment to appreciate the humor and resolve, the humanity that was being shared. "Who are you disappointed with at Parker?"

"Everyone, including myself," admitted Peter.

"Why do you include yourself?"

"I'm not exactly making the world a better place, am I?"

"You didn't create the situation either. Your job is to handle the press based on the information you're given. It seems to me that's exactly what you're doing." Redmon didn't leave a pause for Peter to respond. "Until you know what the truth is—and it's probably very complicated—it seems reasonable to me that you should continue to do your job to the best of your ability, which again, in my estimation, is exactly what you're doing. It's not your responsibility to make decisions for the college. So, let me ask you again. Who at Parker are you disappointed with?"

"Did you just give me permission to use the *I was just following orders* excuse?"

"You know that's not what I meant, and you're avoiding the question," Redmon shot back.

"But I really am struggling to know if I'm doing the right thing, Doc."

"I know," said Redmon treading lightly. "You are in a difficult situation. There are things you don't know, and your mind is very good—*very good*—at filling in the blanks. Maybe you're seeing it clearly, but maybe you're not. Neither of us knows for sure. But there are things we *do* know. There are things we can address, *right now*, that will help you tremendously. So, I want us to stay focused on those things. Who are you disappointed with at Parker?"

"Loch."

"Talk about that."

Peter wanted to talk about Glenn and Billings, William and Josh. He needed to know what to do. *That's probably a conversation for a lawyer, anyway*, he thought, but he needed to get it off his chest. "The thing is, I know they covered up a crime by a wealthy student—it happened before I started working there," Peter continued. "At least, that's what I think I know for sure."

"Peter, we can talk about whatever you'd like, but you came here today because you asked me to make your back stronger and shoulders wider. My concern is not Parker College and their potential legal problems. You may have to deal with those at some point, but they're not *your* problems. My concern is *you*." Redmon was stern like during the early sessions. Redmon could see Peter's frustration building. He leaned forward and sharpened his gaze. "There's still a piece we haven't addressed. A piece that could become very dangerous for you, especially if you're right about the seriousness of the crimes."

"Is this going to be another bicycle moment where I'm the last one in the room who knows what I'm about to tell you?"

Redmon smiled. "We've talked a lot about Loch during our sessions," said Redmon. "The admiration you felt for him as a child. The respect you saw in your father's eyes. The way you feel he protects you from Goodwin."

"You don't think that's real?"

"It sounds very paternal," said Redmon. "Like a father's care."

"You *don't* think it's real," Peter confirmed.

"I think you're protecting *him*, and I think he knows that," said Redmon. "I think he appreciates it. I think he appreciates you as a person and respects the work you do."

"But you think, *I* think, he's my father?" asked Peter. "Or that I want him to replace my father, or something?"

"What do you think?" Redmon asked gently.

"I admire him," admitted Peter, somewhat dismissively.

"I admire Desmond Tutu," said Redmon. "But I'm not sure I'd help protect him if I thought he broke the law."

"Yeah . . . Jesus," Peter was feeling dumb wrapped in shell of disappointment and dipped in humiliation sauce.

"I know it provides you comfort to believe he's protecting you—and that belief has served you well up until this point. It's been helpful, but from everything you've told me about what's going on at Parker, I think, moving forward, that relationship might be dangerous for you emotionally, professionally, and potentially legally."

"I suspect we're about to explore the emotional part," quipped Peter.

"Peter, I know this is a lot to deal with at one time, but it's the reality of where you are," said Redmon taking care to choose the right words. "I think you need to ask yourself, if you left your job tomorrow, would the two of you remain in contact? Would he offer you advice or support? Would he help you financially if you got fired? Would he even tell you, now, if you were in danger of being fired today?"

Every question made Peter sink deeper in his chair. He felt

foolish. He couldn't look at Redmon. Instead, he looked at the floor and shook his head. "I've been a fool," said Peter.

"You have not been a fool, Peter. You found a way to make your situation tenable. That's what you do. That's what you've always done. That why you're sitting here, the accomplished and successful man that you are, and not—well—somewhere else," Redmon continued. "I'm sure he admires you for what you've been able to do for him and the college, but I worry that moving forward, the level of trust you've placed in him could be dangerous for you."

"Wow," said Peter. "Sometimes I think I'm so smart and that nothing can get by me, and then I have a moment like this, when I think, 'how can something so obvious, something so completely ridiculous, seem so real to me?'"

"It's how you cope, Peter. On some level, you've always known what happened with your parents," said Redmon. "You kept it hidden to protect yourself—and I think, probably, to protect the memory of your father. In a way, it's allowed you to live a very different life than the one that directly factored in all your trauma—and I'm afraid we've only just scratched the surface of that."

"You think it's about more than seeing them die?" asked Peter.

"It seems highly unlikely to me that both your parents chose to commit suicide while you were at school—without leaving a note or making plans for you. I'm sure you've thought about this," said Redmon.

"I don't want to have to think about that right now," said Peter.

"That's a future project, but it could help shed light on how you think about Loch," said Redmon. "Loch is a sort-of surrogate that provides some of the things you feel are missing from your life."

"Yeah, I still don't completely get the thing with Loch, yet," said Peter.

"When I say Loch, think proxy. I think he represents all the things you wish you had in your life. Your father was very impressed by him," said Redmon. "When did you meet him?"

"It was an election year; he was running for mayor," said Peter. "So, September or October of . . ." Peter got quiet, and a tear fell to his cheek. "My parents died on October twenty-first, soon after Loch told me that 'I'd do great things one day.' My aunt brought home a manila envelope from the morgue with my parents' personal effects. All that was in it was my father's wallet, their wedding rings, and a "Loch for Mayor" button that I still have in my father's old cigar box."

"You needed someone who believed in you. Someone to be the kind of parent that maybe your father was never able to be. The kind of role model you want to be."

"It seems improbable, impossible actually, that I searched out this opportunity my whole life," said Peter, incredulously.

"I agree," Redmon quickly dismissed that idea. "You've had other mentors in your life, other surrogates. This isn't a new pattern, but Loch was something of a perfect storm. His presence helped coalesce all the factors that brought us to this moment. You said you were drawn to Parker to help him shine in the spotlight one last time, but really, he was probably fulfilling other needs of yours."

"Is this karma?" asked Peter with a hint of irony.

Redmon smiled. "Whatever it is, you should embrace it," he smiled. "One day, but probably not soon, you will be able to see it as a gift, one day when you're feeling healthy and looking back. Peter, childhood trauma wrecks people, but you did what you needed to do to get yourself to this point. To get yourself to a place where you're ready to heal—when you had the capacity, the tools, the energy, the resources to deal with the trauma you experienced all those years ago. Embrace your ability to create a world that provides you with what you needed. It's a unique gift—and it is a gift."

"You're right," Peter said with a laugh. "It'll be a while before I'll feel lucky."

"There's another opportunity you have now. There's a tendency for people who have experienced childhood trauma to feel unworthy and often responsible for the people around them. You must understand that you are worthy of love before anything else can move forward. It's time to accept yourself for the man you've become. You don't need to sacrifice parts of yourself for anyone else."

"So, what does that look like?" asked Peter. "All this self-love bullshit and whatnot?"

Redmon smiled in relief. "Ultimately, what that looks like is up to you," said Redmon before becoming hesitant for the first time in one of their sessions. "Peter, you're never going to have the chance to confront your parents. But you may have an opportunity to confront Loch. You might want to think about what you would ask him, or what you might want to tell him."

"What would the point of that be if it's not really him that I was seeking out?" asked Peter.

"The point is for you to see yourself as the man you've become. That you don't need anyone's approval to be proud of who you are. There are no tests left for you to pass. You've struggled your whole life, Peter, to find the person who would validate you, who would protect you and guide you—and never abandon you. To be your mentor. A surrogate parent who would love you unconditionally. The point of all our time together is to show you that you've already found that person. He is strong, and caring, and intelligent, and determined, and brave, and loving. The person you've been looking for all this time, Peter, *is you*. The point of all of this is for you to see that—understand who you've become and embrace what you've achieved because it defies the odds. Your back has always been made of steel and your shoulders are wide enough to carry any burden. Nobody did that for you. Nobody gave you permission to carry that weight. My whole job with you, Peter, is to get you to see that. There's more work ahead, but the most important thing for you, right now, is to understand how powerful you truly are. There is not a single person in this world whose approval should matter to you more than your own."

31

THE WEEK BEFORE
BACCHANALIA

Upon arriving forty minutes early to the North Lot for his morning news debrief with the brass, Peter reflexively looked for Angela as he stepped out of his car. Of course, she wasn't there. He thought about the truth bomb she'd dropped the day before and how closely it resembled Redmon's advice. Then he wondered where Angela's friendship fit into Redmon's novel ideas of loving himself and exploring his own needs. It seemed inappropriate to think of Angela as anything other than a work friend, but he couldn't help it. *What if she's the reason I was brought to Parker?* He thought. *What if the result of all this misery was to bring soulmates together? That would be an awful start, but we do really like each other, I think.* Peter got distracted by the smell of freshly cut grass. It had been years since he had come upon such a large expanse of newly cut lawn. The unmistakable rattle and hum of a ride-on mower rose over the shallow bluff that separated the North Lot from the Grand Lawn. The intense smell conjured images of spring training and the promise of long summer days. It also briefly replaced his pondering about Angela, fate, and infidelity. *Holy shit,* Peter stopped in his tracks. *Is this what Redmon was talking about? Am I doing that coping thing with Angela? I'm making it into a thing that's not there. Unconditional love. Right? Maybe? Do I want it to be true? Why does everything have to be so fucking hard?*

* * *

Loch, Rosen, Collins, and Goodwin had arrived before Peter and took their places around the table. The room felt light, given the reason they were there. Even Goodwin was lacking a sense of urgency and his normal constipated look. Confusing. *What did I miss?* Peter wondered.

It was a blustery morning, and a huge gust of wind startled the room. Sunshine momentarily streaked past the layers of clouds. Through the rattling south windows, Peter noticed the cherry trees on the lawn were nearing full bloom. Rays of sharply focused light illuminated the pink and white blossoms. Boughs swayed; Peter imagined the light was being carried by the wind. Cherry blossom petals fell like snowflakes against the patches of gray and blue sky. It was beautiful. Loch broke Peter's mild trance by redirecting his attention from the scene outside to the work at hand. There had been a breakthrough in finding Josh's supplier. They'd gotten a tip from someone who saw the same student with William James on the night of his overdose and then leaving Josh's room the night he died.

Please let the source be Glenn. Please, Glenn. Please, have gone to the police, Peter pleaded with the gods, but he knew the room wouldn't be so light if the tip implicated Billings. "I'm not a constitutional law expert," said Peter while looking at the constitutional law expert in the room. "But what you've described doesn't sound like probable cause to me. Can the police get a warrant to search the student's room based on this tip?"

"I don't know about the police," Rosen responded, being the resident expert on student contracts. "But our housing contract stipulates that the college can search a room for almost any reason, and certainly if we suspect illegal activity. We'll be searching the room later today."

Seeming particularly smug, Goodwin asked why Peter had brought them all together so early in the morning. Ignoring the others as he spoke, Goodwin eyed the yellow tin he'd pulled from his pocket. Peter resisted the impulse to ask Goodwin if he needed some alone time with his beeswax and instead decided to see if he could flesh out more information. If Glenn was lying, then Peter needed to protect himself, but if he wasn't, Peter wanted to protect him. He began by saying their news had scooped the reason for the debrief, and the Bacchanalia storyline would surely take a back seat to news of an arrest. Then he floated, "the *Stumptown* reporter, Craven, called me at the end of the day yesterday. He said the cops had identified a student. His story didn't sound credible, and he wasn't asking me for comment, so I wrote it off. It seemed very odd, until now."

"He said the police told him this yesterday?" Loch asked.

"Is his name really Craven?" asked Collins. Everybody

stared at him blankly. "Craven" was the Dictionary.com Word of the Day.

"Yes, and yes," Peter clarified. "Craven told me the police had identified a Parkie as the possible supplier. He went on again about knowing that Josh, William James, and the lawsuit were all linked and that he was going to find the connection and sink the college." The heavy silence filling the room was broken by the popping of Goodwin's beeswax lid. He put the tin back in his pocket, cleared his throat, and looked to Rosen and then Loch.

"What did you say to him?" asked Loch.

"I asked him if he was wearing a tinfoil hat, but now I realize he had scooped us, well, me anyway," Peter said as a matter of fact. "I called this meeting to debrief the Channel 8 interview and to prepare a response to the Bacchanalia storyline, but if an arrest is imminent, that is certainly going to be the story moving forward."

"Why did the *Stumptown* reporter call you?" asked Goodwin. "I mean, if he didn't ask you anything."

"After finding out the suspect was a Parkie, maybe he thought I would know who it was and he could get me to tell him," Peter said. "But the real answer is that I have no idea."

"Did he professed to have evidence linking Josh's death to Noon's lawsuit?" Loch asked Peter to clarify.

"No," Peter said as if he believed none could exist. "He said he was going to find it. I'm sorry, but what am I missing? It must be the same student. Right? I'm assuming Craven is linking the tip he got with some shaky, thin evidence in hope that he found a career-making story."

"This must be stopped!" Goodwin insisted, as he slashed his

index finger through the air, pointing it at Peter before driving its tip into the table with a boney thud. "That idea needs to be stopped! Understood?"

Their suspect clearly isn't Billings, Peter smiled at his obvious deduction. Now that Goodwin believed the police had identified Billings, Peter did understand. Stopping an idea is impossible, of course, but Peter nodded in agreement. "Okay," he said with a dopey grin and a nod. Goodwin had ordered that the truth be expunged from existence. Money can buy people, but the truth is impartial and resilient to coercion. The pressure was forcing people's true nature to the forefront; Goodwin's fragile ego exposed him as a spoiled child ordering his nanny to make the bad dreams go away. His fear made Peter stop worrying about what came next. *Men are fragile. The truth is unconquerable,* he thought. *Stay allied with the truth.*

Peter extinguished the light mood that had greeted him at the start of the meeting. *I'll be gone within a week no matter what I do. It's easier to decide right from wrong when you have nothing left to lose,* he thought while looking around the table and wondering who among them would survive the next few weeks. He contemplated rubbing salt in their wounds by pretending that Craven had told him his tip was "some billionaire." But Loch already looked as if he was composing his resignation letter in his head.

"If there's nothing else for the good of the order—" Loch said and rose slowly from his chair, everyone followed suit. Loch turned his back on the others and started toward his desk, glimpsing the cherry trees as he walked past the window; he asked Goodwin to stay behind. He agreed as he glared at Peter.

The Great Recession had changed the view from the top.

Dwindling resources had caused people to focus on where the wealth was concentrated, and they found remarkable inequity. The wealth of the nation had been used to bail out the misdeeds of a few wealthy bankers who were then "punished" with grotesquely large bonus checks funded by the American taxpayer. It was the stuff of the French Revolution, only nobody was being offered cake. The One Percent was feeling threatened. Even small displays of defiance made people like Goodwin feel nervous. Peter returned Goodwin's glare with indifference.

* * *

Peter grabbed the public affairs' door handle with more force than he'd intended, startling everyone in the office. Angela's eyebrows arched and her head tilted as she turned to Peter in disgust. He apologized to everyone as he entered and walked meekly toward Angela, inviting her to his office. His voicemail light was blinking. Angela noticed him notice and asked if he needed to go play Secret Squirrel. Her usual charmingly sarcastic scowl was replaced with disdainful one.

Not knowing where to begin, Peter apologized for being paternalistic the previous day, explaining that he had been trying to shield her from knowing things that could get her fired—something that was likely going to happen to him within a matter of minutes. Angela was exasperated. "I just wanted to say thank you for being—" Peter didn't know how to finish the sentence.

"First of all, fuck you, for your chauvinistic bullshit, but also congratulations for seeing it when I didn't. I was busy being annoyed at other deficiencies of yours. Second, the next time you think I need protecting, ask me, because that felt shitty.

And when you get fired, or whatever happens, you'd better not pretend I don't exist, because *that*, I am done with. Do you understand me, mister?"

Peter took his talking-to. The doorknob rattled. Collins marched to his office, barely looking at the two as he did. Relieved, Angela said, "Well, if you make it through the day, let's get a drink. To get back at you, I'm going to make you pay because that's what men do, and then I'm going to say other sexist things. I'm going to tell you to go fix something with your manly tool belt that I'm sure you always have with you because you're such a manly man!"

"I accept my punishment," joked Peter, before becoming serious. "Angela, thank you."

She smiled and nodded. "Fuck you," she said, deadpan. "Now let me go. I need to think of inappropriate things to say after I get all drunk and handsy. Make sure you wear something cute."

Peter was glad things were back to normal with Angela.

* * *

Peter contemplated quitting before Goodwin could fire him, but leaving any job during the worst economy since the Great Depression was, well, dumb. Watching his toes skim along rock bottom at least brought the comfort of knowing the fall would not kill him. He had messages from Sam at the *Daily* and Craven from the *STD*, both asking about the letter Josh's mother had written to the student body. They wanted to know when it had been delivered and what the administration thought about it. He knew nothing about the letter. The phone rang as he was reaching for it to call Rosen to see if he knew what they were talking about. It was Sam from the *Daily*, calling again before filing her story with "no comment" from Parker College.

Sam proceeded to lie about having filed a Freedom of Information Act request to the DA's office to obtain a copy of the letter. There was no way for her to have known to file a FOIA request, which takes more than a few minutes to grant, since Peter didn't even know of the letter's existence. He asked Sam to send him a digital copy. "If you want us to comment on the letter, it would be decent of you, or the DA, who most likely wrote it, to let us read it first."

Peter wasn't sure if he was angrier with McMahon or with Sam for being his lapdog. As Peter waited for the letter, Glenn staggered through the main door. Peter brought him into his office, sat him down and offered him water. Glenn looked like a shadow person. "You look awful! What's happened?"

"Remember, I told you that Billings came to me the morning after Josh died?" Glenn looked for the courage to say what he had come to tell Peter.

"You told me you didn't help him. Is that true?" Peter asked gently. Glenn paused. His eyes teared and his hands shook. "Glenn, I'm done with all the lying! You need to tell me what you did. If there's a way out of this, we'll find it. But you have to tell me the whole truth, and you have to tell me *right now,* or I'm done helping you."

"Billings asked me to hold his kit. He told me it was everything he had. He told me after they searched his room that he'd come back and get it."

"So he gave you his needles and whatever?" asked Peter.

"Yeah, only he didn't come back, and then I found out about Josh." Glenn stopped shaking and looked into Peter's eyes. "Billings went to Goodwin and told him it was me that fixed up Josh and Willy. Billings gave me the needle Josh used."

Mark "Chuck" Palmachuk, was the last of the security guards who worked with Glenn. As the last man standing, he was elevated to department head after Mike Marino quit. Palmachuk had a mountain of evidence that connected Billings to Josh and Willy but was told to ignore it during a meeting with Rosen, Goodwin, and Loch. They told him that he would find the heroin and paraphilia in Glenn's room. He was told their evidence was rock solid. Palmachuk went straight to Glenn to get his side of the story. No ambiguity remained; Parker College was being run like a crime syndicate. Loch, Goodwin, and Rosen were happy to have a fall guy. Ruin a life, pass go, collect $25 million. Peter was furious. He tried to clear his mind and find a path forward. Collins had surely seen Glenn come into the office. Peter needed to get Glenn moving before Collins could call Goodwin. *McMahon wants big headlines. He wants it to be Billings. He'll believe Glenn,* thought Peter. *But if Glenn is lying... I hope he's not lying.* "Did you go to the police?"

"I can't," said Glenn.

"Glenn, I'm done with the bullshit. I'm going to take you straight to the DA, right now," said Peter, worried if he could trust McMahon to do the right thing. "If you won't come with me, I'll go by myself. He knows about the night in the apartments, but he doesn't know it was Billings that fixed up Josh and Willy. If you tell him, he'll believe you. Bring the kit. It will have Josh's DNA. If we're lucky, it will have Billings' prints too. It's the only way out of this for you."

"My prints and DNA are on it too." Glenn was humiliated.

"It was too much. I thought I could resist it, but it was just sitting there."

All of Peter's hope flushed from his body in a massive sigh. Peter was becoming triggered. He felt responsible. The tingle began in the back of his neck. He felt his chest constricting. When he looked at Glenn, Peter felt like the little boy watching through the garage window as his parents died. His reality was starting to fray. He had to stop himself. *This isn't about me. This is about putting money over human life. I cannot let this continue. Be strong.*

"It will be okay," said Peter. 'It's still your only option. It will be better if you tell the police your side of things, before they come to arrest you. We'll go together and tell the DA everything we know. They have all the dots; they just need you to connect them. You have to trust me that it's your only way out of this."

"But, I'll get kicked out of Parker," said Glenn as if nothing else mattered.

"Glenn, you do understand that the other option is being arrested for murder. You get that, right? They're going to charge you with reckless homicide. This is as serious as it gets."

The silence made Peter wonder if Glenn was contemplating which was worse or if he didn't understand the stakes. The intensity was still shining in Glenn's eyes. Resolve. It was obvious he had made up his mind. "I'm going to do this alone. I don't want to drag you into it—more than I already have." Glenn flashed a playful smile. "As my dad would say, 'it's time to cowboy up.'"

Glenn stood and extended his hand to shake, but Peter pulled him in for a hug.

"If you change your mind, I'm here for you. Okay? I'll be

here for you the whole time. Let them know I can corroborate your story." He wrote his cell number on the back of his business card and handed it to Glenn." You have to go. Right. Now!"

Before Glenn opened the door, he thanked Peter again and made him promise that after all the dust settled, he'd move back to Alaska and befriend a raven.

32

DENIAL TO ANGER

"If the college brazenly refused to follow electrical code, resulting in a fire that caused a student's death, who would be responsible for the death? It's simple: the college. It's the same legal reasoning that makes Parker College culpable for the overdose death of our son, when it did not strictly enforce its drug policy," began a letter addressed to the student body and signed by Josh's mother and father. It implored students to "take the initiative for curbing drug use, since the administration had failed them." Its crescendo was the statement that she had "encouraged the District Attorney's office to charge the college's leadership, using crack house laws that make it illegal to knowingly rent space for the purpose of using or selling drugs."

The letter's final demand was for the college to "cancel

Bacchanalia or risk losing another student to the ravages of drugs." The letter arrived by courier at approximately the same time Peter was talking on the phone with Sam. Up to that point, relations between the Leonards and the college had been open, cordial, and cooperative. Seeing their only son lying lifeless on a gurney had changed all that. Their generosity toward the college was snuffed out after they confirmed Josh's identity. Letting go of their denial was as hard as getting the initial news of his death. As the Leonards left the morgue, they were met by Assistant District Attorney John McMahon, as Peter had feared. McMahon said he was there to share details from the investigation into their son's death, but he was also there to expedite their transition from denial to anger.

Peter had only sympathy for Josh's parents. Knowing the letter was written by McMahon, however, brought him regret for trusting Glenn's fate to someone who would exploit parents' grief for political gain. McMahon needed a win and sank to appalling depths to achieve it. Under McMahon's watch, Multnomah County was flooded with cheap and potent heroin. His jurisdiction suffered twice the fatal overdoses than any other in the United States. McMahon needed a strawman to prove he was winning the war on drugs, and the small private college in the most affluent neighborhood of Portland was a safer target than the cartels and gangs that were controlling the supply chain. One hundred and forty-eight people had died from heroin overdoses in Multnomah County the previous year, but none of them attracted even passing interest by the press. Not one of them was the subject of radio talk shows or editorials in the *Portland Daily*. But none of them had been a rich white kid from Parker College.

It's not that Peter even disagreed with the letter, it's that he despised a coward. McMahon was afraid to cut off the head of the viper; so instead he'd become a snake oil salesman, hawking Parker College as the epicenter of the region's drug problem. Peter wished he could take back his advice to Glenn. Though he was nearly blinded with anger, he could see the genius in the tactic of coming after the administration through crack house laws. *This is a game changer.* He wondered who would be the first of Parker's inner circle to cut a deal with McMahon and throw the others under the bus. *This will be interesting to watch.*

* * *

After having read the letter, Peter, Loch, Goodwin, and Rosen convened for the second time that morning to find the least damaging path to move the college forward. "There are a few things that complicate sending the letter to the student body as it's written." Rosen began with the painfully obvious, but then ventured into the parts of the letter the others had skimmed over. "For starters, as we know, Josh had been caught with someone else's prescription of oxycodone and was forced to attend NA and threatened with suspension if he was ever…"

"Forgive me for interrupting, but invoking the use of crack house laws supersedes any factual inconsistences in the letter," said Loch, uncomfortably adjusting himself in his chair while massaging his eyelids and releasing a comically loud harrumph. "The statute she referenced was recently amended in the Illicit Drug Anti-Proliferation Act of 2003, which now makes it easier to prosecute event promoters. So, the hosts of Bacchanalia, for instance, could be held criminally liable for illegal drug sales or use. I'm sure Mrs. Leonard came across this little legal tidbit while casually perusing federal statute 21 in U.S. Code 856."

Peter suppressed his laughter, while the others processed what the information meant for their legal liability. Goodwin took his little yellow tin from his pocket and placed it sideways on the table as if he was going to spin it. "What does that mean, exactly? Whom could be held criminally liable for what?"

"It's *who*, not *whom*, and you and I could be held criminally liable if McMahon could prove that we are renting a dorm room, or one of the Parker College apartments, to someone we know is engaging in illegal drug activity—it makes us complicit in that activity and open to felony prosecution."

"How far does the culpability extend?" asked a nervous Rosen, realizing his faux pas only after Goodwin and Loch looked at him with repugnance. "I mean, if this letter gets delivered, I will have staff in the housing department concerned about their liability."

"This letter will never get delivered," said Loch. "And it is unlikely that prosecutors would look beyond the VP level. So, your *staff members* should rest easy, but I'd be worried if I was sitting in this room, or on the Board."

It was perversely satisfying to watch the architects of this vile creation having to confront their own monster. They deserved to be in jail. *Hubris is the thing that turns revolutionaries into dictators*, an editor had once told Peter when he'd used hubris as a synonym for arrogance in a story about a mid-level governmental bureaucrat. *Hubris is its own category of self-delusion. Remember the Julius Caesar quote, "it's only hubris if I fail." That was an arrogant thing to say, but if he lost the battle, it would be the fault of hubris.* This is what was running though Peter's mind as the others were flipping through their mental rolodexes searching for criminal defense lawyers.

The press had the letter before it reached the college. Peter let the others know that it wouldn't matter if they emailed it to students or not, because it will be all over the news and the internet within hours. All that was left to do was mitigate the damage. Because Peter was supposed to believe the lawsuit was fiction, he suggested the college put out a statement of their own, calling for McMahon to do his job and to stop scapegoating the college. He relied on the acting training he'd gotten in college to make his delivery believable. As Loch thought of a response to Peter's performance, Rosen got a text, alerting him to a protest outside the student union. *Stumptown* had already posted the letter to its website and students were rebelling at the idea of Bacchanalia's cancelation. If the administration acquiesced to the letter's appeals, the protestors threatened to call the press and encourage the student body to march naked on the quad.

"Would they actually do that?" asked Peter.

"Probably," replied Rosen.

"Definitely," responded Loch.

"This is a public relations nightmare," lamented Rosen.

Peter laughed, which surprised the others. Loch shot him a quizzical look that encouraged him to go on. "Yeah, sorry, but the DA threatening college leadership with crack house laws through a letter by the grieving mother of a kid who OD'd, while naked students are chanting, 'don't take away our drug party.' Yeah, that's, uh, not a nightmare. That's our 'bulldoze the college to the ground and start over from scratch' reality."

Loch was amused by Peter's characterization. Nobody had slept much in days. The mix of pressure, guilt, grief, and exhaustion created opportunities for gallows humor. He laughed, but ultimately, he knew Peter was right. Going forward, it was all thorns with no roses.

"More students suffer knee and ankle injuries at Bacchanalia playing Ultimate Frisbee than they do from drug- and alcohol-related issues," said a frustrated Rosen. "Couldn't we just compare the number of emergency room visits for alcohol poisoning at the average Pac 12 football game with the number of issues we have at Bacchanalia?"

"Being drunk at a sporting event is as American as apple pie, guns, and obesity," said Peter. "There are no Super Bowl commercials with people taking psychedelics to celebrate academic achievement. We just have to be realistic about where we are. We know the Leonards didn't write this letter, but it's going be everywhere, soon, and we need to figure out how to respond to our most important constituencies. And we have to do it in a way that doesn't look like we're attacking the grieving parents."

"When I last spoke with Mrs. Leonard, to let her know we had received her letter, her demeanor hadn't changed toward me," said Rosen. "She seemed apologetic for the letter. She let me know it had been written at the behest of the DA and with his assistance. Her words."

"A lot of people will find it abhorrent that he's playing politics with grieving parents," said Peter. "If we told the right reporter, it could, at least, put him on the defensive and give us a little breathing room." Rosen wanted to hear more. This was a new world to him. It was like watching open-heart surgery— ghastly, but fascinating.

"I wish you were on my staff when I was running for mayor, but once again, we're not running a political campaign, Peter, we're running a college. Political careers are short, but institutions need to take the long view." Loch looked to Rosen. "Could you convince the Leonards that it's simply the wrong letter to send to students? They are in the unique situation to make an emotional appeal. That's certainly not something the college is going to do. Could you call the mother back and gently ask her to leave the policy prescriptions to the DA and instead appeal to the students as a mother—as only she can?"

"That's perfect," added Peter. "Her goal should be to write something that pulls their heartstrings so hard that it jerks the bongs right out of their hands."

Rosen found Peter's folksy language less amusing than did Loch, but he found merit in the argument. He knew it was the right thing to do, but it didn't make it more attractive to be the one to have to make the call.

"The *Portland Daily* reporter lied to me about how she got the letter," said Peter. "We might get a less damning story there, but I don't know what we do about *Stumptown*."

* * *

Peter called Sam and Craven to explain that Mrs. Leonard reconsidered her letter and was writing a new draft. Printing the version they had, he told them, would be against the mother's wishes. Having already posted the letter to *Stumptown*'s website, Craven changed its headline while Peter was still on the phone: "Letter Never Sent: Parker Censors Grieving Mother." Craven never ran the second, but Sam posted it to the *Daily*'s website in its entirety.

I loved my son, as your parents love you, the second letter began. *There is no greater joy than being a parent. Sharing your child's accomplishments and heartache, sharing first steps and first ice cream cones, stories of first loves and even breakups, and hoping you've learned enough to share a little wisdom during the hard times. One of Josh's happiest days was receiving his acceptance letter to Parker College. He called me at work to let me know he got in. He stuck the letter on our refrigerator with a magnet. Written in marker were the words, 'We did it!' We celebrated at his favorite restaurant that night. I asked him why he wrote 'we,' when it was his grades, achievements, and determination that got him accepted to Parker. He told my husband and me that he couldn't have done it without us. What I'd thought was taken as years of nagging and pestering had been seen for what it was: our best and most loving intentions. It was one of my proudest moments as a parent. Every moment I spent with Josh was a gift, but that moment was even more special.*

A few nights ago, I awoke to a knock on my door. It was a sight that every parent dreads—a policeman standing in the doorway. He told me that he regretted to inform me that my son had died. It took several days for the reality of those words to sink in and to truly understand my boy was never coming home. I will live my life wondering what else I could have said or done to prevent his death—what I could have said to change his mind, what could have helped me see his smile or hear his beautiful laughter one more time. Many of your parents have arranged their trips to Portland to see you accept your diplomas and help you in the next phase in the realization of your dreams. Every one of you is a gift. In the most privileged country in the world, you are the most privileged few. Don't deny the world of the gift of reaching your full potential. Please don't throw your life away for the false promise of a euphoric high. Don't let Bacchanalia destroy another gift. Be safe.

The letter became the most visited page on the *Daily's* website. Students forwarded the letter to their parents, who forwarded it their friends and families, who posted it on Facebook and other social media. The letter went viral. People who had never heard of Parker College were now becoming curious about Bacchanalia and why it might "destroy another gift."

Peter rushed home that night and surprised Ben and Blythe with sandwiches from Gene's Deli, where he also bought a handful of lottery tickets in hope that divine intervention might pay the way out of his situation. He hugged his kids extra tight as they greeted him at the door. Tessa spread a beach towel over the worn carpet in front of the TV, and they made a picnic. Blythe folded paper towels into squares, placed one before Tessa and Ben, and put one on Peter's lap, before sitting crossed-legged next to him and melting comfortably against his side. Peter sat in his cramped apartment, surrounded by his wife and children, certain of only two things: that he loved his family and that, in that moment, he was in the right place.

33

BEYOND THE RAVEN

Peter dreamt he was in the living room of his childhood home, looking down through the window at 1970s ambulances parked in the driveway. He was a small boy in the dream, wearing his adult crisis blazer that hung from his office door at Parker College in anticipation of unscheduled TV interviews. Imitating the robot from *Lost in Space*, he playfully waved his arms and watched the sleeves of the enormous jacket flail before him. His goofing was interrupted by the sound of tapping on glass. Not being able to identify its source outside, Peter looked to see if it was coming from inside the room. Finding nothing, he looked back out the window and was seamlessly standing in the driveway transformed to his current age. The enormous jacket was now snug. A TV camera pointed at Peter, and a reporter was holding a microphone under his chin. The interview was in progress, but Peter didn't know the topic. The reporter's lips moved but no words came out. Peter wondered if he was being interviewed about his parents, or Josh, or maybe Willy. *What if it was about Billings?* He wondered as fear prickled across his back and neck. He tried to remain calm while asking the reporter to repeat the question.

"Why does everyone abandon you?" The reporter was impatient for having to repeat himself. Peter became more confused about the subject of the interview. He still couldn't identify the source of the tapping, which was getting louder and had reached a feverish pace. One of the '70s boxy ambulances had become an aerodynamic modern hearse. The tapping was coming from inside the coffin compartment which was filled with exhaust. Peter struggled to see who was trying to get his attention. *Is it my parents? Can I save them this time?* Drip lines trickled down the window, creating a pattern in the condensation that looked like jail bars. Through the drip lines, Peter could make out the faint outline of an unidentifiable figure moving within the dense exhaust. He wasn't even sure it was human. As Peter rushed to open the door, Glenn Nurse emerged through the smoke. The drip lines on the rear window became the steel bars of an old western-style jail door. Glenn, however, was unphased, peaceful, wearing a contented smile. The jail bars quickly faded into emptiness, Glenn leaned toward Peter and whispered, "Tell them we know everything we came to learn," then he morphed into smoke that swirled to fill the coffin area, rumbling like a tornado, concentrating into the center of the cabin. It accelerated, becoming deafening as it formed the shape of a raven. Having transformed from vapor into feathers and folklore, the raven looked at Peter. Its black eyes blinked, then flashed a blinding light that shredded the fabric of the dream. All that remained in the dreamscape was Peter and the raven. As it spread its wings, a vibrant new reality was created by the wind under its primary feathers. Peter watched in awe as the bird took flight. What had been the dim cabin of the hearse was now a brilliant expanse of ancient forest. The distinctive caw familiar in Southeast Alaska reverberated throughout this new reality. The soaring raven brought light to everything in its path. Rising above the tree line toward jagged mountain peaks, the majestic bird turned to Peter once again and, in Glenn's voice, called for him to follow.

Peter startled awake at 4:09 a.m. and couldn't fall back to sleep. For a while he watched Tessa cozied next to him and wondered if their relationship would strengthen. He then got up for the second time that night to check on the kids. He thought about how unlikely it was that he'd keep his promise to Glenn about moving back to Alaska. It seemed as likely as befriending a raven. The sight of his sleeping children caused his heart to swell with love. Scrunching down on the floor between their beds, he hoped that if the right path revealed itself, he would have the awareness to see it and the courage to follow it. Providing for his family was important, but more than anything, Peter wanted to be a good role model, a good father, to Blythe and Ben.

Clearing his mind and straightening his back, he thought about the strength it took to get though his parents' death and any other trauma that likely occurred. As Redmon had suggested, he meditated on returning to the memory of his parents' deaths as if he were returning to visit the boy who was trapped in that moment. Peter followed his breath in and out until he imagined he could see himself as a boy staring through the garage window into the exhaust-filled car. As if he was there like a time traveler,

Peter took his own young hand and walked the boy away from the garage door. He hugged him, told him he loved him, and that everything turned out okay. He thanked him for getting them through that time. As he sat with the young boy, his gratitude and love swelled, and tears washed over Peter's face. He stayed in that memory with the boy until they both felt safe and secure. Peter was evolving toward a healthier place where he could be the kind of father he never had and provide his children with the kind of love he always wanted. Holding the boy with fierce empathy, kindness, and appreciation, the young and old Peters became one. Feeling their combined strength, Peter believed would bring him the courage to work through whatever came next. The strength was familiar. It was a feeling he had always known but could never identify.

Golden light kissed the windows as the sun approached the horizon. Morning twilight was Peter's favorite time of day. The rising sun was filled with hope, beauty, and promise. Quietly as he could, he tried to convince his aging knees to rise and meet the day. His butt was asleep, and he labored to stand without waking the children. His legs tingled with pins and needles as he walked like Frankenstein's monster toward the door. While hobbling out of the room, he spotted his father's old cigar box sitting atop Blythe's bureau; it was a time capsule where he kept all his precious childhood relics. Curious if his things had been replaced with new treasures like a snakeskin or a fidget spinner, he opened the lid. All the items looked familiar, with a few additions. There was a picture of Ben and Blythe holding crabs over a trap that was balanced on the gunwale of their skiff. It was an explosion of color: orange life vests, yellow slickers, green and blue raincoats, and red crab against a backdrop of emerald water dotted by brightly colored buoys. All Peter saw, however, was the joy on his children's faces. He missed that.

"Mom said that box was for holding your favorite memories," said Blythe in a sweet voice that begged permission that she knew had already been granted. "I wanted to put my favorite memories in there too."

Peter didn't turn around right away but then decided it would be okay for Blythe to see him cry. Jumping out of bed, she hugged her dad. Peter leaned over and kissed the top of her head. "That was a very good idea, sweetie," he said in a hushed voice as he walked her back to bed. "It's still very early though," said Peter as he tucked her beneath her covers. "We'll keep that box right where it is so everyone can put their favorite memories in there. Sound good?"

"Yes."

"I love you, sweetheart, more than you could ever imagine times infinity," said Peter.

Blythe closed her eyes, and her face glowed with happiness. While shutting the lid to the box of memories, Peter noticed the "Loch for Mayor" campaign button. It was heavier than he remembered, the tin thicker. Peter knew he was done at Parker College. He realized he had been fighting battles before knowing which side of the war he thought was just. The anguish and shame he felt at work was reflected in his relationships with his family. He could no longer rationalize his involvement in the direction Loch and the others had taken. Now that he was certain of their actions, he would be complicit. *Do what's right. There's no more ambiguity*, he thought as he walked out of his children's room.

Peter made coffee and watched through the kitchen window

as the sun brought life to the city. A halo of clouds surrounded the peak of Oregon's largest mountain, Wy'east. The sky filled with gentle shades of lavender and auburn as the sun filtered through the atmosphere. Peter admired the ephemeral splendor as shadows gave way to a palette of brilliant colors that brought definition to the mountain's silhouette. There was still an hour left before the alarm on his iPhone was set to go off. Peter tried to relax as he sipped his coffee and wondered about how to handle the day ahead. He subconsciously rubbed his thumb over the pinpoint of the Loch campaign pin as he made his way to the bedroom to turn off his alarm that was sitting on his nightstand.

He had missed a call at 5:17 a.m. There was a voicemail from a number local number he didn't recognize. It was the Assistant DA John McMahon.

3 4

A RECKONING

Angela's echoing greeting of, "Hey, jackass!" startled Peter as he
climbed out of his Subaru, causing him to laugh. A middle-aged
woman with short platinum hair, wearing thick, yellow-framed
eyeglasses and a suede jacket garnished with fringe along its
Western stitching, made sure her disapproving glance was seen
before looking away. Angela scrunched her nose, snarled her
lip, and shook her head side to side in response. "You'd think
somebody who dresses up like Guy Fieri would have a better
sense of humor," she joked. "Now I feel like I just insulted Guy.
I'm going to write him a letter of apology."

"You're dialed up to eleven. Is it because we're friends again?"
asked Peter.

Angela smiled and opened her arms for a hug. The longer

they hugged the tighter they embraced. Their moment of pure appreciation was broken by Angela being Angela. "What's the opposite of a Shrinky Dink? My mind was all flaccid when that thought just popped into my head."

"You're the worst," Peter laughed and blushed as they let go. Instead of dispensing a comeback, he got a bit mopey.

"Are you okay," she asked tenderly to meet Peter's disposition. "Did something happen?"

"No," Peter struggled for the right words. "I just really wanted to thank you."

"What for?" Angela became concerned about the serious turn in the conversation.

"It's hard to put into words. This has been one of the toughest stretches of my life, and you've been there. You've . . . I don't know how to say it exactly. You've been someone I could count on. You've been there."

"Aww! You're really bad at this," Angela said with a kind smile. "It's okay for friends to say, 'I love you.' Are you quitting? Is that why you let me cop a feel back there?"

"You're much worse at this," Peter chuckled and then held back tears. "Our friendship means the world to me. And yes, what I'm trying to say is that I love you."

"Can we hug again? I promise, no jokes this time." They embraced like they knew it would be their last.

"So, seriously, is this it? Are you coming in to quit?"

"Something like that," said Peter. "I don't know how this day is going to end, exactly. I just know it's not going to be pretty."

"That's, um, the type of thing people say in *Lifetime* movies just before they commit crimes of passion," said Angela as they approached the building. "What are you about to do? Quick, say something to stop me from freaking out."

"No violence. It takes the cooperation of good people sometimes to do bad things. I recently got some excellent advice from
a dear friend—a friend who I love—who helped me understand
that I should stop advancing causes that are not in line with my
beliefs. That's all. I'm a lover, not a fighter," he said with a wink.

* * *

Collins was standing with Goodwin in the doorway of his office
as Peter and Angela rattled the door handle. The sound even
made Goodwin jerk his head in a nervous twitch. Goodwin's
stare caused Angela to freeze in place. Nudging herself into
motion, the two walked toward their desks. Goodwin quieted
his voice and finished talking to Collins before telling Peter he
was needed upstairs. Angela tossed her purse on her desk in an
expression of anger that went unaddressed. Peter dropped his
computer bag by his office door and followed behind Goodwin.

They didn't exchange a single word as they walked up the
stairs and through the president's suite. Loch's door was closed,
and Sally didn't look up as the pair walked into Goodwin's
office. *Loch will not be coming to my rescue,* thought Peter as
he shut the door behind him. Goodwin turned in dramatic
fashion as he had six previous times in the past eight years.
What he found this time gave him pause. Peter showed no
signs of fear; he stood with a straight back, broad shoulders,
and vengeful determination in his eyes. Goodwin's face went
gaunt at the sight of Peter's menacing posture; he remained still
and silent. Goodwin fought to compose himself, taking a few
steps in retreat, looking at his feet before grabbing a chairback
for balance.

"What's your relationship with Glenn Nurse?" Goodwin finally asked.

"Glenn was a student coordinator for the voting reform conference," said Peter. "I was his staff mentor, and we became friends."

"What was he doing in your office yesterday?" Goodwin moved to the conference table and leaned over a different chair, grabbing it with both hands as he waited for Peter's reply. The back of Peter's neck began to tingle. He was becoming triggered. Breathing slowly and deeply, he took the steps he had been taught to ground himself. Then, drawing courage from the bravery of the young boy in Brighton, and from his sessions with Redmon, he thought, *I have the strength to do this. This motherfucker couldn't break me with jackhammer.*

"Is Glenn being accused of something?" asked Peter feeling strong and confident.

"Answer my question!" shouted Goodwin.

"I answered your question," Peter responded calmly. "I'm his mentor and his friend. Now answer my question."

"I don't know where your arrogance comes from," said Goodwin. "I suppose you see yourself as some sort of Horatio Alger creation. Is that it?"

"Should I be embarrassed that I wasn't born into wealth and privilege?" snarked Peter.

Goodwin fumed. "I don't like you," said Goodwin.

"That's because I'm a threat to you," said Peter as he walked to the opposite side of the conference table. "I know things that are dangerous to you."

Goodwin became uneasy. He understood the tables had turned, but he didn't exactly know how. "I brought you up here to fire you!" snapped Goodwin.

Peter let out a small laugh. "You really are a one-trick pony. I've never thought about how frightening it must be to know the only thing you bring to the table is your family's checkbook," said Peter. "Your only skill is the ability to sign your name in the lower righthand corner."

"Get out," said Goodwin.

"I don't think I will," said Peter defiantly. "I came here for answers!"

"I said get out!"

"What's your relationship with Carson Billings?" asked Peter as he pulled a chair back from the table and sat.

"Now I see what this is about," said Goodwin. "Someone else looking for a check from my family's account—money they didn't earn."

"You didn't earn it either, Alistair, and I don't want it. Does that horrify you? It must. You can't fire me again, and you can't buy me. You've got no bullets left," said Peter. "I know someone else who wouldn't take your hush money. Someone who knows even more than me."

"Your friend Glenn Nurse is dead! He died of an overdose," Goodwin's eyes were cold and vacant. It pleased him to break the news to Peter. "He was found early this morning. He used the needle that was missing from Josh Leonard's arm. The case is closed."

Peter slumped his head. Goodwin waited patiently. Finally, he knew something Peter hadn't. He'd gained the upper hand without writing a check. It made him proud. He felt clever. Peter lifted his head slowly.

"Let me tell you about Glenn." Peter's voice was calm and steady. "He loved this college. His education transformed his life, but Billings fed his addiction—and you're complicit in that. I know you don't think about people like Glenn as you travel the country with your tin cup, asking daddy's friends for money, but he's the reason they give. He's the reason I wanted to work here. He understood this place in a way you never will. A way you never could!"

"That's enough out of you," said Goodwin, surprised by Peter's lack of emotion.

"I will tell you when it's enough!" demanded Peter. "I'm not done here, *Alistair*."

"I said *that is enough!*" Goodwin shouted and brought his open hand down on the conference table. Peter stood. He was several inches taller and a few dozen pounds heavier than Goodwin. The fear in Goodwin's eyes was palpable; he moved toward the phone on his desk.

"You don't tell me what to do anymore," Peter responded as he slowly walked toward Goodwin.

Goodwin reached for the phone. "I'm calling security." His hand trembled as he picked up the receiver.

"How did you know Glenn used the same needle as Josh, unless Billings told you as part of his alibi?" asked Peter.

Goodwin placed the receiver back into its holder. His eyes lost focus as they stared down the cliff he'd just stepped off. His hands continued to shake. Goodwin reached into his pocket, jangling his fingers through his coins to find his yellow tin—*pop*.

"What do you want?" asked Goodwin.

"The truth. I've been lied to from the second I walked onto this campus. All I want is to look into your weak, pathetic eyes while you explain to me why you let people die so you could collect Billing's blood money."

"You think you're so very noble." Goodwin's words came from a dark place Peter had not yet seen. "Right and wrong, black and white, it's all very simple in your world, isn't it?"

"I'm not letting you pin this on Glenn," said Peter calmly.

"Who's going to believe you over me?" Goodwin snapped. "We know about your weekly visits to the psychologist's office and your money troubles. It will be easy to paint you as unstable and desperate. It will be easy for the police to believe that you're trying to extort the college. That is what you're trying to do, isn't it?"

"Deep down you're just a little child looking for daddy's approval, aren't you?" Peter was still calm. "He gave you every advantage in life—and look at you. Pathetic. He must have been so disappointed. Getting you into Harvard. Getting you this job. He probably died wishing you were the pool boy's kid."

"What do you want from me?!" snapped Goodwin.

"Glenn was my friend," Peter said calmly. "I want you to explain why you let him die!"

"Drug addicts die every day," said a calculating Goodwin. "We gave him a chance. If Parker hadn't provided him with a substantial aid package, he would have died as a factory worker, or coal miner, or whatever menial job he took."

"Collateral damage? The cost of doing business." Peter raised his voice, stepped closer, and talked more rapidly. "Like letting a billionaire sell drugs on campus. If he killed a few people like Glenn and Willy and Josh, at least they're not the ones contributing to the endowment."

Goodwin was outraged. "That's right! What? I suppose it would have been better to let him rot in jail?" snapped Goodwin. "Carson Billings comes from a good family. He has had every possible advantage."

"Just like you."

"Yes, just like me. There is every reason to think he'll turn his life around, but I suppose it would have been justified, in your mind, to let all that potential go to waste. Why? Would that have made things right? Would watching the media parade him through the town square, tarred and feathered, have corrected all the inequities in your little world? Another triumph of the takers over the doers. I'm sorry to destroy your little fantasy, but it's families like mine and Billings' who established this country and give people like you places to work."

"So the doers get to choose who lives and who dies?" asked Peter. "Is it that simple? You covered up Billings' crimes because being born with money gives you potential?"

"Yes. It's that simple, and I would do it again," Goodwin seemed to inflate with pride. "The winners are chosen before the race is run, and that is why you, my sanctimonious friend, are, and always will be, a loser."

"Just say it, and I'll go away," Peter said as he crumbled. "Say you hid Billings' crimes because money is all that matters. I need to know the truth because I can't live in this fucking fantasy world anymore." Peter's shoulders slumped, and he put his hands in his face. Goodwin swelled as Peter deflated. It was time to stomp out the weak and move on.

"Yes, let me say it again. I did what I had to do to help Billings succeed," said Goodwin as he moved closer to Peter. "That is how life works, and people like you and Glenn are collateral damage—pawns. I do find it ironic, however, that you disregard that the outcome of my deal with Billing—a deal that you find so reprehensible—will make the college more accessible to the people who you pretend to care so much about. Do you know how many scholarships $25 million will provide!"

Peter took a few beats before standing up straight. His demeanor completely changed—like an actor after the director yelled "cut." Goodwin wasn't sure what had happened.

"We already had you, Alistair, but admitting to the conspiracy, and including the dollar amount, that was fucking epic!" Peter chucked, adding in W. C. Fields affect, "Hoisted by his own petard!" Goodwin was confused by what seemed like Peter's relief. "Glenn wasn't the only one who knew about the coverup," continued Peter as he walked to the east-facing windows.

"What are you talking about? What's going on here?" asked a bewildered Goodwin.

"When I said I knew others who didn't take your hush money, I wasn't talking about Glenn. You told campus security to protect Billings at all costs—to protect your investment. Mike Marino and Mark Palmachuk didn't take your money either. 'Come straight to me if there's ever a problem with Billings. It will be worth your while, but no one can ever know.' That's what you told Mike. 'No matter what happens, don't go to the cops; come to me if Billings breaks the law.'"

"I don't have to explain myself to you," snapped Goodwin.

"I'm not asking you to," said Peter. "I'm just repeating Marino's testimony to John McMahon. That's what he used to get the warrant for me to wear a wire. And you just confirmed the whole fucking thing, my self-aggrandizing friend."

"What's going on here?" stammered Goodwin.

Peter pointed to the East Lot. "See that van? It flashed its lights to let me know they have enough to arrest you."

"You're lying," said a timid Goodwin.

"Flash your lights again, please. He missed it," said Peter.

The van flashed its lights.

"Turn on your windshield wipers," said Peter with a chuckle as they obeyed his instructions. He turned to Goodwin, "Well, that's probably a coincidence. Flash your hazard lights if it's a coincidence."

The van's hazard lights flashed.

"Oh, look, lucky you," said Peter as he turned. "Hopefully your jury will be made up of *doers* who understand you were making the tough decisions that keep America great."

"Not reporting a crime on your own property is different than breaking the law," Goodwin said as he shuffled back from Peter.

"Save it for the jury. You knowingly leased a dorm room for the purpose of using and selling drugs. And frankly, I don't know that much about the law, but I'm pretty sure you just admitted to breaking them all. You singlehandedly turned Parker College into a crack house," said Peter as he unbuttoned his oxford shirt while standing by the conference table. He removed the wire from under his tee-shirt and pulled the transmitter from beneath his waistband. Peter tossed the microphone and the tiny transmitter on the table. "I asked the cops not to come for you until I left the building. I really want to see you in jail, but I thought I'd give you time to consider options that would be less embarrassing to the college than your trial."

Peter didn't look back as he exited Goodwin's office, hoping that if he ever saw Goodwin again it would be in video of his perp walk on CNN. Sally was stiff and conscious of her every move, like when someone with a camera tells you to act naturally. She knew Peter came to Goodwin's office to get fired. It was easier to ignore them on their way out, especially the ones she liked. Sally kept her eyes fixed on her computer screen until Peter reached for Loch's door handle.

"He can't be disturbed," Sally stood as she uttered the words she had been told to say.

"He'll want to hear this, Sally," Peter said with a sincere smile that failed to put her at ease. Loch sighed at the sight of Peter, then looked away as he stacked papers that were spread across his desk.

"Goodwin's about to be arrested. I wanted to let you know it was me who encouraged Glenn Nurse to report everything to McMahon. That was a fucked-up thing you did," said Peter waiting in vain for a reaction from Loch. "McMahon called me this morning and told me about Glenn. He told me all the nice things he'd said about me and got me to wear a wire. Goodwin confessed to everything. They'll be up here in a minute to arrest him and question you."

"Do you feel like you made the right decision?" said Loch, dryly.

"I do," Peter said without hesitation.

"Good," said Loch. "Well—"

"I told him that I didn't know what you knew or when you knew it," said Peter, trying to be reassuring.

"I didn't ask you to protect me before, and I'm not asking you now," said Loch looking at Peter for the first time during their conversation. He tightened the muscles around his eyes and let out another sigh.

"I took off the wire," said Peter as he showed his open and untucked shirt. Loch frowned. In none of Peter's imagined scenarios did Loch become defensive or shrink from confrontation.

"I said what I came to say. I thought I owed you that much." Peter turned to leave.

"I didn't know the whole time," admitted Loch. "I believed what they told me, at first."

"Why did you let it get this far?" Peter's anguish hung from each word. He was still hoping for a solution—a way he could fix things—a way to protect Loch and his legacy—a way to bring Glenn back. A way to undo the whole fiasco.

"It had already gone too far by the time I knew. Twenty-five million dollars could do a lot of good," said Loch. "I was blinded by it. Ironically, I was trying to help people like Glenn. The people who'd benefit most from Parker being need-blind."

"The college benefits most from being need-blind," Peter shot back.

"The college doesn't exist for its own ends," Loch returned. "It exists to keep alive the humanities and the liberal arts tradition."

"The development department has three times the staff as the humanities department."

"What's your point, Peter? Why are you still here?"

"My point is that I wanted to believe," Peter caught himself from saying *in you.* "I wanted there to be something left to believe in." Peter wanted to scream at Loch and accuse him of failing Glenn, Josh, and Willy, but most of all for failing the Charles Loch who ran for mayor of Boston. *I want you to know how much it hurts to feel abandoned again,* thought Peter. *To feel abandoned.* That phrase echoed in his mind. It was the moment Redmon had wished for him. Loch was never more than an empty promise, a Maltese Falcon that led Peter to find his own self-worth. Peter felt both light and heavy, smart, and dumb—it was the psychological equivalent of looking for your glasses and finding them on your nose. On his way out the door, he reached into his pocket and tossed the mayoral campaign pin to Loch.

"You said your father was a union guy?" said Loch as he held the pin, feeling its weight. Peter nodded. "When I was campaigning, I always looked for someone wearing union insignia. We were courting unions, heavily. They carried a lot of clout back then. I would have walked straight to him, shook his hand, and then probably talked about collective bargaining and about my strong union support. It was a bonus when there was a kid. I'm sure I talked about education and safe streets and closed by predicting that when you were mayor, life would be better because of all the wonderful things I would have accomplished. I probably patted you on the head and told you I had faith that you'd attain some lofty position one day." Loch let out an ironic laugh as he watched for Peter's reaction. The compassion that poured from Peter's eyes surprised him.

"You were spot-on that day. Convincing," said Peter. "You know, I came here hoping to work for that guy. Loch, the mayoral candidate, the defender of the working man. Knowing now that I did, knowing you're the same guy I so admired all those years ago, is one of the great disappointments of my life. What's the saying? Never meet your heroes."

35

FINDING HOME

The *Columbia* steamed north between Vancouver Island and the Canadian mainland toward the choppy waters of Queen Charlotte Strait. It was beautiful, but not yet Alaska. Peter rested comfortably on a deckchair under the solarium's heat lamps. He had a mug of coffee and that morning's national edition of the *New York Times*. On the front page, below the fold, was a story about Parker College that Peter had not yet read. He scanned the deck for another reason to procrastinate while trying to coerce himself to read what he knew would be pitiful attempts by the college to spin the scandal. He felt certain they would admit no wrongdoing, and it would drive him mad.

Near the end of the covered area, a pair of camping neophytes struggled to pitch their tent against the occasional gusts of swirling wind while most other campers were already napping under the shelter of theirs. "Blue poles, blue loops; gold poles, gold loops," Peter wanted to shout to them as they struggled with the instructions. The man's shiny, loosely fitting wedding band made Peter think, *honeymooners*. Amygdaliform was the Word of the Day, which made him wish the woman's engagement ring had an almond-shaped diamond. What a perfect entiree. "Oh, what a beautiful amygdaliform diamond," he'd say, and then offer his advice on pitching the tent. It seemed like wasted effort without Angela there to chuckle. *She's what I'll miss most about Parker College.*

Peter felt no panic while anticipating the three days he was about to spend alone on the *Columbia*. Free time was becoming less intimidating as he was learning to replace the mental busywork of seeking threats with the gentle observance of his thoughts. Working with Redmon gave him the freedom to get lost along the inroads of his mind. He was learning the explorer's secret that the biggest concern is not losing your way home but finding a place you'll love more.

There was no job waiting for him in Juneau, only the warmth of his friends and the hope of a future lived more consciously. Peter was getting to know the nurturing part of himself that had helped get him through his hardest challenges. There was a lot more to learn, but he was grateful to be on the path. It was up to him now, and no one else, to choose his way forward. Peter and Tessa had to draw from their retirement funds to pay the mortgage in Alaska and keep the rest of the family in the apartment through the school year. The money wouldn't last very long. He'd need to find work quickly to keep them afloat and be able to plan their next new life." There were a lot of hard decisions ahead.

Done procrastinating, Peter finally flipped the newspaper and read the headline: "Need-Blind Ambition: Billionaire, College Leadership Complicit in Student Deaths." Even though he'd been avoiding the news coverage, Peter had been awaiting this story with a dollop of morbid curiosity. Angela had shared that Collins worked with the reporter. "I kept hearing him say, 'I cannot confirm, nor can I deny that fact.' He is literally the dumbest person I've ever met," she'd said. Peter laughed aloud, remembering their conversation.

The *Times* was weighing like a lead blanket on his lap. He had no faith that Billings and Goodwin would be held accountable for their crimes. *I really don't want to know. Combined, Billings and Goodwin are worth billions, which puts the odds of them suffering any consequence at a few billion to one*, he thought as he settled in to read the article.

The newlyweds had cracked the code of tent assembly, and to celebrate their accomplishment, they shared an ironic high-five that warmed Peter's heart. *They're good together*, he thought, as they walked away from their tent without anchoring it down. Trouble. Peter watched them snuggle hug as they walked toward the galley as their tent clung precariously to the boat in the gentle breeze. Mild swirling drafts jostled the tent, scraping the aluminum poles against the deck. He hoped they'd hear it and look back before a gust lifted the four pounds of nylon and aluminum alloy like a box kite and tossed it into the sea. Peter folded his paper in thirds and placed it under one of the heavy chair legs as he stood to help the newlyweds secure their tent. As soon as he stood, a forceful blast caused the flag to change directions so quickly it cracked like a whip. The tent toppled and rolled past Peter, knocking over his chair, scattering his newspaper like an explosion. The wind swirled again, causing the tent to change directions and take flight right in front of Peter. He jumped, snatching a golden pole that had been fed though a blue loop. The others on the deck broke into spontaneous cheers and laughter at the exciting rescue.

As Peter fought against the wind to return the tent to its owners, he saw his disassembled newspaper being strewn in all directions. Pages were blown hundreds of feet in the air, while others were plastered to every unmovable object on the deck. Reassembly would be like putting shaving cream back in the can. Peter was amused by the other voyagers chasing loose pages around the ship. He watched a section floating on the ocean's surface, slowly sinking into the water. *In a few days it will decompose into an unintelligible mush*, thought Peter. *There's probably a good lesson in that.* As the excitement was dying down, Peter noticed a raven flying north, soaring above the tree line toward jagged mountain peaks. It looked back, and like in his dream, it let out a caw that chilled Peter to the bone. He didn't try to make sense of it. He watched it fly away as the newlyweds took control of their tent.

"Was that your paper?" Asked one of the newlyweds.

"I'm not worried about that," said Peter as he smiled and nodded, helping the couple load their backpacks into the tent, then bracketing it on both sides with deckchairs. "That ought to hold it," said Peter. The newlyweds were relieved that their lodging for the next few nights was safe and secured. They beamed, already having an adventure to share with their friends, and Peter felt like he had accomplished more good for the cause of humanity in that thirty seconds than he had throughout the duration of his employment at Parker College.

"The least we could do is buy you a new paper," offered one of the newlyweds.

"Oh, that was yesterday's news," said Peter, knowing he wouldn't find another *Times* onboard. "There must be a water-under-the-bridge joke I'm missing."

Peter did accept their invitation to breakfast, feeling like a third wheel as he followed them into the galley. They were moving to Juneau and happy to have an ambassador who could give them the lay of the land. He shared the red/blue political divide between the Valley and Downtown but accentuated that being Alaskan trumped all other affiliations. He shared his favorite trails for short and long hikes and his favorite Forest Service cabins to rent for overnights. His eyes sparkled when he shared his favorite local delicacies: springs rolls from Pete's in the Nugget Mall, and Jerry's Meats smoked salmon spread. "I eat it on Wheat Thins until I feel sick. Then I hide it, so I don't eat myself into a coma." Then he shared a few of his favorite stories that exemplified the other simple pleasures of life in Alaska.

"The way you talk about it really confirms our decision to move!" The new bride said with a contented smile. "If you could boil it down to one thing that makes it so special for you, what do you think that would be?"

Peter thought for a moment, then smiled, "The ravens."